A man appeared
in the threshold . . .

Tall and broad, a shadow backlit by the twilight outside, his dark traveling cloak caught by a sudden gust and billowing out behind him, showing a form as powerful and sleek as the dog standing between her and the door.

Feeling as if she were being turned inside out in the space of a heartbeat, Priss could only stand rooted to the floor, as if she were being held by the force of his gaze. Here was trouble—in his eyes beneath straight brows curved downward at the outer corners. Beautiful eyes of vibrant, unfathomable blue, glinting sparks of fury and impatience and a guardedness that seemed tangible.

But, oh my, he was the most fascinating man she had ever seen.

Other **AVON ROMANCES**

EVE BYRON

MY LORD DESTINY

AVON BOOKS ◆ NEW YORK

AVON BOOKS, INC.
1350 Avenue of the Americas
New York, New York 10019

Copyright © 1999 by Connie Rinehold
Published by arrangement with the author
Library of Congress Catalog Card Number: 99-94810
ISBN: 0-380-80365-8
www.avonbooks.com/romance

First Avon Books Printing: October 1999

AVON TRADEMARK REG. U.S. PAT. OFF. AND IN OTHER COUNTRIES, MARCA REGIS-
TRADA, HECHO EN U.S.A.

Printed in the U.S.A.

WCD   10   9   8   7   6   5   4   3   2   1

To my loopy sisters—all forty of them—
diamonds twinkling in the litter of fallen pieces of sky.
I wish I could name you all here
but you know who you are.

To my editor, Lucia Macro,
who is a joy to work with.

To Gini Rifkin, Audra Harders,
and Mary Frances Stark
with profound thanks for many things.

To mom with love.

And to Gail Smith, Kay Rustermeyer,
Jeanne King, Ilse Box, and Renee Sloan
from Medical Lake High.
I've never forgotten you.

*There are more things in heaven and earth, Horatio,
than are dreamt of in your philosophy . . .*

WILLIAM SHAKESPEARE, *HAMLET*

MY LORD
DESTINY

Legend

The St. Aldan line would flourish and survive. It would endure as he would not. And one in a future time would love as Myrddin had, deeply, profoundly, magically. Myrddin saw the chosen one as clearly as if he stood in his path, waiting for him. A man who believed in nothing but what he could see and touch, standing beside a woman who had lost herself in fear and uncertainty. They would come together, completing the circle he and his lady had created. Within, they would find true beauty, true magic, love as it was meant to be.

Myrddin walked on, feeling his age increase with each step, feeling his existence fade with every breath as all of his kind had faded over the years since Arthur had passed into Avalon. As all sorcerers became legends rather than a part of the modern world. It was best, he knew. Best for mankind to accept the Creator, to know that all things came from one source. Arthur had tried to make them understand how all things came from the same thought, but they could not comprehend such a concept. Humanity was too young, the minds of men too constricted by incomprehensible fears to understand that all things in the universe dwelled within the same circle and were fashioned by the same hand. But ofttimes, man had to take a step back before he could take two forward.

If only he could go back, back to the sanctuary he had conjured, back to the woman who waited for him. But he was fading too quickly to see the journey through and would drift in the ether long before reaching the woman he loved.

She had begged him to remain, to leave the St. Aldans to aid themselves, even as she understood that he could not abandon those of his blood in their time of need. And so she'd bid him farewell with a promise to wait—forever if need be.

A comforting word—forever. It recognized no conditions, set no limits. It was the promise of eternity that had united much of the world under one faith. A promise older than the earth upon which he walked. A promise upon which love was built.

Even now he and his lady were bound together by the symbols of forever: the trees in a circle, trees that nourished creatures of the earth and produced air that sustained all life.

He'd fashioned the symbols with painstaking care, one for him and one for her, both circles, each different, yet fitting together as two people fitted together in love.

Sighing with more weariness than he'd

thought possible, Myrddin chanted his most powerful spell, his words carried back to the place of his birth by the wind to bind his promise to his family. He'd left his medallion with the master of St. Aldan, knowing his relative would hold love in safekeeping for those who needed most to feel and experience the magic that dwells in the heart.

The true magic. The only magic.

And in the great Somewhen, his lady's medallion would be found and joined with his ring to bind two hearts together in love. It was his gift to his kinfolk, a family that would rise to greatness in the old land, preserving what was best of the old ways while gently strolling into the new age. They would need love and understanding to carry on the traditions and preserve the legacies of the past.

Myrddin began to walk toward the horizon, driven by hope that he would, after all, reach his sanctuary that none but the chosen could see, that he would once more find rest in the arms of his lady, his life, his love.

But his form faded and wavered as all that he was became a part of earth and sky, drifting toward forever.

Chapter 1

Castell Eryri, Wales
1820

"**D**amned to perdition," the Reverend Price said in his usual monotone.

Damned. Gavan St. Aldan scribbled the word on a sheet of foolscap in front of him. He'd propped his head on one hand minutes—or hours?—ago to keep it from lolling to the side should he fall asleep. *Damned to boredom.* He drew a line from the phrase and with a flourish wrote "Bored." *Bored to tears . . . bored senseless . . . bored stiff.* The words sprouted from his quill with blots of ink at first, then fading as the tip dried.

"Curses and legends indeed. You are perpetuating the danger they present, my lord. You are jeopardizing the well-being of everyone in the district with your tolerance."

What was the reverend talking about? Gavan stifled the urge to ask as he sank his quill into the inkpot and widened his eyes to keep them from falling shut.

4

"Can you not see that by allowing Whitmore to dig about and explore old burial mounds, you are encouraging your people—the very people for whom you are responsible—to return to the old ways?"

Whitmore. Gavan scrawled. Finally, Price had come to a point of sorts. A rather dull point, but a point nonetheless. He really should have foreseen this when he'd given his blessing to Whitmore to search for "artifacts and truth" as the man had put it. Such idealistic fervor was . . .

Tedious . . . Pitiable . . . Enviable . . .

Frowning at the last word, Gavan crossed it out. Whitmore, in his opinion, was definitely not to be envied. Liked, definitely. He'd taken to Mr. William Whitmore immediately for his open manner and even more open admiration of Gavan's rather plain sister. A man who saw the beauty beneath the surface was rare indeed—a fact evidenced by Gwyneth's spinster state at the age of twenty-eight.

Whitmore had arrived a fortnight past with hat in hand to request permission to explore the St. Aldan holdings. By the time they had completed the meal Gwyneth had offered in the name of hospitality, Gavan had granted their guest free rein of the district. Since then he'd seen precious little of his sister and the family hound, who preferred to follow her and Whitmore about outside rather than sit quietly at Gavan's feet while he worked over plans for his newest projects.

"And where is your sister now?" Price

asked in a rather pathetic imitation of outrage.

Gavan's head jerked as he snapped his eyes open and favored the vicar with a cold stare. Tolerant of the clergy he might be, but no one below a king questioned a St. Aldan.

Price backed up a step, toppling into a chair as the backs of his knees hit the seat.

"Please do sit down, Mr. Price," Gavan said dryly, and returned to doodling on the paper.

Price regained his feet and strode toward the desk. "Begging your pardon, my lord, but I must again inquire as to the whereabouts of your sister, if I am to protect her immortal soul."

"Lady Gwyneth is out." *In love*, he scrawled the width of the paper. "With my blessing. Do you question that?" he asked with calm detachment, not giving a damn what the vicar thought.

Price sputtered, his mouth flapping like a banner in a gale. "I *must* question it," the tall string of a man said with more passion than Gavan had thought possible. "It is my duty to protect the souls of my flock, whether they like it or not."

"Like what?" Gwyneth asked as she sailed into the library in a flurry of bright skirts and even brighter cheeks, her cape billowing around her. "Has someone sinned again, vicar?" Halting beside Gavan, she leaned over to buss his cheek as Daisy slid to a halt on his other side and nuzzled his arm for a pat.

Gavan glared at the greyhound in accusation at her defection. If the dog had been here instead of gallivanting with Gwyneth, he could have at least played fetch with her while suffering through Price's rant.

"I don't precisely know, my lady. Have they?" Price fixed a penetrating glare on her.

"Oh dear, I see I am found out," Gwyneth said. "I knew I shouldn't have taken the last of the chocolate this morning. What sin would that be? Gluttony or greed?"

"You mock the Lord's word?"

"No sir, I would not mock God, but really Mr. Price, you are so diligent and somber you invite a bit of jest."

Somber. Gavan scrawled along the edge of the page. *Irritating. Pompous*—

Gwyneth reached across Gavan and pulled the quill from his hand to write on the paper. *Get rid of him. Life and death!*

As she slipped the quill back into his hold, Gavan shot a glance at his sister and frowned at the realization that the high color in her cheeks was more from haste than excitement, the shine in her eyes more from distress than exuberance. Of course with Gwyneth's penchant for drama, life and death could be anything from spilled milk in the kitchen to famine throughout the land.

"Of course, you are correct, my lady." Price drew up to his full height, an action that seemed to stretch him to even more height. "But, surely you understand why I must. If not I, then who will save us from ourselves?"

Daisy imparted her opinion with a low growl.

Gavan tossed the quill onto the table, preferring to deal with whatever had brought on Gwyneth's anxiety than with Price's ever-present air of doom and gloom. Gwyneth, at least, was entertaining and always presented him with a challenge in devising a way to calm her. "You have an entire parish, sir, and we are but two. Would your time not be better spent in the village?"

"I am dismayed, my lord, that you should take the danger to us all so lightly. You, of all people, should be aware of the constant threat imposed by the old ways."

It had been in Gavan's mind to encourage Whitmore for the sole purpose of debunking the old beliefs once and for all, but he wouldn't tell Price that. The man would never leave him in peace then, and Gavan would be continually wrestling away old and unwelcome memories better left unearthed and unremarked, even in his own mind—

The reverend cleared his throat and raised a haughty brow at Gavan's wandering attention. "It is my duty—and yours—to see that they remain buried in those dreadful mounds, yet you allow Whitmore to unearth them one by one. Have you no concept of what would happen if his activities should revive the Druid beliefs? It is quite bad enough that you have refused industry entrance into St. Aldan and instead have planted trees where valuable minerals might be mined. Prosperity is what we should be seeking for our people. Nature can quite take care of itself."

"You mean that *God* will take care of nature, don't you, sir?" Gwyneth asked quietly, her anxiety apparently bowing out in favor of defending Gavan's pet project.

"Well, of course I do, but it is up to those of us in authority to carry out His wishes."

Whirling, Gwyneth planted her hands on her hips and advanced on the vicar, her ire at full mast. Daisy bounded to her feet and kept pace with her, ears pricked and sleek head erect. "Are you suggesting that my brother might not be doing God's work in his efforts to preserve the land? And as for William digging up the burial mounds—you are in error. None of us is so callous as to disturb the dead."

As Price's mouth again flapped, Gavan quickly sketched an apparatus that might keep the vicar's jaws from falling out of joint. If he didn't miss his guess, Gwyneth would dispose of the vicar's unwelcome presence within the next thirty seconds, thus saving Gavan the trouble of dragging the man out by the scruff of his neck.

"If you are so troubled by our misdeeds, sir," Gwyneth continued, "then perhaps you should repair with all haste to the parsonage, where you may pray for our souls in comfort." She grasped Price's arm and ushered him to the door. "I trust you can find your way from here?"

Price tossed an entreating glance at Gavan over his shoulder before Gwyneth slammed the door in his face.

"Do you remember the old legend of Myrddin the Sorcerer?" she asked quickly, as she turned in a flurry of skirts to face Gavan, the vicar apparently forgotten.

An old legend? This was her urgent matter? "I recall well over a thousand old legends. Would you care to be more specific?"

"*The* legend!" Gwyneth said in a loud hiss and cast a furtive look at the door. "*Our* legend. The one inspired by Myrddin himself."

Stifling a groan, Gavan prayed he wasn't in for another of her performances, complete with chants of dragons and sorcerers and rings of stone. And somewhere in a shadowed corner of his mind, old pain began to writhe at the memory of the torment the "family" legend had wrought in his father.

Torment that had plagued Gavan with images and sounds from a past he could not revoke in spite of reason and logic and maturity.

He forced the reminders of that long-ago time aside and watched Gwyneth stride to the far end of the great hall, the only room in Castell Eryri still untouched by progress, if one didn't count the large library table at which Gavan sat working on his maps of St. Aldan and the drawings detailing his plans to replenish the forests in his domain. In his extensive renovations of the castle, he hadn't been able to bring himself to touch this room where kings had sat, conferring over concerns of war and peace and where so much of the St. Aldan spirit seemed to thrive in the ancient tapestries and hand-hewn furnishings. Modern conveniences and wallpapers and carved paneling that enhanced the rest of the castle would look sadly out of place in here—

"Do not ridicule this, Gavan," Gwyneth said, her voice striking the old stone walls and seeming to multiply as it carried through the air. She raised her arms in a flourish. "The time has come. The signs have appeared. *The book has been found.*"

Oh no, not that. Gavan suppressed his sudden sense of dread with his usual mockery, though he would voice neither, respecting the limits to which he could scoff at his sister's beliefs, especially where "the book" was concerned. Of all the legends threaded through their history, the one regarding a tome supposedly written by Myrddin's lover was the most oft repeated and believed. It was also the most absurd. A book over a thousand years old would be dust by now and hardly an instrument for bringing old spells to life. More likely, Whitmore had uncovered the journal of some wanderer, or the written ramblings of a self-proclaimed philosopher. Wales had a way of inspiring eloquence.

Such a book would have a way of inspiring otherwise sound men to dementia in pursuit of the impossible.

His mouth twitching with the amusement he'd convinced himself he felt over the subject, Gavan quirked a brow at her exaggerations, admiring the flair with which she presented them.

"Owan is dead, Gavan," she said with a lowering of her head, her arms falling to her sides beneath her cloak.

Gavan's brows snapped together, though he was hardly surprised. The old druid had claimed a full century of living, and Gavan had often wondered what kept him going. Still, Owan had been an important part of his life, and Gwyneth's, having taught them the old language and passed down the stories of their people to the young master and mistress of St. Aldan as tradition had dictated for hundreds of years.

Druids did not write down their history, but entrusted it to each successive generation through the spoken word. But the old ways had been dying since the dawn of Christianity, and only a few thought the tales more than a good story to tell on a winter's night.

Only a few . . . like his father. And Gwyneth. She had heard the history and learned the beliefs, accepting her duty to carry the past into the future.

Absurd. A waste of time. Yet, Gavan indulged her because the ritual was important to her. Because she had little else in her life but a castle to run and a brother who lived firmly in the present, refusing to entertain his own flights of fantasy. Because Owan had trusted him and Gwyneth to carry on the traditions and preserve the history of the land and its people by passing on all the lore to them, teaching them of their origins and weaving the legends associated with the district and the St. Aldan family into their awareness.

And because old Owan had been like a father to Gavan and Gwyneth when their own had retreated into a pit of despair.

As long as his sister honored rather than

practiced the old rituals, treating them as history rather than religion, he would continue his indulgence. For that decision, Owan had been responsible by teaching Gavan to respect individual beliefs rather than judge all by the acts of one.

Still, Gwyneth's forays into ancient legends struck him like an affliction for which there was no treatment beyond forced amusement and mockery and continual reminders that Gwyneth was not their father. That, for all her feather-headed notions, she had too much sense to fall prey to the lure of magic and miracles. In any case, to forbid the old ways would be to encourage secrecy. At least this way, he had some measure of control.

Gavan sighed. "I will see to the preparations for Owan's burial," Gavan said, hoping to divert her.

"It is done," Gwyneth said. "William and I took him to the secret burial mound last night. We thought it best that no one know where his body lies, what with Mr. Price's attitude and how quickly the zealots are to stir."

Gavan struggled against an odd thrust of hurt that he had not been told. For all his mockery of the old ways, he had cared for Owan and would have said farewell to his old teacher. Yet Gwyneth was right; Owan deserved to rest in peace in the place of his choosing. It wouldn't do for his remains to be unearthed and prayed over by those who would try to save—or to condemn—his soul even after death.

He jerked his head up as the full meaning

of what Gwyneth had said caught up with him. "Last night? You were out all night?" He slammed his fist on the table as he shot to his feet. "With Whitmore?" he asked in a deadly calm voice.

Gwyneth spread out her elbows and planted her hands on her hips beneath her cloak, making her look like an angel whose wings were slipping. "You are not paying attention," she said as she glared at him. "Or have you conveniently forgotten our legacy?" Without giving him an opportunity to reply, Gwyneth raised her arms. "Take heed, Gavan, as I remind you of what you work so hard to forget," she said and launched into the story all St. Aldan children learned along with the family name and the boundaries of their land.

"We are named St. Aldan in honor of the mother of Myrddin—the greatest of the wizards, who brought a true king to the throne and majesty to the land," she intoned, obviously bent on distracting him from his brotherly duty to her honor by reciting the whole blasted tale. "Our land is named St. Aldan. All within our keeping, but the castell itself are named St. Aldan so that none forget the history that so many wish to take from us."

Gavan sank back into his chair, yielding to her determination to finish her recitation before he decided upon whom his wrath should fall—Gwyneth or Whitmore. Secret burial ceremonies notwithstanding, Whitmore had no business allowing Gwyneth to remain out all night, and Gwyneth should have come for

Gavan immediately upon discovering Owan's death.

"Myrddin was born right here on St. Aldan land, and returned often," Gwyneth said, raising her voice an octave. "His heart was here . . . as was his love. After Arthur was killed in battle, rumors abounded that Myrddin went mad, or was imprisoned by an evil sorceress, or traveled to other lands. But he did not. He found a special place in these very mountains, where he and his lady hid away from the rest of the world. A place so secret that none but the chosen can see."

Daisy glanced from Gwyneth to Gavan, then dropped where she stood and folded her paws over her nose, apparently as resigned as her master to enduring another of Gwyneth's performances.

Gavan listened with only half an ear, knowing where every pause, every emphasis lay in the narrative. The litany lost something in the translation from old Owan's singsong voice, uttering the words in a mix of common speech and old Welsh to Gwen's perfect, aristocratic pronunciation of the King's English.

He picked up the quill and began to sketch an idea for a new project he had in mind, determined that this time he would neither remember nor feel the sharp bite of his memories.

Gwyneth muttered a phrase of disapproval in the old tongue that he understood well. The rebuke for his lack of attention was as much a tradition as "the telling" of pagan wisdom imparted to generation after generation of a family that had eschewed the old ways with the first stirrings of Christianity in the land. A dichotomy Gavan had never understood.

He fixed a bland expression on his face as he allowed the quill to drop from his fingers—the best he could do while facing a wraith who sighed and tapped her foot in exasperation.

Gwyneth nodded at his show of attention and began to pace as she picked up the thread of her tale. "But Myrddin left his woman and his home to help our family, which, it is said, was his own. He knew that the old ones were disappearing, their powers vanishing to extinction in the light of Christ. He knew that to leave his sanctuary was to begin to wane as all the others had done, so he cast a spell over the woman and the sanctuary of his heart, rendering both invisible to all but the ones meant to see. The ones who would understand and be enriched by the sight."

Sanctuary, Gavan scrawled across the whole of the sheet of paper after surreptitiously retrieving his quill. Must he wait until he inhabited his own burial mound to escape the torture of listening to the same old story?

"But, Myrddin fell prey to age and infirmity and did not return to his lady," Gwyneth said loudly to catch his straying attention. "And while she waited for him, she completed journals of his prophecies, so they would not be lost. There was no one for her to tell, you see." She turned back to him so abruptly, her cloak snapped in the air and twisted around her limbs as she halted to glare at him. The fabric settled back into place, the hem falling to the floor. Watery light from a window set high in the stone wall cast her shadow across the floor, long and thin like a finger pointing at him.

How did she do that? he'd often wondered when she would manage this or a similar eerie effect. No doubt his sister practiced long hours while the rest of the household slept.

"Myrddin had a charm—a circle he'd fashioned during his idyll"—Gwyneth waved her hand at Gavan's ring—"and left his portion of it with the first Earl of St. Aldan, charging him to use it to set the family apart from ordinary men and ensure our survival. His lady had the rest of it—a medallion crafted by Myrddin himself for her—a circle that completed his. A symbol of love and all that was meant to be . . ." Her hand fell to her side in a melodramatic gesture of despair and a silent moment of grief for love lost too soon.

Gavan instinctively rolled the ring on his finger and traced the design—their family seal—used for centuries as a symbol of the legacy left behind by a mythical figure in their family tree. Those who believed the old stories also believed the St. Aldans were enchanted.

Enchanted indeed, Gavan thought with a snort. Shrewd, yes. Strong and powerful, without question. And perhaps they were lucky, though many before him preferred the word "blessed." Life proceeded without change for each successive generation, holding the lands and the title, honoring the tapestry of their history that so artfully blended truth and legend, taking an active hand in the prosperity of their lands by setting their own code of proper behavior. They governed wisely and rolled up their sleeves to labor beside whoever required aid. They saw to their own and rarely concerned themselves with the outside world. The mountains of Snowdonia were world enough for the St. Aldan's . . .

All but one, who sought a world that did not exist except in his own mind.

Gavan inhaled sharply and focused on his sister. Nothing could be served by that particular thought.

Gwyneth's silent moment passed; she raised her head and fixed him with a stare that never failed to rattle him, as if she knew of his irreverence and would call down the wrath of dragons upon him. Yet her voice was soft, a whisper almost, as if the words would break if not treated with delicacy. "Her medallion would be found by one who honors old things, and it would be passed to another who fears herself. The book would be found and cause great strife. And when the parts of the circle come together, two who are lost will be found, and they will discover the joy and completion denied Myrddin and his lady."

A pretty story if one were a starry-eyed maid, Gavan thought wearily as he glanced down at the ring—a rather nice circular design of Celtic braids and a tree sprouting from a smaller circle in the center. "The circle of my ring is complete," he stated, unable to completely humor his sister.

"A delusion fostered in a mind constricted by order," she snapped. "Really, Gavan, you

would not be so bored with life if you allowed
your mind to fly."

"One bat in the belfry is quite enough, Gwyneth," he replied, repeating an old tease. "You
'fly' quite enough for both of us."

"Do you not comprehend?" she shouted in
exasperation. "William—one who honors old
things—found the book with the lady's charm
inside. He asked Owan to translate the ancient
language." Her voice lowered to an ominous
whisper. "But Owan is dead, and we must
now allow destiny to rule us. *We* are the ones
intended to complete the circle. *We* are the
ones who must allow the book to lead us and
teach us the magic of—"

"Um-hm," Gavan mumbled as he drew con-
centric rings all over the paper. He knew what
Gwyneth was about to say. The magic of love,
indeed. It was all well and good for those who
believed in such fantasy. Gavan did not. Love
had no existence outside of wishes and old
legends. His own experience with love had
proved to him that it was indeed as much a
delusion as belief in sorcerers and magic
swords.

Only love for his sister was real and solid.
A comfortable, sometimes exasperating feeling
of closeness and caring rather than earthshak-
ing emotion and debilitating need. If romantic
love existed, much less endured, there would
be no need for stories and dreams. Life would
be enough.

But Gwyneth did believe in it, as she apparently believed that Myrddin's prophecy
was meant for her. Whitmore's appearance

and subsequent unearthing of an old book no doubt added texture to her dreams. Thankfully, Whitmore seemed equally enamored of Gwyneth and had only yesterday hemmed and hawed in a clumsy effort to request Gavan's permission to court her.

Gwyneth ran to him and knelt before him, her hand covering his, her plain face infinitely expressive. Gwyneth could speak volumes with a single look. "Myrddin said that all will come together as it was foretold. That we would learn the true nature of magic. He said to let it happen, to let the dreams come into our hearts. To embrace them and pursue them, one at a time, until they come true. Then we shall know what joy truly is." The last word trailed off as a tear meandered down her cheek.

Gavan reached out and wiped the single drop away. "A nice touch," he said gently. "But such things are for those who believe, like you, Gwyneth. Don't translate the book you found. Don't destroy your fantasy with the truth."

Ironic that he encouraged in Gwyneth what he refused to consider for himself. That he wished for her all the bliss of innocence he'd lost so long ago.

"Oh! The book." She rose abruptly, pulling her hood over her head as she hurried toward the door. "I must go to London. The coach will be outside by now."

Gavan blinked, disoriented by the sudden change in subject. "What?" He lunged from the chair, stepped over Daisy, and caught up to her in long strides. "What the hell is in London?"

"The truth. Life." She opened her arms wide as she swept down the corridor. "Danger."

He caught her arm as they reached the entry hall. "You are not going to London. There is no reason. There is never a reason to leave here."

Sighing loudly, she favored him with a pitying look. "I often wonder if you weren't a changeling, Gavan. But since you look exactly like our sire, I know you are not."

He waited, knowing her pause was a harbinger of one nonsensical declaration or another.

She turned just before reaching the threshold. "Your destiny is at stake. Our very lives are at stake. It is obviously up to me to save us all."

He covered the length of the hall at a run. "Gwyneth," he called with a warning note none ignored save his sister.

A pair of footmen raised the bar and pulled open the arched double doors that led out into the courtyard. Endless gray shrouded the sky outside. Trees dropped under the steady deluge of rain. Beyond the drawbridge, cottages seemed to huddle into themselves as thin wisps of smoke disappeared before they could rise above the rims of the chimneys. Not a breeze stirred, as if the air itself were gray and heavy in mourning for the end of summer.

Gwyneth stepped outside and halted, keeping her back to him. "The time has come for

the circle to be completed. If it is not, we will
die as Owan did."

"I can think of worse ways to die than of
old age," Gavan said dryly. "And I fail to understand what London has to do with it."

"Owan did not die of old age," she said
softly. "He was murdered." Without waiting
for his reaction, she hurried to the coach waiting a few feet away from the entrance to the
castle proper and climbed inside, not waiting
for assistance.

The words hung in the air like the calm before a storm, chilling Gavan with the flat way
she had delivered them. Cursing in the old
tongue of his ancestors, Gavan did not question why a footman held his greatcoat out for
him, or why he reached for it and strode out
to the coach. He yanked the door open and
climbed in, pushing Gwyneth's skirts aside as
he sat across from her and noted her valise on
the seat beside her.

"What are you doing?" she asked with pro-
nounced nonchalance as he held the door
wide for Daisy to jump in.

He favored his own valise placed on the seat
he occupied with a cynical arch of his brow.
"It would appear," he said dryly, as Daisy settled happily on Gavan's feet, "that I am going
to London. I strongly suggest that you spend
the journey telling me why."

Chapter 2

❦

"**W**e are taking William to his sister," Gwyneth said, as the coach lumbered and swayed over the slog of twisted and muddy mountain roads. "He will be safe there while the book is being translated."

Gavan shook his head in an effort to rearrange the varying bits of Gwyneth's explanation into logical order. "If we are taking William to London, why is he not with us?" he asked.

"He is masquerading as a postillion," Gwyneth said as if it were the most logical thing in the world.

"To keep him safe?" Gavan ventured, certain that must be why a guest of Castell Eryri would be posing as a servant.

"Well, of course to keep him safe. I thought he should hide in the boot but he wanted to be able to fight should the need arise. He is still smarting over being bested by his attackers. Hopefully, we have left so abruptly that no one had the opportunity to follow—"

"Stop!" Gavan roared over the clamor in his mind. *Fight? Attackers? Followed?*

Gwyneth snapped her mouth shut.

The coach lurched to a halt.

Daisy yawned.

Nodding in satisfaction, Gavan leaned his head out the window. "Whitmore, inside . . . now!" he rapped as he held up his hand to stay whatever argument Gwyneth might pose.

Cold, damp air entered the coach on William's heels as he hurried inside the coach and struggled to remove his wet coat before sitting down next to Gwyneth.

With a long-suffering sigh, Gavan pushed him down on the seat and leaned over to pull the door shut. "Is it possible," he said, settling back against the squabs, "for one of you to enlighten me without resorting to riddles and high melodrama?"

"It's quite simple—" William began.

"Gavan, we really must keep going," Gwyneth interrupted.

"Not until I receive a coherent explanation."

"Order the driver to move on," Gwyneth said with a mutinous tightening of her mouth.

"It *would* be best if we keep moving," Whitmore said quietly.

Stifling the urge to throttle both of them, Gavan jerked on the cord attached to a bell in the driver's box—one of the inventions he enjoyed devising when boredom set in. It made so much more sense than rapping one's knuckles on the roof of the coach.

Gwyneth sighed with exaggerated relief when the coach rolled forward with a lurch, as if the driver, too, felt her urgency. More likely, the poor devil was anxious to get some-where—anywhere—dry and warm.

Gavan angled into the corner and propped a leg on the seat. Another boring evening at home was beginning to look more appealing by the minute. "I suggest that one of you tell me what is going on . . . from the beginning." He fixed an uncompromising stare on his sis-ter and then on their guest.

"As I said, we are taking William to his sis-ter in London," Gwyneth repeated, the words tumbling out rapidly. "Her name is Priscilla, and she is a woman of business—isn't that marvelous? I can't imagine being so indepen-dent as to live alone and do what I pleased, but I certainly would like to try"—she tossed William a quick smile—"although being mis-tress of one's own household would be almost the same thing, I should imagine . . ."

Gavan sank deeper into the squabs, pre-pared for his sister's customary manner of lib-erally salting her explanations with whatever thoughts or wishes or illusions she happened to have at any given time. At this particular moment, she seemed to be heavily influenced by the illusion of love.

He didn't know whether to be alarmed or pleased. The illusion was nice while it lasted, but in his experience it could have a rather nasty end.

"She makes hats, Gavan! Wonderful hats! How nice it must be to be so creative."

Gavan rolled his eyes. Gwyneth had quite enough creativity for ten people though hers

was of thought, which produced nothing save
an amazing number of inspired ideas and the
odd entertaining moment. This moment, how-
ever, was exceedingly tedious. He didn't give
a hang about William's sister or her headgear
when there was still the matter of their mad
flight over mountainous roads because of a
supposed murder, some fantastical notion that
they were in danger, and an even more absurd
expectation of some sort of a fight, none of
which seemed immediate enough to keep
Gwyneth from verbal woolgathering.

Of course, Gwyneth had no need for urgency now that she'd bamboozled him into
the coach and on a harebrained jaunt to London.

Cursing himself for not seeing it coming, he
idly rubbed his thumb over the family ring,
allowing Gwyneth to prattle on while he organized the thoughts scattered by the whirl-
wind that was his sister. Since they were
trapped in the carriage for four days or more
on a journey for which he still didn't know the
reason, he had plenty of time to sort through
it all. Apparently, Whitmore's family was
worth at least half an hour of monologue—

". . . their father died, you see, and left William and Priscilla with nothing but a plantation neither of them wanted. Priscilla wanted
to return to London and live in solitude . . ."

Well every family had the odd knob, he thought
and wondered who held the distinction in
his—himself or Gwyneth. But then, any family
who claimed descent from Merlin—or Myrd-

din to be more precise—and presumed to name virtually everything in sight "Aldan" after the wizard's mother was sure to have more than one eccentric in each generation—

"Their mother had no wish to remain in the West Indies; an amazing woman, their mother. She said that if she was to live out her days as a widow, it would be while doing what she'd always wanted, which was to have a shop of her own. William had become disgustingly wealthy during his adventures . . ."

Gavan propped his head on a closed fist and thought that Whitmore's family topped his for being an altogether balmy lot. If Whitmore was so bloody rich, why did the mother choose to work and the sister to become a recluse? For that matter, why would Whitmore choose to wander when he could build his own little world with a home of his own and his family around him? The Whitmores were landed gentry, or had been and could be again. The sister and mother could move about society—

"*Violà*" Gwyneth said suddenly and loudly with a grand sweep of her hands.

Gavan jerked his head up and glanced around as he shook off his preoccupation. "*Voilà* . . . what?" he asked and grimaced. One should never ask his sister anything unless one truly wanted to know the answer.

"Why, they all returned to England. William purchased a shop in Mayfair for his mother, where she sells the lovely hats and fripperies Priscilla makes in her cottage outside the city, and William continues to putter about ruins and libraries, of course. They are all dreadfully happy and doing exactly as they wish. Isn't that wonderful?"

"Wonderful," Gavan said dryly as he nudged Daisy with his foot, wishing the dog would share her secret for sleeping so peacefully during Gwyneth's monologues. "May I assume that all this has some bearing on"—he raised his hand and ticked off each point he thought should be addressed now that Gwyneth had reached the end of the saga of the Whitmore family—"let me see . . . ah yes, you did mention that you suspected that Owan was murdered, did you not? And then you mentioned an attack, and that our safety might be in question, and I believe this all has something to do with a book?"

"Have you not heard a word I've said, Gavan?" Gwyneth said peevishly. "William found Myrddin's book and the token his lady wore, and so it is quite apparent that we are the chosen ones who will realize the sorcerer's legacy—"

"If we are not overtaken and murdered first," Gavan said, more convinced by the minute that he should order the driver to return to Castell Eryri, where he could dose Gwyneth with a good sedative.

"That is a problem," she said gravely. "Until Owan's death and the attack on William, it never occurred to me that the book would be so important or that anyone could be so wicked as to—"

"May we have a little hush, Gwyneth?" Whitmore said softly.

Gwyneth hushed.

Gavan clenched his jaw to keep it from dropping open and favored Whitmore with a nod of approval. For that alone, he would grant the man his sister's hand in marriage.

William met Gavan's gaze with a steady one of his own. "Owan *was* murdered, my lord . . . smothered, I believe—"

"Of course Owan was murdered," Gwyneth said. "We found him with oilskin wrapped about his head, and I hardly think that he did that himself. Just before he died, he distinctly gasped that he'd been murdered. He also gasped out the name of the fellow in London whom we are to contact."

"Owan had agreed to translate the book for us," William said, a voice of reason in the midst of confusion.

"It is in the old language, you see," Gwyneth added.

"No, I do not see," Gavan said impatiently as he struggled with shock at the revelation that proved Gwyneth's claim of murder, regret that he'd not taken her news more seriously, and anger that the old sage had not been allowed to end his life in peace. To lose Owan to a natural death was one thing, but to lose him to an untimely and violent end was quite another.

Gwyneth leaned forward and laid her hand over his. "I know, love. It is difficult to deal with such a thing. And I'm more sorry than you know that you could not help us bury him." She sat back and regarded him with a sadness he'd seen in her eyes many times over the years, as if he was an object of utmost concern and anxiety to her. "But then you would not have been able to go in any case, since you have been unable to find, much less see, the secret place where Myrddin and his followers spend eternity. You would simply have seen William and me disappear into the mist." She shifted in her seat and shook her head sadly. "A terrible, terrible pity that you do not believe in anything but what you can see and hold, though I am at a loss as to why and how you changed. When we were children you had no trouble at all believing in magic. Why it was you who showed me the secret places on our land and first acquainted me with the legends—"

Gavan sliced his hand through the air to silence her. He was not about to again discuss the state of his beliefs or lack thereof. Mists and magic and secret places indeed. He knew where the place was and knew what it held. He'd just never shared his knowledge with Gwyneth. "You and I were both schooled in our native tongue," he said wearily. "Why could you not translate the book?" he asked.

"Because," she said with aggrieved patience, "the book was written more than a millennium ago, Gavan. We learned Welsh in the schoolroom as it is used today, which means that you or I would have great difficulty in translating it. The language is quite different from what we are accustomed to, not to mention that fewer and fewer Welshmen actively speak it. And you know how many of our countrymen have adopted English ways and don't even live in Wales any longer. There is one such in London—a scholar, like William—who is secretly a Druid, according to Owan."

"Owan did say that the letter on the first page indicated that the book was written by Myrddin's lady while she waited for him to return to her," Whitmore interjected.

"Owan was ruled by a tendency toward wishful thinking," Gavan said. Simple logic contradicted such assumptions as Whitmore, Owan, and Gwyneth were making. Science had not yet developed a way to save books from the ravages of time.

"What Owan couldn't discern upon first examination," Whitmore continued as if Gavan hadn't spoken, "was whether the book contains more of Myrddin's prophecies, the greater of his spells, or simply the lamentations of a lonely woman."

"Simply!" Gwyneth said indignantly. "You suffer the wretchedness of losing the one you love and see how *simple* it is. That poor woman must have gone through the agonies of hell waiting for a man who would never return . . . and to fade a bit at a time with none to comfort her rather than meet a peaceful death, surrounded by her own kind. Just ask Gavan how dreadful that is."

Stifling a groan, Gavan rubbed the bridge of his nose. "Pray, do not ask me," he said with a warning glare at the couple sitting across from him. "My sister overstates an incident that affects nothing but her own imagination." He favored Gwyneth with a look that warned he would not dredge up the only folly he had committed in his life. A folly for which he had the excuse of youth and gullibility. He'd fallen "in love" and had quickly fallen out again when the lady who was to be his bride proved how shallow the sentiment was. Love did not conquer all. It had neither vanquished her distaste for his way of life nor his disgust that he could have so easily been deceived by beauty and a falsely sweet nature.

"I most certainly do not overstate," Gwyneth said indignantly. "I vow you exist in virtual solitude in your castle, your life only a shadow of itself, while you indulge in nothing but work. All because a woman—"

"Enough! You will tell me what the bloody hell is going on and leave magic and true love and fading sorcerers out of it."

Daisy raised her elegant head and regarded Gavan with a chiding look for interrupting her sleep, then lowered her head again.

Whitmore shifted and pressed a finger to Gwyneth's mouth, effectively silencing her retort. "Unfortunately, magic and sorcerers—or rather the belief that they once existed—play a part in this business, but I will try." Lowering his hand, he leaned forward and faced Gavan. "We found the book and took it to Owan for translation," he said in a flat voice. "After we buried Owan and while Gwyneth was speaking to one of the villagers, I was attacked with a rope from behind." He loosened his neckcloth to reveal a welt circling his throat, then retied the knot without fanfare. "We are going to London to remove ourselves from danger and to take the book to the man Owan spoke of—"

"With his dying breath," Gwyneth added with a perfunctory nod.

"We can stay with my sister, which should be safer than putting up at an inn in the city, and afford us some time to sort all this out. Priscilla is a bit of a recluse, and her home is tucked out of the way of ordinary traffic."

"Thank you," Gavan said with heartfelt appreciation for Whitmore's succinct summation. "Now, I believe it would be best if we dropped you off at your sister's and returned home. I will make a report to the local constable and conduct an investigation into Owan's death—"

"Murder, most foul," Gwyneth corrected.

"—and you can return to St. Aldan after you have your translation," Gavan finished, as if she hadn't spoken.

"*I* am remaining in London," Gwyneth said. "I can help, and I wish to know William's sister and mother." She turned her head toward Whitmore. "She will be returning from the Continent soon, will she not? In any case I am most fascinated by them."

Gavan arched a brow at her. Help indeed. If ever there was such a thing as a benevolent curse, Gwyneth was it. Whitmore would no doubt finish his business in a fraction of the time and with a good deal less trouble without her dubious aid. Yet Gavan could not voice his opinion. He never could. For all her flightiness, his sister was a tender soul too easily bruised by the harshness of the world as proven by her continued insistence that Gavan's contretemps with love was responsible for the way he lived. He would not hurt her with his opinions—

"I know what you're thinking," she said. "And you are making all the wrong assumptions about whom I aspire to help."

"Perhaps, but I will no doubt be much happier in my error than if I know the exact nature of your aspirations," he countered.

"Impossible," she said with a delicate snort. "You don't know the meaning of the word 'happy.' You are the most cynical and jaded man I have ever known, and one so afflicted cannot be happy without aid. It is you I wish to help, Gavan. You should have the manners to accept with good grace."

"If I required aid, I would accept most graciously," Gavan said and laid his head back to stare at the roof of the coach. This was not a discussion he ever willingly entered into with his sister. But Gwyneth was sadly blind to the true nature of his disinterest in social and romantic pursuits. The truth was that he had found nothing to interest him beyond his responsibilities to St. Aldan.

"He will not listen," Gwyneth said sagely—to Whitmore, he presumed. "But I daresay that he will learn soon enough how misguided he is." Her skirts rustled as if she were arranging them more comfortably about her. "I fully intend to remain in London for a time, Gavan. Since our destinies are now being ruled by events too far in the past for you to change—though I am certain you will try—it would be prudent of you to do your duty as my brother and remain to watch over me. You know how easily I can fall into mischief."

"I know how easily you fall into manipulation," Gavan said with a roll of his eyes. *And how easily I fall for it even when I see it coming*, he silently admitted. Still, he could not bring himself to see the light of excitement in her eyes dimmed. Their life at St. Aldan was confining to a woman of her exuberance. Perhaps a few days in London would not be amiss. For Gwyneth, he supposed he could suffer the theater and the shops she would no doubt wish to visit. If he let it be known they were in the city, they would likely receive invitations to routs and musicales by the score.

Of course to remain in the city also meant he would be obligated to look over the current debutantes for the position of his wife—the only responsibility to St. Aldan that he had not fulfilled. Once in London, he would have no choice but to at least make an effort to find a woman willing to trade her hand in marriage for the distinction of bearing the heir to one of the wealthiest earldoms in Wales. A quiet young woman, perhaps lacking in funds and therefore, choices, he thought cynically. One who preferred to read or paint rather than gad about in society.

It seemed rather a waste of energy to try when he knew nothing would come of it. Yet, after over fifteen centuries of prosperity it would be a pity for the St. Aldan line to "fade away as Merlin had" as Gwyneth had said often enough.

Sighing heavily, he closed his eyes and reluctantly revised his plans to include a search for a mate and the mother of his heir. While he was at it, he could also see about acquiring a mate for Daisy. The humans in the family were not the only ones obligated to preserve tradition by breeding.

Finding a mate for Daisy would be the easy part. Success in finding his own companion for life strained his imagination beyond reasonable limits.

In all of the Upper Ten Thousand, there probably was not a single woman with a nature sensible enough to see in St. Aldan what he saw.

Mountains—the highest in England. Lakes with mist rising in the moonlight and glowing luminescent in the early hours after dawn. Green valleys in the summer and craggy peaks mantled with snow that glistened white in the winter. Trees that blazed with hues of fire in autumn and meadows that danced with a riot of flowers in the spring.

The last lady to consider marriage to him had said that no woman could be happy in such isolation unless she was completely without hope for better prospects . . . or completely mad.

Chapter 3

"**I** was mad to agree to this," Priscilla said as she situated an ostrich feather on the brim of the half-finished hat perched on her head, hoping to find inspiration by seeing it on a human rather than a faceless wooden form. "Ostrich feathers quite overwhelm the stuffed robin Lady Marton insists must be on her hat." Sighing, she cast a longing look at the note she'd received from her brother two days past.

Willie would be coming to see her as soon as he had a book translated by an old Druid in some Welsh village. He was quite up in the boughs about his find, if his hurried scrawl and disjointed sentences were anything to go by. Of course given Willie's conception of time, "soon" could mean anywhere from a fortnight to a year, depending upon what further studies the translation prompted him to make. Still, a book that might contain the lost prophecies of Myrddin the Sorcerer as recorded by Myrddin's lady . . . it was enough to tempt her to hie off to Wales to see it for herself. How intriguing to hold in one's hands the proof that Myrddin was not simply a fable. . . .

Why, holding in her hands proof of Myrddin's life, and his great love for his lady, might renew her belief that magic and true love replete with undying devotion and high romance truly existed. It would be nice to believe again. Life had lost some of its brightness when she had lost faith in such things—

"You are not listening to me," Mr. George Simms said as he gave her an annoyed glare. "My patience wears thin, Priscilla."

"Really?" she murmured as she sent a reassuring grin to her maid Jenny hovering just outside her workroom, then returned her attention to her latest creation. "I fail to see why it is your patience at risk. I have listened to you once a week, every week, for the past year and know your conversation by heart. You wish to marry me. You are certain I must be rescued from a life not worthy of me. You can save me and my family from the disgrace I most assuredly heap upon them by being in trade." She met his gaze and lowered her hands to her lap, leaving the feather hanging precariously off the narrow brim. "You see, I have listened; I just don't happen to agree. Perhaps it is you who have not listened. . . ."

Her voice trailed off as she wondered if she should go to Wales rather than wait for Willie to tear himself away. At least then she would not have to strain herself so to convince George that she *did not* love him and therefore *could not* marry him. He was so dogged in his belief that she did and therefore she could and should.

"I have listened," he shouted, then quickly lowered his voice, "and if you made a modicum of sense, I would consider your arguments against my proposal. I am well situated, both in my future and my social position. When my uncle cocks up his toes I will inherit his lands and his title, further adding to my wealth. You will live in a grand house. Neither you nor your mother will have to subsist in such a common manner again."

Priscilla smiled absently and returned her gaze to the looking glass propped on her worktable. "Common? You must be in error. It seems to me that the way I subsist is most uncommon, and I assure you that both my mother and I are quite happy about it. We see no reason to change simply to please your sense of propriety."

"I fail to see how you and your mother can possibly be happy about it. Your father was landed gentry. Your brother is Midas reincarnated; every bit of refuse he digs up turns to gold in his pocket." He smiled, clasped his hands behind his back, and rocked on his heels, a veritable image of satisfaction. "You will not know true happiness until you take your proper place in society. Trust me in this."

"Truly I cannot, George. We own everything we have. We are not dependent upon anyone else for our livelihoods." *We are not forced to entertain the grim expectation of the death of a relative so that we may live as we wish*, she added silently, employing the caution she'd cultivated over the years rather than hurt George with such a statement. She'd hurt enough people to last a lifetime.

George frowned, opened his mouth, closed it, and flushed crimson.

Sighing, she stared at the looking glass, rather than face George's distress. "I'm sorry, George, but you know it is true. Mother and I are not only comfortable, but we are quite happy as we are."

"If your mother were here instead of traveling about the Continent looking for materials for your shop, I'm certain that she would urge you to consider my proposal . . . and no doubt your brother would offer his blessings." He grinned triumphantly, as if he had just found the perfect argument. "When did you say he would be arriving? I will speak with him." Nodding, George sat in a chair and drained the glass of sherry he'd left on the table at his elbow, as if he were toasting his own clever mind.

"Willie's note said he should arrive in the next fortnight, if he is not detained, but I know better than to expect him until he is standing on my doorstep. Since he has discovered something quite incredible, I daresay he might not come for a month or more." Stifling the urge to shred the dratted ostrich feather, she examined it closely with an eye toward trimming it down. A pity, she thought. It was a magnificent feather that would have filled her with pride had she been an ostrich.

"I do believe, Priscilla," George drawled, "that your brother might enjoy his pursuits more if he did not have to fret about you and your mother. I suspect he interrupts his jaunts for the sole purpose of checking on your well-being. If you were married, he would be free to indulge his passions, as is proper for a man."

"Willie indulges his passions as freely as he wishes; trust me in this," she retorted. "He knows Mummy and I are entirely capable of taking care of ourselves and visits only when the mood strikes him. I promise you that we do not burden him overmuch."

No matter what odd paths Willie might travel, he'd always made certain that his family was secure, though that did not include unnecessary worry. For that she loved him most of all. It was a rare thing to know someone had faith and trust in her and loved her enough to allow her to follow her own path. If there were another man in all Christendom who possessed the same qualities, she would most definitely fall in love with him and marry him. But she had known only one other such as Willie, and he was married—not that that had stopped her from loving him. . . .

A love that was most certainly *not* meant to be.

She smiled fondly as her hand found the pendant dangling from a ribbon around her neck, an antiquity Willie had discovered tucked inside the book and sent to her "for luck." It held the memory of a magnificent dream, he'd said, elaborating at great length in his message. A memory that would come to life and find fulfillment. He'd said that the pendant itself was purported to symbolize a spell of great power.

Willie had written that the piece wrought in fine gold in a design of trees in a circle, their roots meeting in a smaller center circle representing the sun, signified life never-ending. Except that the trees did not comprise a complete circle but fell short by one, leaving a space at the top of the pendant. Willie had said that the space was hope, the nearest kin to faith.

A lovely sentiment and one she believed in, but not for her. Only once had love touched her, and she thought that perhaps she had squandered her chance for that special magic by seeking to destroy it for two others.

Perhaps she should consider George's proposal, she thought, forcing her mind to follow a different direction. From what she had seen, men such as her brother and the man she had loved so long ago were thin on the ground indeed. And George was rather handsome, with his blond hair and brown eyes and trim frame, and he was bright and earnest. Their children would be quite lovely and clever. . . .

Children—the only prospect that had ever prompted her to consider marriage. How sad. She was pretty and resourceful and not in the least dim, yet she had a regrettable lack of emotion where men were concerned. Perhaps she had become frigid in her disappointment with love.

Dimly, she realized that George was speaking again—or was he still speaking?—not at all a good sign. How could she marry a man who could not command her attention?

"Priscilla, I love you quite madly," he said, startling her with his presence by her side.

She gasped as he hauled her out of her chair and swept her into an embrace, his mouth covering hers before she could utter a sound. Instinctively, she raised her hand to hold the hat in place. If it fell from her head, the pins would fall out and she would have to start all over again arranging the decorations. . . .

She willed herself to remain still, to allow George this one liberty, to see if perhaps it would become exciting. She closed her eyes and opened them again as George prolonged the kiss. Would it never end?

He skimmed his mouth over her lips and then her cheek, finally coming to a halt at her ear. "I should have planned this a long time ago," he murmured. "I should have seduced you and shown you how well we will suit one another in marriage." He kissed her ear and her eyelids and her nose, then angled back to meet her gaze.

"Planned? You *planned* this?" she asked, unsure whether she ought to be outraged or amused, and not particularly caring either way.

"Of course," he said. "One does not take such an improper step lightly. One must be fully cognizant of the risks one takes. But it was a worthy gamble. Surely you realize that you enjoyed it."

"It was . . . nice," she lied after careful deliberation, hoping it was the kind thing to do. The only thing she realized was that not once had she released her hold on the hat, and she could hardly wound his pride by telling him that.

Surely a kiss should make one forget about such mundane things.

As he released her, she quickly sank back onto her chair, anxious to escape his hold before he planned another such *risk*.

She shook her head sadly and wondered how she could tell him that she had admired his actions in sweeping her off her feet—off her chair really, but that was beside the point— that it was romantic and complimentary to think that she could make him lose control. She'd always known that any man she loved would have to be of intrepid nature. A man who kissed her because he had no choice, because he *had* to, because he would die if he didn't. A man who didn't give a fig if it was proper or not to sweep her into a passionate embrace, sweeping her so far away from hats and pins that she would want her hands to be on him and only him.

George hadn't swept her very far at all or she would not have cared about the silly hat or the pins. If he loved her as much as he insisted, he would not have cared about risk or gambles or whether it was worth it. Love had to happen. It had to be deep and overwhelming and beyond even the most eloquent description.

She had no trouble describing George's kiss, much less her feelings for George himself. The kiss had been disappointing; she had so hoped that it would shake the earth for her. George was disappointing as well; who could possibly feel unbridled passion for a man who had to *plan* his caresses?

Poor George, she thought as she felt the weight of the pendant at the base of her throat. "I'm so sorry, George, dear, but I really do not wish to marry at all. I believe that I am not meant for marriage, you see."

"Blast it, Priscilla! You are four-and-twenty years old. I cannot credit that a spinster would harbor such a ninnyhammered belief. You should be pleased and grateful that a life of ease and comfort is offered you. You should be content to have the opportunity for a quiet and ordered existence."

"Yes, so you've said more than once," she replied blandly. In fact, she had heard it so many times, it no longer had the power to infuriate her. Now that she thought of it, that pompous and degrading statement was the single most prominent of all the reasons why she had refused his hundred or so proposals.

Glancing impatiently out the bow window, Priscilla was relieved to see that the molten gold light of late afternoon was being replaced by a silver-blue glow that fell in a lace pattern through the trees surrounding her home. It was her favorite time, the transition between day and night, which she shared with no one but herself as she suspended all activity for a few precious moments and soaked up the peace, allowing her mind to wander where it might.

"It is becoming late, George," she said, giving him a regretful smile. "I think we have strained your sense of propriety quite enough for one day—"

"No," George said harshly. "I'll not be dismissed this way, Priscilla." He grasped her arms and once again hauled her up from her chair. Her hand immediately flew up to the hat as his mouth crashed down on hers in another kiss.

Oh dear. It really was annoying when George got a thing into his head and went on and on about it. Yet, despite her irritation, she remained still in his arms, telling herself to be patient, that it would be over in a moment and he would leave—

The earth shook. The air exploded with sound.

Her mouth slid away from George's as her gaze sped to the window.

Hoofbeats thundered on the main road outside her property. Galloping hoofbeats. Many of them. Wheels rumbled and squeaked, and shouts rose above the clatter.

She pushed George away and ran to the window.

A huge coach coated with mud swerved off the main road and careened toward the house . . . directly toward her.

She watched in wide-eyed horror as the coach advanced at terrifying speed. Panic froze her in place as horses squealed and the driver stood in his box, hauling back on the reins. She opened her mouth to scream, yet no sound escaped as the team of six reared to an abrupt halt bare inches away from the mullioned panes of glass.

From the corner of her eye, she dimly saw George grab the fireplace poker and raise it high as men tumbled out of the vehicle and ran toward the house.

Jenny ran into the room and screamed as the door crashed open.

Fear clawed up into Priss's throat as a greyhound charged inside, barking frantically. A man appeared in the threshold, tall and broad, a shadow backlit by the twilight outside, his dark traveling cloak caught by a sudden gust and billowing out behind him, showing a form as powerful and sleek as the dog standing between her and the door.

She couldn't seem to move as she stared at him, at the face obscured by shadow, at his utter stillness as he stared back at her, casting some sort of spell over her with his presence.

"You will move aside," he ordered.

She stepped aside, unable to do anything but obey that dangerously soft voice. And then she gasped at the sudden realization that he supported the sagging body of another man.

"Willie!" she cried in alarm as she ran to her brother, the spell shattered and dispersed in fragments of impressions as she bent to examine her brother's battered face.

"Hullo, Priss," he slurred through a cut and bleeding mouth. "I'm here."

With a curse, the man holding him up brushed past her and lowered Willie into the chair George had occupied. "You," he called to Jenny, "get hot water and soap and bandages. And you"—he pointed at Priscilla—"see to your brother."

A woman dashed to Willie's side and sank

to her knees, her gaze only for him. "Do not faint," she ordered. "I forbid it."

Willie grinned and winced in pain. "Men don't faint; we keel over."

Priss let out a breath of relief. Bruises and cuts aside, Willie was all right. He always jested when he was all right. Still, she leaned over the woman to get a better look.

" 'S all right, Priss," he said. "I wouldn't lie to you."

No, he wouldn't. She gave him a tremulous smile and stared harder, just to be sure, then turned as Jenny returned with a pan of steaming water in her hands and several linen towels draped over her arm.

Priscilla took the pan from her, set it on the table beside the chair, and began to tear a length of linen into strips. Incredibly, the woman kneeling at Willie's feet stared up at her with the most piercing scrutiny Priss had ever experienced.

Feeling as if she were being turned inside out in the space of a heartbeat, Priss could only stand rooted to the floor, as if she were being held by the force of that gaze.

The woman nodded and smiled brilliantly. "I am Gwyneth," she said, as if that explained everything. "Please do allow me to tend to William. I really need the practice, you see. I assure you that he looks far worse than he is." She gently slid a piece of cloth from Priss's grasp and dipped it into the water. "I believe you might be of immense help to my brother, Gavan."

The wording seemed odd to Priscilla, as if

it meant something she did not comprehend. Dazed, she glanced at the other man, seeing no injury unless one counted his disheveled hair.

Dark hair, like midnight, gleaming with blue lights, like stars gleaming in the ether.

She shook off the thought, chastising herself for entertaining nonsense when clearly trouble was afoot. Opening her mouth to ask a thousand questions, she snapped it shut again. Everyone was safe. There appeared to be no urgency other than seeing Willie taken care of. Later, she would ask questions, when she had a better idea of what to ask first.

"I am unhurt," the stranger said, breaking the spell cast by his commanding air and wholly male countenance.

Her gaze swept over him and settled on the arm he held stiffly to his side. "You are not unhurt," she said hoarsely through suddenly dry lips, and stepped close to him, reaching up to slip his coat off wide shoulders and muscular arms. "Your breathing is quite shallow. Your ribs must pain you."

"Get away from him, Priscilla," George commanded from the far end of the room.

The stranger's gaze abruptly shot over Priss's head to the source. The woman—Gwyneth—continued to dab at Willie's face as if nothing had occurred.

Priss glanced over her shoulder and stared . . . she'd forgotten about George.

He stood backed into the corner holding her fireplace poker high, his face bleached of color and beaded with perspiration as his gaze skipped from her to the dog standing in front of him, teeth bared. He licked his lips and raised the poker higher as he took one small step away from the wall. "What is the meaning of this . . . this intrusion?"

Willie snickered and grimaced.

Priss shook her head in disbelief at the man she had only a few moments past thought to be tolerable. "It's all right, George. No one here will hurt me." For some reason she cast a quick glance at the tall stranger. "I assure you," she continued, hoping she spoke the truth. "I would be most grateful if you went home now," she said firmly.

"Yes, do go home, George," Willie slurred. "I can take care of m'sister."

George's chest puffed out. "I would be neglect in my duty to Priscilla if I did not remain until order is restored. Your manner of arrival indicates—"

"Out," a deep baritone said from behind Priss, so deep and so smooth that it seemed a caress in the air.

George's gaze skittered nervously from the stranger to the greyhound.

"Daisy, back," the voice commanded. Immediately, the dog backed away and sat, her gaze never leaving George.

Fascinated, Priss watched the stranger step toward George with a languid gait that seemed more dangerous than a full-out charge.

George inched toward the door, keeping his back to the wall at all times, and disappeared into the gathering shadows outside.

"Good riddance," Gwyneth muttered as she continued to wipe blood from Willie's mouth.

"Coward," Willie stated flatly.

The stranger—Gavan—halted, his back straight and stiff as he slowly exhaled.

"We must see to your ribs, sir," Priscilla said, and again reached for his coat. "Your coat and shirt must come off."

He removed her hand and scowled at her down the length of his clearly aristocratic nose. "I will take care of it."

The dog made a grumbling sound in her throat, as if peeved with her master.

"Priscilla is right, Gavan," Gwyneth said without looking up from her task. "That beastly man kicked you in the ribs. Do be a good boy and allow her to investigate."

Willie snorted in a mangled attempt to laugh.

Priss stared up at Gavan and was again caught up in the spell of him, in the harshness and danger of his unique male beauty, harsh and dangerous and full of secrets. *Untouchable,* she thought, as if he had only recently fallen to earth and had not yet become a part of it. He stood still and watchful, his lean, muscular body obviously honed by physical labor and carried tall and straight with assured power. Enough power to hold the world at bay while he chose which elements to reject and which to devour . . .

Like a predator who shared his lair with no one.

Unfortunately for him, he was in her lair now. Taken aback that she had entertained what seemed to be a threatening thought, Priss struggled to present her company with a genial smile. "Willie, perhaps you should properly introduce us before I nurse your friend back to health," she said, hoping to restore some order to her disheveled mind. There, that hadn't sounded too inane.

"Gavan St. Aldan, Earl of St. Aldan," he said with a short bow, then winced as he waved a hand toward Gwyneth. "My sister Lady Gwyneth."

"Thank you, sir," she said politely. "I am Pricilla Whitmore. Now that we have been introduced, though not quite properly, I must insist that you allow me to bind your ribs." She swallowed down the sudden mortification at speaking so to a complete stranger, much less an earl.

Again his eyes darkened with a turbulence that might have frightened her if she had not known he was injured and likely incapable of inflicting too much damage. "My indulgence of impropriety does not extend to removing my shirt in public," the earl said stiffly.

"And if a rib pierces once of your lungs, I suppose you would die happy, knowing you did so in all propriety," Priss blurted, unable to stop the flow of words. "I was raised on a plantation in the Indies, sir. Male slaves worked in the fields with very little covering them. I have a brother. I doubt that your chest is any different from others I have seen, and if it is, I should appreciate the further education the sight would afford me. Now, you have the choice of removing your coat and shirt or suffering in arrogant silence just to prove you can.'' Heat climbed from her toes to her face as she continued to glare at him, too rattled to summon up a shred of apology for her temerity.

Silence fell in her workroom as all gazes fastened on the earl.

Breath seemed to whoosh out of him. Was that a glint of amusement in his eyes?

Without another twitch of expression or sound of outrage, the earl removed his coat and shirt, arrogantly took his time in neatly folding them and draping them just so over her worktable, before standing stiffly in the center of the room, his gaze aimed right between Priss's eyes.

Priss's eyes widened at the sight before her. She might have seen a male chest or two, but not like this one. Hard plates of muscle covered a lean frame one could only be born with. Muscle that layered over wide shoulders and powerful arms descended in ridges to a narrow waist. Muscle covered with smooth flesh bronzed by the sun, as if he actually worked outside. Flesh sprinkled with a dark dusting of silky hair that wedged down . . .

She wrenched her gaze upward to his face. Her mouth dried at the look in his eyes. Here was trouble—in his eyes beneath straight brows curved downward at the outer corners. Beautiful eyes of vibrant, unfathomable blue, glinting sparks of fury and impatience and a guardedness that seemed tangible. Eyes that showed nothing of the man but turbulence without definition.

Her gaze swept from high cheekbones defining a lean face to a sharp blade of a nose, slightly bumped near the bridge, to a sensual mouth, tight with tension, and a strong jaw, darkened by stubble, down to a neck tightly corded with tension.

Pain, she recited silently. He was in pain. He needed care, not admiration.

But, oh my, he was the most fascinating man she had ever seen.

Chapter 4

Impertinent wench. No one but a mother had the right to speak to a grown man in such a way. And even a mother would not discuss body parts so openly.

Miss Priscilla Whitmore was a piece of work. She appeared as appallingly dotty as Gwyneth, and the disorder in which she obviously lived and worked offered proof that he could not be far off the mark. And she was too calm and accepting of them barreling into her life unannounced. Any other woman would be nattering away, asking too many questions.

Why hadn't she? They had erupted into her home, battered and bruised, with Gavan all but carrying her brother like a sack of wheat, yet she had asked no questions, exhibited no hysteria. She hadn't screamed or surrendered to panic. She had been quiet, her gaze just vague enough to indicate careful thought rather than idiocy.

He mistrusted anyone who thought so carefully that instinctive reactions were subdued.

She made Gwyneth seem almost normal,

though his sister's "be a good boy" had se-
verely strained his sense of dignity. It was one
thing to indulge such banter in private, but the
Whitmores were strangers. He stifled a snort
at the memory of Miss Whitmore speaking to
him as if he were in fact a boy, needing a severe scold.

Just to prove he could indeed. He was not
in the habit of beating his chest for the sake of
male conceit. Nor was he in the habit of defending his actions to himself, yet here he was,
keeping his mouth pressed firmly shut to
avoid doing so with Miss Priscilla Whitmore.
A St. Aldan did not have to defend his actions
ever. He only had to weigh them carefully and
implement them to the good of all.

He grimaced at the sound of his thoughts.
He *was* an arrogant sod.

Gavan clenched his jaw as Miss Whitmore
struggled to wind long strips of linen tightly
around his torso, binding his bruised ribs securely. It might have afforded him some relief
from the jabs of pain if her breath hadn't kept
brushing against his chest . . . his sides . . . his
back . . . not to mention the plume jutting out
from the absurd hat perched on her head
threatening to tickle him to bursts of invol-
untary laughter.

She might look odd and behave even more
oddly, but she smelled like heaven. Like the
mountains of home in the spring when rain
was a strawberry-sweet promise in the air. Or
when the sun glowed in the sky like a lantern
behind a silver curtain just before the first
snow of winter. . . .

He forced those thoughts from his mind and fixed his attention on her peculiarities. In appearance alone, Priscilla Whitmore was a sight to behold, with her voluminous smock covering her gown from neck to ankles. At least he assumed she was clothed beneath the wrinkled cotton, littered with bits of feathers and lace and threads—or was it some kind of animal hair?

Gown or hair—he didn't want to know. If Miss Whitmore had a pet, it was bound to be as unconventional as its mistress.

A long strand of tawny hair spiraled down her cheek and over her breast—or what he assumed was her breast. It was impossible to discern through her oversized garment. She could be fat or thin or anything in between. The observation that she was pretty crept into his mind like an afterthought.

He hadn't noticed her face, what with the distraction of her surroundings. Chaos everywhere. Fabrics and life-size wooden and plaster heads and every imaginable frippery in existence were stacked on shelves and chairs. Flowers and herbs hung from ceiling and window hangings—drying, he supposed. Papers and drawings were tacked on walls and littered over the huge table set in front of a large window that would admit sunlight most of the day. Tall candelabra stood on the floor with no apparent order, and candlesticks gathered along every surface that was not otherwise in use. For light, he deduced. Obviously, she worked at night. That she had been receiving the cowardly George in her workroom, it could be assumed that she rarely did *not* work.

A quality he would admire if he was in the mood to admire anything about the chit.

He bit back a groan as the blasted strand of hair whispered teasingly along his side. If she didn't finish soon, another part of his anatomy would need strict binding.

His breath stalled. She was merely wrapping his ribs, not seducing him, yet he was responding . . . and he was beginning to ache in a place far south of his injuries. His stomach muscles clenched as her hair again brushed over his flesh. The woman had no sense of propriety at all in insisting he stand half-naked in her workroom.

"Your hair," he gritted in a low voice. "Please . . . remove it from my person."

She paused and frowned, as if reasoning out how she could remove anything without unraveling her work.

He lifted his hand and brushed the tendril away from her face, his knuckles brushing her neck beneath her ear. Soft skin, warming beneath his touch, inviting him to linger and explore.

She raised her head and met his gaze with eyes the color of crystal blue water as she skimmed her tongue over parted lips.

His eyes narrowed on her mouth, his breath stalling at the temptation to replace her tongue with his. . . .

She swallowed and pressed her lips together.

Hell.

He flipped the offending long strand of hair

over her shoulder and jerked his hands away.

She lowered her head and began to wind faster. The ridiculous hat she sported—for whatever reason he could not guess—slipped to the side of her head. She didn't bother to right it.

A hard tremble jolted through him from belly to chest as the feather swayed over his nipples. "Bloody feather," he said in a whispered croak, and nudged her head a few more inches away, fighting the urge to push her away entirely and throttle her in the process.

A sigh trembled from her lips as she gave her head a little shake, dislodging the hat altogether. It fell to the floor and remained there.

With a final wrap and tug, she took his hand and placed it over the top of the binding to hold it in place. Her fingers were warm, gentle as they brushed his side just above the bandage. He clenched his fists at his sides, denying the sudden need to hold her hands against him, to feel them move over him . . . all over him.

"I believe this will keep you comfortable," she finally said as she tore the long tail of linen in half and quickly wrapped the two ends in opposite directions, then tied them securely at his side. "Will this knot get in your way?" she asked.

He glanced down at the flat knot, at her hands adjusting it this way and that. Nice hands, with long fingers and short nails and a good bit of character in the dry skin and the calluses on the sides of her pinkies and forefingers.

"No, it will not be in my way," he said, surprised to hear the sound of his voice in the silent room. He turned his head toward Gwyneth and Whitmore at the realization that they had been quiet for some time now.

They were unabashedly staring at him as if he were an oddity to be gaped over. Daisy sat with tilted head, regarding him with somber eyes.

As Gavan fixed them with a cold glare, Whitmore arched a brow and grinned with the portion of his mouth that was not split and swollen. Gwyneth favored him with a sweet smile that portended pure mischief.

Priscilla continued to fuss with the knot.

He stepped away from her with a jerk and took the few steps back to the table as fast as he could. "The knot is quite comfortable," he said tersely, and reached for his shirt. "Perfect, in fact," he added, as she eyed it dubiously. "To disturb it further would be to damage a work of art."

She dragged her attention away from his side and favored him with an ingenuous smile. "You really think so?" she said, as if her entire state of well-being depended on the answer. "Surely you exaggerate, sir."

A quick wit, he thought, *as well as impertinent.*

She inhaled sharply, as if catching herself in some unacceptable act. "I suppose it will do," she said as she gave the knot one last lingering examination. "Yes, it is quite . . . adequate."

"Thank you," he said simply, hoping it would put an end to the matter.

She blew upward at a stray lock falling over

her forehead and hastened to the chair on the other side of the table, leaving the hat lying ignored on the floor. "Willie, are you quite all right now?"

"My pride is far more battered than my person," Whitmore replied dryly. "I should have been able to flatten that puny blighter."

"Good. Now that you and Lord St. Aldan are taken care of, you will please tell me what this is about," she said haltingly as she firmly fixed her attention on her brother.

Finally, she asked. Gavan's thought was quickly chased by confirmation of his earlier observation. Miss Whitmore calculated everything even, it seemed, inquiries into why her brother and his companions arrived looking as if they'd been in a tavern brawl—

"I collect that you were in a brawl?" Miss Whitmore continued.

"Of course," Gavan said with a straight face. "We thought it would break the monotony of the journey." He rolled his eyes as she appeared to consider the logic of his statement.

"We were attacked!" Gwyneth said with an indignant glare at Gavan. "Right out in the open, not a day's ride from here."

"The oldest trick in the world," Whitmore said. "Appeared to be in trouble with a phaeton broken down in the middle of the road. Should have known that men dressed so roughly wouldn't own a phaeton."

"But it was a very old phaeton, William," Gwyneth argued. "It did not surprise me a bit that it had broken down, and that poor man looked near death."

Whitmore smiled indulgently at Gwyneth. "We had no choice but to stop. Either that or mow them all down." He sprawled back in the chair and stretched out his legs with a relieved sigh. "We gave them a good fight all the same."

"Yes, you did," Gwyneth said. "And while half their number—why there must have been more than a dozen of them—"

"There were eight," Gavan said to the ceiling as he pulled on his shirt.

Gwyneth fluttered her hand. "Yes, well, eight or a dozen, they were very large men, quite frightening. While they were engaged with you, Gavan, our driver, and the postilions the others were ripping through the coach, searching, for what I cannot say."

"I would imagine they were searching for Myrddin's book," Priscilla said with a distracted air as she fussed with a bit of ribbon on her table. "In his last letter to me, Willie said that it was quite valuable—"

Gavan shot her a sharp look, amazed that she would think of what they had all missed in the frenzy of the attack and beyond. Did she miss nothing?

"The book!" Gwyneth exclaimed after a stunned pause, her hand flying to her mouth as she jumped to her feet and averted her suddenly flushed face. "Oh dear heaven, we must see if they got the book!" She ran to the door and pulled it open.

Cursing, Whitmore struggled to his feet.

Cursing more vehemently, Gavan strode out behind them in his shirtsleeves, Daisy trotting gracefully at his heel. How could any of them have forgotten the damned book? It had been the bane of his existence for four days—a bane he'd planned to eliminate at first opportunity. He wondered if it was too much to ask that their attackers had done the job for him.

It was pitch dark outside, a heavy mantle of clouds obscuring moon and stars, rendering his sister and Whitmore nothing more than shadows moving in the night. Gwyneth brushed the driver away and lunged into the coach. Clothing flew as she tossed her portmanteau out the door, then his.

"William, where did you hide it?" Gwyneth cried frantically.

"Right there. I tore open a seam in the cushions and slid it inside, then sewed it shut again."

"You *sew?*" Gwyneth asked as she continued to search the cushions, barring the entrance to the coach with her body.

Gavan reached inside the coach, grasped his sister's waist, and hauled her out, then groaned at the sharp stab in his ribs. "You will go inside now," he ordered around a gasp. "I will search for the book as soon as someone has the presence of mind to bring out a"—he sensed a presence by his side, caught the sweet strawberry scent, and blinked at the sudden illumination of the yard—"light."

"I lit the lantern hanging by the door," Priscilla said, "and brought you another." Without ceremony, she handed the light to him and hurried to the other side of the coach. "William, you are in no condition, and someone must keep Lady Gwyneth inside. Lord St. Aldan and I will find the book and bring it to you."

"Not if I can help it," Gavan muttered under his breath. If the book was to be found, he would reduce it to ash before it caused any more trouble. It had evidently been the reason for Owan's murder and the earlier attack on Whitmore. Now his sister's life had been put in danger because of the damned book. All of their lives might have been forfeit for what would likely turn out to be a piece of nonsense. Prophecies indeed. Life would happen as it would without the ramblings of an old Druid who had fancied himself a wizard . . . if he had even existed.

His eyes narrowed as Gwyneth left the coach and urged Whitmore into the cottage without a single whimper of protest. And was it his imagination or had the flush on her face turned to red blotches—a sure sign that she was fibbing about something?

He might have worried about that if Priscilla hadn't immediately approached the open door of the coach and prepared to climb in, effectively banishing all thoughts with her strawberry scent and golden hair looking like a halo in the light of the lantern. "Do you know what it looks like?" she asked absently.

"Like a book, I should imagine," he said unable to resist the temptation. Without ceremony, he eased past her and climbed in, leaving no room for her to maneuver. He didn't want her inside, brushing against him, filling every breath with her scent. Nor did he want her to witness him sitting down inside to catch a breath and beat back the pain in his ribs. He damn sure didn't want her to discover the book and hand it over to her brother.

If their attackers hadn't found it, then Gavan would make bloody certain that Whitmore and Gwyneth believed they had.

It was gone.

Gavan found nothing but the odd bit of clothing scattered by the criminals in their search. He'd even extended his hand all the way inside the upholstery of the seats on the chance that the book had slid deeper into the padding during the journey.

Backing out of the coach, he stepped down and brushed horsehair and wool from his hands and sleeves . . . and collided with Priscilla.

She stumbled backward, and the lantern fell from her hold with a spatter and hiss into the puddle as she began a swift descent into the mud left by the rain earlier in the day.

He turned to catch her and yanked her to her feet, the momentum slamming her against his chest. Air whooshed out of him as pain immobilized him.

"Oh, I am so sorry," she said breathlessly.

He bit back a scathing reply and willed calm. Why didn't she leave? Why did she continue to stare up at him, as if he were a specimen she had never seen before? He realized that she had little choice. He was still holding her close, her hips pressed against his, her breasts flattened against his chest.

His hands tightened on her waist, a small waist. His thumbs brushed her rib cage, which flared up into generous breasts still pressed against him. Her hips were more than a suggestion beneath the sides of his fingers.

His body stirred and began to rise in hope.

He swallowed and told himself that the only hope he entertained was for his sanity to return.

He forced his fingers to open, to release her, forced his feet to carry him back, out of reach, forced his mouth to do something other than anticipate the feel and taste of hers.

"Go inside," he said, meaning it to be harsh, surprised that it was gentle.

She tilted her head, her hair tumbling around her shoulders in wild curls gleaming silver in the waxing moonlight. "Yes," she said, and smiled, an angel's smile hinting of secrets untold.

"Tell them that the book is not here." Still he could not look away from her.

"No, not the book," she agreed softly, and turned away, leaving her thoughts unspoken.

Yet he heard it as a sigh on the night air rustling through the trees, a suggestion that perhaps something else was to be found . . . something far more compelling.

Idiocy. Raking his hand through his hair, he nodded at the driver and strode toward the house. The only thing compelling him was his desire to forget the damned book and escape the clutches of the mad hatter.

Chapter 5

He had to find the book. He could not rely on hirelings again.

His men had failed. The perfect opportunity to take the book, and they had lost it. It should have been simple, with the earl's party reinforced only by a driver and two postilions. Eight men against five and one fluff-brained woman.

He paced the length of his room at the inn, mentally comparing it to the spaciousness and rich appointments of his own home. A home far more fine than he had expected in a place as provincial as Snowdonia, though he had quickly reached the conclusion that men of his station were treated so well in recompense for the paganism to which the natives clung in spite of their attendance to his teachings on Sundays.

Their gifts aside, he would take their legends and myths and sorcerers and destroy them for the greater good. And then he would convince them that such abominations had never existed. Men were ever reluctant to perpetuate faith without proof that it was justified.

But he knew better, and someday they would, too. Someday, when their heathen ways faded beyond memory and their heathen language died from lack of use.

He had to find the book.

He stopped dead in the center of the small parlor attached to his room. His men had searched bags and trunks in the boot of the carriage and the occupants themselves—all the obvious places one would carry a book if it were not valuable. But this discovery meant fame and fortune for Whitmore. It meant the turning of legends into history and a truth that would deny mankind its ultimate salvation.

For the villagers, it meant something evil and sinister. They would go back to their magic and pagan rituals. They would abandon all the promise he and others like him had brought to them in favor of immediate gratification. The evil would spread and destroy them all. They would turn their backs on the gentle faith he brought them and embrace what they could see and touch and hold.

No! They would not. They were *his* flock, and he would keep them safe and if a few others suffered, so be it.

He would find the book.

And in the end the people would rejoice for the victory he would secure for them.

Priss sat at the far end of the plank table in her kitchen, as far away from her brother and his guests as she could without eating her sup-

per in the yard. Never had she felt so lost and
lonely as she began to feel the ordinary sensations of warmth from the fireplace and ov-
ens, smell the rich aroma of stew and fresh
bread, hear and comprehend the conversation
of the others as they bemoaned the loss of the
book and how to find it again.

At the moment, she couldn't care about the
book. Not with the earl sitting across the table
from her, watching her intently beneath half-
lowered lids. She could barely speak properly,
much less trust herself to make it out of the
kitchen without mishap.

Something had happened to her, as she'd
bound the earl's ribs and later stood within his
hold with no thought of moving away. For
that one single flicker of a moment outside,
she'd felt a sense of rightness and well-being
so complete that she hadn't dared to breathe
or to move for fear of losing it. Even the earl's
abrupt dismissal of her hadn't shaken it loose.
Somewhere deep inside her, the feeling clung,
flaring with warmth and vitality every time
she looked at the earl or heard his voice or
simply thought of him.

It was just awareness of a woman for a man.
She'd felt something like it before. Yet, it
hadn't been quite the same. This went deeper,
so deep that she couldn't grasp it, as if there
was a part of herself she didn't know. As if all
the truths she'd established for herself and her
life were incomplete, and she'd been fooling
herself during all the long years of discovering
what she wanted, and finding where she be-

longed, and building her life on those foundations of belief.

She couldn't like the earl for that. Nor could she like him for his cavalier attitude about the disappearance of Willie's book.

She forced the thought forward, needing to think of something else, something tangible. She shouldn't mourn the gradual shrinking of that special feeling, but welcome it. It *had* been simple attraction coupled with the anxiety of seeing her brother hurt. Who wouldn't respond to the earl's presence? She doubted she'd be considered normal if she hadn't expelled a few sighs over him . . . over his touch.

Balance returned gradually as the conversation began to make sense to her. Willie was speculating on the effectiveness of hiring Bow Street Runners to find the culprit who had stolen the book.

"And where would they search?" the earl asked.

"In St. Aldan North, where it all began," Gwyneth said hotly.

The earl's eyes clouded with a bleakness that added humanity to his otherwise indifferent manner. But then it was gone, and Priss could not be sure she had seen it at all.

"Let it go, Whitmore," the earl said flatly. "It obviously *is not* meant to be, contrary to my sister's belief. Find fame and fortune elsewhere."

A scathing reply leaped to Priss's lips—further evidence that she had returned to herself. Quick retorts were always leaping to her tongue whether she welcomed them or not. It had taken her years to cultivate the art of thinking before speaking, an art that she employed now by choking her words down with a hasty bite of fresh bread. Willie could take care of himself.

"Do not dare to suggest such a thing," Gwyneth said, her entire countenance bristling. "William has no desire to profit from his discovery, and you know it. He searches only for personal enlightenment."

"Quite noble to be sure," the earl said gravely, with an exasperated glance at his sister. "I meant no offense."

"None taken," Willie said absently.

"I'm so sorry, Willie," Priss said. "I know how much that book meant to you. I would have liked to see it myself."

Or perhaps not, she thought, as a strange quiver raced up her spine. Perhaps it was better to forget the book. What good would it do her to know that magic truly was real? And there would be other finds for Willie. Gwyneth would continue to believe in the legend she'd related at the beginning of the meal. The earl would go away. . . .

And Priscilla could settle back into the safety of her assumptions that if magic and true love did exist, they were not meant to exist in her life.

"We will retrieve it," Gwyneth said firmly. "There is no question."

"God forbid," the earl said. "It's better this way," he added with a firmness that suggested a conceit so vast he could not imagine ever being wrong.

"It is not better," Gwyneth insisted. "We were meant to have the book, Gavan. Our ancestor left it for us."

"I seriously doubt that Myrddin existed, much less that he was our ancestor."

"No? Then pray tell me why we and all of our lands carry the name of his mother?"

The earl's mouth quirked only enough to convince Priss that he was capable of producing an expression other than boredom or mockery or hauteur. "I daresay we carry the name of someone's mother," he said with a trace of wryness. "And you know that the prefix of St. was added by a later and most pious ancestor to show that our name had no connection to Myrddin or his mother. In any case, it is inconsequential. The book is gone, and I, for one, see that as a blessing. It saves me the trouble of disposing of it—"

"How can you even think of doing such a thing?" Gwyneth cried. "It would be a crime to—"

"My point precisely," Gavan said harshly. "Quite enough crime has been committed already over that piece of tripe. And I do not need our people running about the countryside in white robes chanting absurd spells and performing meaningless rituals. They will be too tired to work the next day, and we will have to allow the miners to come in to improve our economy—"

"I've heard it all before," Gwyneth snapped. "We can take care of our own. We do not need outsiders coming in to spoil the land and promise riches to the people, then leave it again when the minerals are gone. I have no idea how you can know such a thing would happen. Our history wants preserving as much as the land, and surely the earth's riches are infinite—"

"Like the supply of wood is infinite?" Gavan asked, a light sparking in his eyes. "Is that why we now send to America for lumber? Because our trees instantly replace themselves when we cut them down?"

Priss leaned forward and offered Daisy a tidbit of meat. "I cannot imagine that things such as trees and minerals last any longer than civilizations," she mused.

The earl's gaze shot to her, his brows rising, as if she had either said something incredibly profound or incredibly stupid.

Yet as he continued to regard her, his gaze began to smolder with reminders of what had happened outside. Reminders she didn't want, of dropping the lantern and forgetting everything—the driver and footmen and two postilions, the fine, mud-spattered coach and cattle and the circumstances under which her visitors had arrived. Forgetting everything but him.

At least she'd had the presence of mind to send Jenny out to tend the bruises of the earl's men and situate them in the groom's quarters next to the modest stable Priss had added on to her property. Dimly, she heard the voices of Willie and his companions swirl around her as she fed one bite after another to the earl's dog. Daisy, he'd called her—a ridiculous name for such a noble beast—

The sudden silence captured her attention.

Lifting her gaze, she smiled apologetically at her brother's quizzical gaze, opened her mouth to apologize for her inattention at Gwyneth's amused smile, and snapped it shut again at the earl's impassive glare, though how he could glare and be impassive at the same time was beyond her ability to explain.

Willie cleared his throat. "I believe that Lord St. Aldan wishes you to cease feeding his dog from the table, Priss."

She snatched her hand away before Daisy could take the morsel of bread from her fingers. "Oh . . . you have but to say so, my lord."

"I did . . . twice," he said flatly. "Daisy gets a special mixture of grains and meat."

"Then I apologize," she said, and immediately removed her gaze from his, not at all liking the way every acknowledgement of his presence—by looking at him or listening to his voice made her feel as if she were floating in the ether with only him as her companion.

"I told Gwyneth and Lord St. Aldan that they were welcome here," Willie said, jarring her back to earth most unpleasantly.

She breathed deeply and forced her mind to form the proper response rather than blurt the first thing that hopped onto her tongue. She wanted to refuse, to make any excuse, transparent or otherwise. She would never manage with the earl within sight and sound . . . and reach. "Of course, Willie," she heard herself reply. "The cottage is as much your home as mine, and with fifteen rooms we shouldn't be at all cramped. I've never understood why they call this a cottage when it is so large. Why, in the islands a cottage is only one or two rooms . . . sometimes three. . . ." Realizing she was babbling, she trailed off and mentally went over which bedchambers were aired and made up and which were stuffed to the rafters with materials for her hats, as well as the things she'd never gotten around to putting away when she'd moved into the cottage.

"Oh, one or two rooms here would be considered a hut or a hovel," Gwyneth explained helpfully. "Though the ones at St. Aldan are very well constructed and appointed in spite of the images one conjures at the name."

The earl turned his chair enough to allow him to stretch out his legs, then stared at the ceiling in a display of aggrieved indulgence Priss could not like. It presented an image of him she did not want to have. An image of a man who plainly adored his sister and would grant her anything within his power and beyond.

A kind, gentle man.

More fantasy. He was cold and stiff with conceit, thinking that anything he decreed was right for everyone.

"I fear we must accept your hospitality for tonight, Miss Whitmore," Gavan said as if she were on the ceiling rather than across from him. "Tomorrow, I will see about letting a town house so that Gwyneth and I can be closer to the entertainments of the Little Season."

"Whyever should we do that?" Gwyneth asked with a blink. "We are far safer here than out about in the city, and there is still the book to consider—"

"The book is gone," Gavan said tightly, "and therefore the danger is gone." He shifted to regard his sister with a look of cold, unyielding steel. "Since we are here, I will arrange to find a male suitable to breed with Daisy, and we will attend the Little Season, where I might endeavor to find a wife...." His mouth flattened as if he were annoyed by his contribution to the discussion.

"... suitable to breed with you?" Priss finished, outraged that he would speak of dogs and wives and entertainments in the same breath.

His expression darkened into a frown of disapproval as his brows snapped together in startlement at her retort.

She didn't care. This was the man over whom she had almost lost her composure and restraint. That he would speak so casually of finding a wife only an hour after staring at her as if he would kiss her senseless with the slightest provocation increased her ire and unfortunately added hurt to the turmoil.

But he hadn't kissed her. He'd sent her inside as if she were a naughty child.

She felt like a mongrel who had been rejected out of hand. She'd proved it with her improper remark about breeding. Before she could utter another thoughtless piece of nonsense, she popped the last of her bread into her mouth.

"A wife?" Gwyneth scoffed. "Better you

search for love, for you will find no one suitable without it."

Again bleakness flickered in the earl's eyes, quickly replaced by scorn. "I haven't a lifetime to spare searching for such a fickle and unreasonable emotion."

Priss almost envied him his certainty.

Gwyneth shook her head, as if the subject wearied her. "Yes, well, my life will not be complete until I see you choke on your cynicism. Nevertheless, I prefer to remain here," she added with a firmness of tone and purpose that mirrored those of her brother. "I have no desire to hobnob with polite society—you know how I hated the crush and the posturing during my Season. I would much rather spend the time with Priscilla; she and I are going to get along famously with one another, I can tell. In any case, I have not packed the proper attire." She nodded triumphantly.

Gavan's brows snapped together in consternation, as if the idea that he had overlooked such an important detail was beyond his ken. "We will obtain what we need in the shops," he said firmly.

Gwyneth sagged in obvious dismay.

"Only if you plan to remain for the entire Season," Priss blurted without thinking. "Even if you pay an exorbitant sum, it will take a modiste more than a week to assemble a suitable wardrobe, and I daresay it is the same with the tailors. They are extremely busy at the moment."

His frown returned and deepened into a

fierce scowl as he mumbled something under his breath. A curse most likely.

Priss reached for another slice of bread and concentrated on smearing butter over every crumb.

Gwyneth immediately brightened. "How provincial we are," she chirped happily. "It has been so long since we ventured from our tower, we have no conception of what goes on in the outside world."

"It's a bit more than a tower, Gwyneth," Willie said with his usual attention to detail. "More like a kingdom in itself, complete with ancient castle, even more ancient villages, and a society that is almost completely dependent upon itself. Why even the name invokes visions of isolation and dragons sleeping beneath the dungeons."

The description awakened in Priss old dreams of heroes and knights and noble quests, none of which she cared to entertain.

"I don't believe we have any dragons in our history," Gwyneth said absently, "but our ancestor, Myrddin, did wake a pair of them once."

It seemed to Priss that St. Aldan had a very live dragon in the form of its master.

The earl's mouth curled upward in a slight smile as he regarded his sister with a look of wry fondness and something else that resembled grief, though it was too fleeting for Priss to be sure. "No dragons," he said, and rose. "Though after several days of careening over hill and dale in that coach, I will become one if I do not get a proper night's rest."

Confused, Priss glanced from the earl to his sister and then to Willie. What on earth was going on? Not a single thing had been resolved except that she would have unwanted houseguests for the night. *One* unwanted guest, she amended. Gwyneth was welcome as long as she wished to remain. In fact, Priss would love to know the earl's sister better. Gwyneth's quirky nature and open manner were quite appealing, and Priss rarely had the pleasure of another woman's company. And since it appeared that something was brewing between Willie and Gwyneth, she really ought to learn more about her.

"Miss Whitmore," the earl said, startling her, "I am most appreciative of your kind invitation, though it must seem otherwise to you."

"Yes, it most certainly does," she said, and wanted to stuff her napkin into her mouth. His attempt at graciousness was too impressive for her to resort to rudeness.

Apparently his overbearing lordship agreed. His gaze found hers, brows arched and mouth pressed into a flat line of yet more disapproval.

"I will have Jenny show you to your rooms," she said weakly, unable to bring herself to offering an apology for telling the truth.

"No need, Priss," Willie said. "I'll do it. Which rooms have a clear path to the beds?"

"Oh, the ones past yours." She grinned at him, sharing a long-standing jest. "I have not yet made my way that far."

"William told me all about your rooms,"

Gwyneth said as she rose from the table and took Willie's arm. "He said that one must approach them as if one were on a treasure hunt in a barrel of litter."

"Yes, he has ever bemoaned my lack of order," Priss admitted with a chuckle.

"What I cannot fathom is how Priss can find the smallest thing in her clutter in a matter of minutes when I'm sure I couldn't find an elephant if it were standing in the middle and trumpeting at its loudest."

"I told you that it is organized clutter, Willie," Priss said as she took his other arm. "The only time I can't find anything is after I have attempted to straighten it all to fit yours and Mother's conception of order." She strolled, three abreast, with Willie and Gwyneth, from the kitchen into her workroom, leaving the earl to bring up the rear with his dog.

Halfway across, she lowered her arms to her sides as she halted and stared down at the floor. Lady Marton's half-finished hat lay amidst a scattering of pins, the brim bent from the weight of a foot, the bird collapsed on its side atop the crown of the hat. The feather languished a few inches away, broken in the middle.

She raised her hand to her mouth as she stared blindly at the remains, at the bird that wobbled, fell off its felt perch, and slowly rolled against a large, booted foot.

Oh dear heaven, the hat she'd held on to all during George's amorous assaults was lying forgotten on the floor of her workroom. Worse, she'd impatiently brushed the hat from her head while binding the earl's ribs, then promptly forgotten all about it. At the time, she'd barely noticed what she was doing—cruel proof that the earl had made her forget herself, as well as everything else of significance. But now, the import of her actions struck her like a blow from behind and left her reeling. She didn't want to contemplate what it might mean, much less face the earl just then. She didn't want to face him again ... ever. To avoid looking up from his fine boots, over impressive thighs, narrow hips, and the chest that had already disturbed her more than enough for a lifetime, she quickly bent over to retrieve the hat, thinking to place it back on her head and pretend it had been there all along.

His hand collided with hers as he reached down to retrieve it. Her gaze raced to his as his breath hissed out and his hand shook. His face paled; his eyes clouded with pain.

Immediately, she straightened and reached for his arm to help him rise. "You must remember your ribs," she admonished, as the hat fell from her fingers.

"I am fine," he said hoarsely.

"The only thing about you that is fine is your pride," she snapped, and took his arm, helping him rise whether he liked it or not. If he didn't soon get out of her sight, she would likely forget her own name.

With a swift kick to the side, she sent the hat skimming across the floor and hastened to join Willie and Gwyneth at the foot of the stairs. To perdition with the dratted hat.

Abruptly she halted to fetch candles from a side table situated along one wall of the entry . . . and collided with the earl yet again—a comedy of errors she could not appreciate. "I'm sorry," she said simply, and wondered what exactly the apology covered.

"Are you indeed?" he asked, seeming as if he would say more. Instead, he took a candle from her unresisting fingers, brushed past Willie and Gwyneth, and climbed the stairs, only to pause at the landing and toss an inquiring glance at her over his shoulder, Daisy standing patiently by his side.

What now? she wondered. Could he not just leave her sight without all the fits and starts? She needed him to disappear, to leave her in peace to gather the tattered remains of her composure.

"The last room on the left," Willie directed.

Priss said a silent prayer of thanks that her bedchamber was on the ground floor next to her workroom, at the opposite end of the cottage. At least she would not hear the evidence of his presence in her home through the walls, or, heaven forbid, bump into him in the morning before she had fully emerged from the dregs of sleep.

The earl did not move as he stood high above her in a wide-legged and most commanding stance. "It occurs to me that you might not wish to have a dog as a guest," he addressed the air over her head. "Daisy can sleep in your stable, if you prefer."

"I wouldn't dream of sending a well-behaved creature like *Daisy* to the stables . . ."

Her voice trailed off as she realized what she'd said and how it must sound.

The earl's brows rose, and again his mouth twitched. She didn't bother to see more and tossed a frantic glance at Willie.

Her brother pursed his lips in a silent whistle and fixed his gaze on the wall. No aid from that quarter.

Gwyneth chuckled. "Good for you, Priss—may I call you Priss? You see, Gavan, I've told you we need to go out and about more often. I am taking liberties with our hostess's name and you have been a bit . . . well . . . like yourself when the miners are threatening to invade our district." She leaned conspiratorially toward Priss. "He takes being lord of all he surveys quite to heart you see, which is necessary for a man with his responsibilities." She spread her arms wide and lifted her gaze to empty air. "But alas, my dear brother leaves home so seldom and takes his duties so seriously that he thinks he is lord of all he surveys no matter where he stands."

Dropping her arms, she again leaned toward Priss. "I do hope you will make allowances. I assure you he is quite tame and behaves as he does in an effort to take care of *everyone* he surveys. I swear he must have been born like this. His sense of duty even extended to changing my bands after our mother died in childbirth and to raising me after our father sank into one bottle after another when we were still children. Poor father," she sighed, "I have never been able to understand what sent him into such a tragic state, which

I believe led to his death a few years later. Gavan knows, I am certain, but he will not speak of it. He is quite protective of me, you see, and likely thinks the truth will send me into a decline."

"Gwyneth." It sounded like a growl, yet not of menace. It was too low, and spiced with a tone holding more love than censure. She turned toward him, just barely managing to press her lips together to keep from laughing at the crimson flagging his haughty cheekbones.

His glower might have been frightening if his lips weren't twitching. "One more word, sister, and I will relate to all who will listen one or more of your lamentable habits."

"Well, I'm certain you would never tell anyone such a thing," Gwyneth said with a sniff and a twinkle in her eye. "Besides, I've already told William about my lamentable habits. He assures me that we all have them and must adapt."

Priss absorbed the conversation in dismay. How easily the earl fell into banter with his sister. How human he seemed. How sweet and tender. She didn't want to know that about him even if he only brought such qualities out of the cupboard for Gwyneth.

She really did want him to be his overbearing lordship, so she could dismiss him from her mind. At the moment she would settle for dismissing him from the room before she acquired any more flattering revelations about him.

Chapter 6

"**I** suppose I should warn you about Gavan," Willie said as he sprawled in the chair, a large cat draped over his lap. He'd sought Priss out only moments after she had tossed out hurried "good nights" to her guests and escaped into her workroom. Before Willie had even settled, Precious had appeared from wherever he'd been hiding to receive the strokes due him from one of his favorite humans.

Though Willie's expression was more serious than she would like, his appearance for one of their late-evening chats reassured her that some things never changed. It might even convince her that the sense that she had changed in some indefinable way owed more to the hectic schedule she kept just prior to and during the Season than to the presence of a man too handsome and intriguing for her own good.

"No, you shouldn't," she said, diverting from asking how he came to address the earl by his given name. She really couldn't care less. In any case, she needed no warnings about the earl. Her own instincts provided more than enough portents of doom where he was concerned.

All that Willie had told her in the last two hours was disturbing enough. He had recited the St. Aldan legend—though she had the feeling that he had omitted a detail or two—related how he and Gwyneth had developed "an extreme fondness" for one another, and given a full accounting of murder, mayhem, and mishaps since discovering what he termed "the greatest find of the century." What else could he tell her that would cause her any more alarm?

"Gwyneth thinks that Gavan is the chosen one as foretold in the legend," Willie said.

"I'm very happy for him."

"After Gwyneth met you she became convinced that you are the one meant to be his salvation."

Something rather startling trembled through her at that. Something so ridiculous that it did not deserve comment. "I've noticed that she has a talent for high drama."

"Yes, well, I'm not in the habit of entertaining legends and fables as anything more than a source of amusement. Historic research has yet to prove a single legend I've ever heard." He poured another draught of brandy into his glass. "But in this case, I must admit to having some doubts. Murder and assault are *not* amusing." His voice hardened, revealing the Willie who had traveled the world and endured—and overcome—unimaginable dangers and hardships in his quest for both wealth and historical truth. For all his placid manner, he was not a man to cross.

"Forget the book, Willie," she said, in honor of the fears lurking in the back of her mind since his arrival that afternoon. "It is not worth any life, much less yours."

"Yes, well, I'm afraid it is no longer that simple, Priss." He drained his glass and set it down on the table at his elbow. "We must find whoever attacked us, and the only way to do that is to know what is contained in the book."

"But it is lost," she reminded him, "and one can only assume in the hands of the criminal who accosted you."

"It is lost, I agree, but I am not at all convinced that it is in the hands of a criminal. I did not observe any sense of triumph in our attackers; nor did I see any of them with the book as they ran off."

She stifled a most unladylike exclamation. Her brother was entirely too observant for her peace of mind, and if he did not see his attackers carry off the book, then they most likely hadn't. For that matter, the earl had appeared to disbelieve their success as well. He had seemed quite bothered that he had not found the book. Another path she did not want to explore. It would help if the earl did not keep popping up in the forefront of her thoughts.

"Willie, you are not leaving this house," she said, knowing all too well how his mind worked.

" 'Fraid so, love. Unless I find the book still

in the coach, though since you were with Gavan the entire time he searched, I can neither hope that he overlooked the book, nor can I suspect that he destroyed it as he has often threatened. Besides, if Gavan had disposed of the book, he would have said so. I've never known a man so certain about himself."

Neither had Priss, though a few hours was hardly enough time to reach such a conclusion.

Leaning over, he smoothed his hands over the cat's silky coat. "I have to leave, Priss—the sooner, the better. Whoever overheard Gwyneth and me talking to Owan about the translation also overheard me say that I had begun copying it to prevent a lot of handling of the fragile pages—a circumstance I don't want the earl to know about for fear he would try to destroy the duplicate pages. Unfortunately, I managed to copy only a portion of it before the attacks began. Whoever is responsible for those will be after me for the pages, and I don't want to be the cause of more trouble for the St. Aldans."

"And you must also retrieve the book because it is important to Gwyneth," Priss said in a monotone. "You love her." Envy bit her deeply as she said it. Envy and happiness. Gwyneth was perfect for Willie. Her eccentricities would keep him from forgetting to live in the present. She would remind him to laugh.

It would have been nice to know what it was like to love someone suited to her. But she'd once loved the wrong man and had forsaken any hope of finding the right one.

"I love her," he said simply. "I love her enough to do whatever I must to protect her, and I have a nasty suspicion the only way to do that is to find the book and the man who is willing to kill for it, as well as have the pages I copied translated."

With a last stroke of the cat stretched out on its back, its legs straight up in the air, Willie strolled around the room. "I know you won't like this, Priss, but I have to ask you to keep Gwyneth here. Of course that means that Gavan will stay, too. He is quite primitive in his belief that no one can protect the ones he loves as well as he."

And who will protect me from the earl? Priss wondered, as panic struck her from all sides. She understood Willie's concern for Gwyneth. She also understood that to be under the same roof with Gwyneth's brother was to invite disaster . . . or heartbreak. She wasn't any good at dealing with her often unruly emotions, and the earl inspired far too many on such short acquaintance. How on earth could she avoid him on a daily basis when the slightest hint of his proximity seduced her into visions of touching him and learning him and—

No! She would not allow herself to be so bewitched by a handsome face and an impressive form. She'd been only sixteen the last time a man had affected her so strongly. She could not accept that she had learned nothing in the last eight years. Her heart was well fortified; she was certain of it.

"Priss?" Willie crooked his finger under her chin and urged her to look at him. "There is no chance that they could let a decent town house now that the Little Season has begun. The better inns will be full to the rafters as well. You live off the beaten path. Here, Gwyneth and Gavan are among friends, and Gavan can control the situation."

And me, she thought with a roll of her stomach. He was already controlling her with a word, a look, a touch.

"I'm not telling you where I'm going or why," Willie continued, as if she had agreed. "If Gwyneth had any idea, she'd hare off after me, her protective instincts flying at full mast."

"Yes, she would," Priss said weakly, knowing it was true, because she would do the same thing. A thousand protests marched through her mind, yet she could not seem to give them voice. She didn't want Willie to know how the earl affected her. How could she when her reactions continually waffled between irritation and fascination?

"It won't be for long, Priss. I promise."

"I suppose you should warn me about the earl after all," she said with a resigned sigh. Forewarned was forearmed, though how could one arm against the betrayal of one's own base nature was beyond her. She'd been trying for years and had discovered in one evening that success was assured only when tempted by the likes of Mr. George Simms.

Her brother turned back to her and grinned. "I already did, though it's more a warning about Gwyneth, I suppose. She believes without doubt or question that you are the other heir to Myrddin's legacy." Clearing his throat, he launched into a fair imitation of the music and lilt of the Welsh accent. " 'Two who are lost will be found and they will discover the joy and completion denied Myrddin and his lady.' "

His voice seemed to recede and echo as a warm frisson crept from her scalp to her toes like the foam of a wave rolling onto shore, tingling, energizing. She sank back in her chair and shivered with the sense of being outside of herself, becoming a part of something she didn't understand.

"It's wrong," she croaked. "We aren't . . . I'm not . . . *he can't be.*" That last bit startled her with its implication that she actually questioned whether it was true or not. There should be no question. Of course it wasn't true. As much as she'd like to believe in magic and legends and what was meant to be, she had enough sense to know that it was simply the illusion one wandered into to escape weariness or worry or loneliness.

"Tell Gwyneth," Willie said. "She might listen to you, though I doubt it. She has it in her head that you are wandering aimlessly in your search for love and fulfillment and that her brother *is* a lost soul."

"I have never searched for love, I am quite happily fulfilled, and it is up to the earl to decide whether he wants to be found or not," Priss retorted as her mind screamed "liar." She'd long ago come to the conclusion that one often saw love simply because one wanted to— not at all a sensible way for one's heart to conduct its affairs. Far better to allow such things to happen than to pursue them. Since the death of her father, her future had been on a steady course only because she had applied that bit of philosophy to every aspect of her life. She took each day as it came and fretted only about what she knew she could control.

"Besides, he's an earl, and I am little more than a shopkeeper," she whispered more to herself than to Willie, as if the argument she'd just waged with herself hadn't been settled at all. "It's impossible." Shaking her head, she focused on her brother and tried desperately to shake off the sudden fantasies upon which her imagination took flight.

How completely aggravating that she should entertain such fantasies even for a moment. How completely puzzling that she had. Since the disasters she'd created in the name of love years ago, she should know better than to harbor such impossible dreams, especially with regard to a man she had only just met.

"Yes, well, I can't imagine you and the earl together," Willie said. "You would likely kill one another within a week." He regarded her with a grave look that always heralded advice. "There's something between you, Priss—momentary fascination is my guess. It was as plain as day. Be careful you don't give in to it."

Momentary fascination . . . yes that had to be it. Of course it was, she thought with satisfaction. Anything momentary could be resisted until it passed. Still, she'd much rather it passed without the object of fascination underfoot. Her cottage might be very large, but the earl had a way of filling a room.

"Now you tell me," she said sourly. "After you've brought his most overbearing lordship into my home and subjected me to your intrigues. Willie, I am in the midst of the busy season for my hats—" She silenced her protests. There was no point in worrying Willie. Once he was gone, she would simply rely on the earl's nature to overrule Willie's wishes. She could not imagine that the earl would remain her guest simply because she requested it.

Willie glanced away as if uneasy. "I suppose I must confess that I've left a note under Gwyneth's door asking that she and Gavan remain here and detailing the reasons why. Gwyneth will give it to him in the morning after she finds it and will no doubt throw a tantrum if that's what it takes to make him agree."

"You wretch—" She'd seen the earl's adoration—and indulgence—for his sister. Willie was the same with her. If something was important to Priss, Willie moved heaven and earth to see she had it, which was precisely why she should do what he asked without question or argument. She should, but then again perhaps this was a good time to take advantage of her brother's indulgence of her. She could make it up to him in some other way. "Willie, I beg you to find another way . . . *please*. If they remain here, I daresay Gwyneth will be the only one not driven to dementia. And as you said, the earl and I would likely kill one another within the week."

"I am hoping I will be gone only a week—a fortnight at most." Willie shrugged. "Just go about your business and keep them well fed. Judging from Gavan's reactions to you, I imagine he would like to avoid you as much as you wish to avoid him." He tossed a grin over his shoulder as he pulled the door open. "Gwyneth would say that ignorance is indeed bliss, and I daresay you and Gavan both have a wish to court ignorance regarding one another at this point. I'll try to get word to you." He slipped outside, leaving his ludicrous advice to linger in the air.

Avoid the earl? He was far too overwhelming to ignore.

"Be safe, Willie," Priss murmured in the sudden silence and stared blindly at the hat lying so forlornly on the table, at the bird she'd fashioned so painstakingly from cloth and feathers and which looked quite as wretched as Precious had after becoming caught in the rain and falling into the mud in his mad dash back to the house.

She poked at the remains, then circled the room, ferreting out furbelows from cupboards and shelves that she might use to salvage her creation, then sat at her table and added them to the piles assembled in the order in which she would use them. She would go about her business, she told herself firmly. Only the bare minimum of politeness would be required. Surely the earl and his sister would understand her need to work long hours at this time of year. She would repair the bird and revive

Lady Marton's hat and then begin another. All would be well.

She was *definitely* all right and would continue to be so. She'd not had company for a very long time. Her home was not the usual shelter for nobility. Of course she was rattled, and her mouth had run away with her more than once. The earl invited plain speaking. Unfortunately, her speaking was usually careless and often silly, but if she were very inventive, she could convince herself that falling so easily into her habit of speaking without thinking was understandable. The circumstances were quite out of the ordinary.

The man was quite out of the ordinary....

The man, she reminded herself, would be underfoot for as long as she could keep him here, she thought irritably as she vowed to establish limits on what she would do for her brother in future. Really, Willie was asking too much . . . and he knew it, which emphasized the seriousness of the situation regarding the dratted book. No wonder belief in magic had died out. It created entirely too much trouble in one way or another.

She and the earl indeed. Such a thing would turn the devil to prayer. Gwyneth was as balmy as the earl was arrogant.

She closed her eyes and sent a fervent prayer upward that Willie would return soon. Very soon.

Until then she would simply have to be more cautious about what she said and did. No more long stares at the earl. No more unwanted impressions of his better nature. No more admiring his face and form, or speaking without laying a great deal of thought in front of her words. He could be as arrogant or as engaging as he wished, and she would not allow herself to be affected one way or another. If she were very vigilant, she might survive with at least some of her dignity intact.

Chapter 7

 ~~~~~~~∽∾∾∽~~~~~~~

At least no one was present to witness his fall from dignity, Gavan thought as he rolled carefully to the edge of the mattress and slid to his knees on the floor, using the strength in his arms and the testers to pull himself to his feet. Apparently, the only way he would be able to get about without crawling on all fours was to remain mobile until his bruised ribs healed.

Every time he'd fallen asleep, he'd rolled onto his injured side and seen stars exploding behind his eyelids. He'd tried to rise in the usual manner, but he'd been lying down long enough for stiffness to seize his muscles. Straightening, he groaned as his body screamed in protest.

Perhaps a brandy would help. Surely no one would be up and about at this late hour of the night.

Miss Priscilla Whitmore was the type to have nothing more potent than elderberry wine in her cupboard. No matter. Enough of any type of spirits could induce stupor in a man.

Stupor would be nice, he decided. At least he would be oblivious to the thoughts of Miss Whitmore that lay in wait at every turn of his mind. If fortune were with him, he might remain insensible enough not to notice her at all. Whitmore could pour him into the coach tomorrow, and once he and Gwyneth were settled at an inn, she could nurse him back to sobriety.

With painstaking care, he reached for his trousers and eased them on—not a simple feat while standing and holding on to a tester for balance. Sleeping unclothed had not been particularly brilliant. But then he always slept unclothed, and he had been relatively limber when he'd undressed.

Sighing with relief, he secured the fastenings, groped for a clean shirt in his bag, and managed to pull it on. After what seemed like hours, he left his bedchamber and felt his way down the darkened hall to the stairs. The last thing he wanted was to awaken anyone in the household, particularly the mistress.

The mistress—a misnomer to be sure. Miss Whitmore needed a keeper.

He refused to acknowledge that the position enticed him with some rather provocative images of how he would "keep" her.

He reached the bottom of the stairs without mishap, grateful that said mistress confined her clutter to certain rooms of the cottage. If the other bedchambers Whitmore had spoken of were anything like her workroom, one could fall down, break his neck, and rot before someone stumbled over the corpse.

He abruptly halted and bit back a curse at the light pouring from the open door leading into the workroom.

She sat at her worktable, her chin propped on her hands, regarding the silly toy bird perched on a jumble of whatever, as if it were sharing secrets with her. She still wore the smock, and her hair was wound in a disheveled bun atop her head. He blinked at the sight of a black cat draped across her shoulders and purring so loudly he could hear it from the hall.

And so the source of the hairs on her smock was solved. Of course it would be a black cat. How could he have imagined anything else?

"What do you think, Precious? The ostrich plume or the smaller feathers layered upon one another?"

He squinted to focus on the thing in front of her and discerned the tattered body of the hat. To her left sat the plume, still sadly broken in the middle. Beside that was pile of small feathers. "I sense that the bird and the plume have formed an attachment by now," he said, prompted by some vicious imp of mischief. "It would be a pity to separate them."

"Oh!" Her head jerked up, her gaze flying toward him as her hands pressed against her chest. In the next breath, she turned back to the hat. The cat swished its tail once and eyed him suspiciously, but did not otherwise move from its position on her shoulders.

"The ostrich plume," she said vaguely. "It was quite costly . . . no, I think it is quite beyond repair."

"I will replace it," he said as he strolled into the room, "since I am responsible for its destruction."

"It cannot be replaced; it took me days to locate one of this size." She favored him with a too-bright smile. "The hat was quite hideous in any case," she added.

"Perhaps it would better serve the birds. It would make a decent nest." He halted halfway into the room and studied the nooks and crannies spilling out all manner of lace and ribbon and renditions of nature's creatures.

Her eyes widened as she stared at him, then down at the bird. "Oh. Yes, of course. I can't imagine why I didn't think of it." Her hands fluttered over the materials set out in piles across her table in no discernible order that he could see, selecting items from one then another and creating a new pile.

Provocative hands that had drifted through his dreams with visions of erotic caresses, the callouses on her fingers a provocative texture on his chest, his belly, his—

What was he doing? He wanted a drink, not temptations involving the peculiar Miss Whitmore. "I don't suppose you have brandy."

Her brow knitted as her hands flew over the felt foundation of the hat. She hesitated so long, he wondered if the question were too difficult for her. "There . . . on the table," she said haltingly, as if she feared the wrong reply could topple nations. "Please feel free to take it to your bedchamber."

A dismissal if ever he'd heard one. Contrarily, he closed the distance to the chair and carefully reached for the half-empty decanter standing next to a used glass, indicating that either Whitmore had been here before him or Miss Whitmore was a tippler. "Have you another glass?"

"In the cupboard," she said without looking up.

He bit back a sharp remark as he glanced around. There were cupboards lining an entire wall.

"No, in the small sideboard by the window," she corrected.

Dubiously eyeing the sideboard, he waited to see if she would again change her mind. Thankfully, she said nothing more.

Having located only a crockery mug in the sideboard, he grimaced and splashed brandy into the mug, then carefully lowered himself into the only chair not occupied by clutter. At least she had good taste in brandy, he thought, as he downed half the contents of the mug in one burning swallow. This should ease the pain nicely before he consumed enough to float away in his cups.

Miss Whitmore worked on as if she were alone in the room, the silence interrupted only by small sounds of scissors snipping and thread being pulled through the heavy felt. Blond strands fell one by one over her shoulders as she bent her head and squinted at her handiwork, while she reached now and then for one bit or another from the various piles marching along the surface of the table. Not once did she remove her gaze from the monstrosity over which she labored.

Apparently she knew exactly where each item was amidst the chaos in front of her. Practice, he supposed. Either that or she had another set of eyes somewhere beneath the mounds of lush, curly hair, gleaming in the candlelight like spirals of spun gold.

Hair enough to clothe a man as she rode him in passion.

He gulped the rest of his brandy and poured more. He could take the decanter to his room as she'd suggested. Yet he remained in the chair observing her, intrigued by the dance of her hands over the feather that was magically taking shape before his eyes. A dozen other hats were scattered about the room in various stages of completion, perched on wooden models carved in the size and shape of human heads. One shelf held what appeared to be molds with felt and beaver skins draped over them and assuming the prescribed forms.

Obviously she worked very hard and did not delegate the menial tasks to underpaid workers—odd since Gwyneth had said she was quite successful. "Do you work at night often?" he asked, and wondered why.

"Often," she replied.

"I see," he said, completely at a loss and feeling suddenly and unaccountably awkward.

"You do? Wonderful. It's working then." She held up the hat and turned it for his inspection.

It looked like a bird's nest, the ostrich plume

wound into a loose coil with the stuffed bird balanced on the edge. Below, a butterfly fashioned from ribbon seemed suspended just above the brim. If the creation was what she referred to, then it definitely was working. The hat was surprisingly attractive. And whimsical. Disturbingly whimsical.

As whimsical as her expression as she arranged the hat on her head and stared intently into the looking glass propped up on the table.

"I can't imagine why I didn't think of it," she said absently as she continued to fuss with the feather, the bird, the butterfly.

A perfectionist. She would worry a thing until it was worn bare. No wonder the feather had looked so frayed earlier. But she was also gifted, as evidenced by the result of her efforts. The frayed feather and battered bird looked surprisingly nice in the new design.

And he was tipsy from lack of sleep. How a hat fashioned like a bird's nest could look nice was beyond him.

"Quite fetching," he said. It was, in fact, brilliant, considering what she'd had to work with.

She met his gaze with a pleased smile that widened her mouth and called attention to gentle lines radiating from the corners of her eyes. Smiles and laughter—neither was rare to her.

She is happy, he realized. Happy, living virtually alone on a secluded lane in the country outside London, working her fingers to calluses day and night, amidst no semblance of order, speaking very little, thinking too much, and having no vanity whatsoever.

The seclusion and work he could understand. The lack of order and her quiet, hesitant manner suggested a total absence of discipline and perhaps a calculating mind.

One absurdity piled haphazardly upon another, like the clutter in this room, he thought with disgust at his continued analysis of her character. Such attention implied interest, and nothing could be further from the truth. The sooner he escaped her company the better.

His attention snapped back to the object of his conjecture as she calmly sat on the chair behind her worktable and removed the hat. Pins flew from the bun on her crown, releasing random curly strands of long, appallingly disheveled hair. Yet it shone richly like burnished gold, obviously clean and full of health. In fact, disorder aside, everything in the room appeared quite clean.

She is an enigma. An enigma he didn't want to solve.

He had far better things with which to occupy his thoughts, namely murder and theft and the problem of convincing Gwyneth once and for all that she lived in the real world and should relegate her belief in all things mystical to the midden heap.

No doubt Miss Whitmore believed in all things mystical.

He lowered his head and breathed in the aroma of fine French brandy yet all he could smell was strawberries. Sweet, ripe strawberries, like Miss Whitmore's lips . . .

"You have no dining room," he said, grasping the first thing he could think of to divert his thoughts. He'd wondered earlier why they'd had to eat in the kitchen.

"No."

He waited for an explanation, suddenly needing to know why her house was as odd as she was. "Why?" he finally asked.

"The dining room has been the parlor since I took possession of the property."

"And where was the parlor before?" A reasonable question, though he had no hope of receiving a reasonable answer.

"This room was the parlor."

"Why did you not make the dining room into your workroom?"

"Because I wanted my bedchamber attached to my workroom."

Frowning, he glanced around, reluctant to ask the next obvious question. Spying a door, he assumed that it must lead to her bedchamber. "What was your bedchamber before you took possession?" he had to ask.

"It wasn't."

He was not going to ask. He refused to ask. "Wasn't what? A bedchamber?" Raising the mug to his lips, he again downed half the contents.

"It wasn't anything but the yard, I suppose. I had a room built on."

Deciding it would accomplish nothing but to give him a headache, he refrained from entertaining any more obvious questions. The obvious was lost on Miss Whitmore, no doubt gone straight over head and out the door. And the sooner he was out the door, the better for his sanity. He rose abruptly from the chair and stood paralyzed by a sharp stab of pain.

She sighed and set the hat aside as she rose from the table. "If you must insist on moving so carelessly, I will have to summon your sister to bully you into behaving," she said.

He favored her with his best "lord of all he surveyed" glare as he fought the urge to protest her assumption that Gwyneth bullied him. The truth was that his sister did bully him on occasion, but only because she was his sister and only when he allowed it.

"Come with me," Miss Whitmore ordered, and headed straight for the kitchen.

"I dread asking where, and why," he muttered.

"I am going to make you some special tea that will ease your muscles and help you sleep."

"No . . . thank . . . you," he gritted out, annoyed that he was following her.

"It is only tea with herbs. I am not going to drug you." She paused and tossed a glance at him over her shoulder. "I do have some laudanum if you would—"

"A frightening thought," he said dryly. "I might awaken from oblivion to find you've turned my bedchamber into a greenhouse."

"I don't think so," she said as she rummaged through the shelves in the pantry, gathering jar, crock, and small cloth bag, like a witch assembling ingredients for a potion. "I already have a greenhouse."

He groaned and pinched the bridge of his nose.

The scent of strawberries wafted in the air. He sniffed and opened his eyes. Miss Whitmore stood right in front of him, her arms full of the makings for tea, her face close as she peered up at him in concern.

"Perhaps I should make your bindings tighter."

"My bindings are fine . . . perfect." He would never survive her ministrations a second time. He wasn't certain he would survive her closeness now. Not with her beautiful eyes wide and inquiring on him and her lips parted and her breasts only a few inches from his chest. . . .

She only stood there, staring up at him.

"The tea?" he prompted.

"Yes, of course." She blinked and brushed past him, her breasts and hair grazing his arm.

His body rose at the possibilities his mind had been rejecting all evening.

"Lady Dane has greyhounds," she said as she set the ingredients in a line on the plank table just as she'd laid out her materials for the construction of the hat, her attention seeming completely focused on her task as she opened the crock and sprinkled a dash of some sort of powder into a small pot. "She told me last month that she had two grown males, one of which had sired a litter. She will have to find someone to take them in." She opened the cloth bag and pinched off a bit of what appeared to be a leaf and added it to the bowl.

Greyhounds . . . Daisy . . . he'd said he wanted

to breed her. He shook his head, horrified that he was beginning to pick up the odd threads of her conversations so easily. "I will look into it," he said gravely.

Picking up the jar, she attempted to remove the lid. Nothing happened. She situated the jar between her body and her arm and used the other hand to pull. The lid came free, the action jerking her backward against him.

He caught her with a "whoof" and held his breath as her bottom pressed against his groin. If the collision hurt his ribs, he didn't feel it, though another portion of his anatomy felt distinctly pained.

"Mint," she exclaimed, and dashed toward the door.

Cursing, he followed her outside without question. God only knew what trouble she might get into outside. Keeping her silhouette firmly in sight, he trailed her past the stables and the house where his driver and postilions were quartered and then to a building set to the side of the stables. A building made of glass and filled with shadows.

He found her bent over what appeared to be an herb garden in the greenhouse, plucking leaves from a small plant.

"Mint," she explained as she straightened. "It soothes . . ."

"God knows I could use soothing," he commented, as his eyes adjusted to the darkness. He studied his surroundings, impressed by the diversity of plants and flowers growing in pots and beds of soil set into wooden boxes.

"Oh, well then I should collect some . . ."

Her voice receded as his mind seemed to close all doors to rational thought in favor of breathing in the scent of fertile earth and the strawberry freshness of the woman in front of him. His libido responded to the sight of her bottom swaying as she again bent over to pick through the plants. He clenched his jaw against the temptation to step up behind her and again feel—

She straightened and turned . . . too close . . . dangerously close. "Do you see anything else you might like?" she asked as she swept her hand over the small garden that should not have been yielding anything at this time of year.

Perhaps she was a sorceress. It would not be difficult to believe with her smock flowing white around her like the robes of a high priestess, seducing him with the memory of the lush body he'd discerned beneath the cloth. Moonlight refracted through the glass and cast a silver aura over her wild curls, holding him in thrall. "Yes," he said hoarsely, and stepped closer to her. "I see something I must have."

She seemed incapable of movement or breath as she stood before him. "What?" she asked in a breathless whisper.

He lowered his head slowly as his hands reached for her, as he breathed deeply of her scent, as he stared at her mouth. "Strawberries . . . I want strawberries," he said softly.

She looked up at him.

He looked down at her, at her complexion glowing in the soft light, her face a beguiling play of shadows over piquant features of delicate chin and small nose . . . and wide, tempting mouth.

She seemed to grow taller—rising on her tiptoes, he realized, reaching up to him, to his mouth as her eyes drifted shut.

The night narrowed and curled into itself, enclosing them in dark velvet and sultry warmth and something he couldn't name. Something he couldn't touch or hold or see. Something that held him instead, as it whispered in a language felt rather than heard.

He lowered his head as his hand flattened over the base of her throat beneath her high collar, feeling the pulse of life speed into a beat of passion, feeling the contrast of metal, warm against her flesh and the softness of the velvet ribbon tied around her throat, feeling the intricate design of a medallion burn into his palm as his mouth closed over hers.

She sighed and trembled and whimpered as if in protest, yet her mouth accepted his, caressed his, granted his tongue entrance to taste and learn her secrets.

She was warm vibrance in his arms. She was strawberry wine to his senses.

She wrapped her arms around his neck, releasing the leaves she'd gathered. They scratched the skin at his nape, yet he didn't move, couldn't release her, couldn't stop discovering and feeling more than he thought it possible to feel.

His arms tightened around her, holding her so close not a sliver of air could pass between them, imprinting the feel and shape of her onto his body, knowing somehow that it would be with him for all time.

Nothing else came to life between them but tender exploration and the discovery that they were beyond themselves in that moment, that the world had stepped aside for this moment, that they were part of something that could not be explained—

Gavan's mind roared in protest at such unwilling, such unacceptable thoughts. He ripped his mouth from hers and felt the pain in the absence of her breath mingling with his, pain in the sudden cold in the air and the metal beneath his palm. Pain, in the return of reason when he would have lingered a while longer—

Madness. Nothing more. It was his ribs that pained him. It was the bite of autumn that chilled him. It was the stir of desire too long absent.

Lust.

Nothing more. Nothing profound. Nothing . . .

"Go inside," he said, meaning it to be harsh, surprised that it was gentle.

She tilted her head, her hair tumbling around her shoulders in wild curls. "I dropped the herbs," she said, and smiled, an angel's smile that hinted of secrets untold.

Need. He needed to know those secrets.

Rebelling against such idiocy, he focused on the medallion he'd pulled from beneath her collar, tracing the design as he ordered his hands to release her, his feet to step away, his arousal to wane. Yet still he held her as he studied the near circle of oak trees wrought in fine gold, the center beneath their bases open, revealing a circle of delicate flesh . . .

"Where did you get that?" he asked, feeling as if he'd been struck in the chest with a battering ram.

She slid her tongue along her lips—such inviting lips, full and tilted up at the corners. "Willie sent it to me a fortnight past," she said breathlessly. "He . . . found it . . . said it was magic."

Gavan stared as his hand rose of its own volition, tracing the design, feeling her pulse warming the fine metal. It could not be . . .

A token crafted by Myrddin himself for his lady—a circle completed. A symbol of love and magic and all that was meant to be. . . .

A coincidence, he told himself. Welsh jewelry was rich in history and tradition. There had to be hundreds of pieces designed just like this.

He had never seen one . . . but then he hadn't been looking.

The only spell he was under was weariness and the long-neglected needs of his body. The only magic in the medallion was the artistry of the man who'd crafted the piece. Everything but the enigma wrapped in the body of a woman could be easily explained—

A shriek rent the night silence.

Chapter 8

What the hell?

Miss Whitmore glanced toward the house. "Gwyneth," she gasped as she pointed to the form of his sister silhouetted in the open window of her chamber on the second floor.

Gavan brushed past her, pain knifing his side as he lengthened his stride. Leaves from a large plant slapped at his face. He kicked a pot from his path. His balance shifted as Miss Whitmore darted past him and just avoided colliding with a potted thing that seemed more like an octopus than a small tree.

She glanced back at him and cried out as he lunged toward her and snatched her from the peril of running into the nasty end of a rake.

He gritted his teeth and tried to catch his breath as she slipped from his grasp, grabbed the rake, and ran for the door. "Dammit! Do not go into the house alone," he shouted.

She disappeared out the door, a blur of white wielding a weapon with bent tines, looking like an avenging angel who'd lost her wings.

Blasted female. She was asking to be locked in the attic.

Her smock billowed around her as she ran past the stable.

"Gavan! Priss!" Gwyneth shrieked again.

Cold fear raced through his veins as he tried to run and could only take long strides. He stumbled over a rock. His foot sank into a puddle mushy from the day's rain.

Stretching his body to the limit, he managed to catch Miss Whitmore at the kitchen door and yank her back. Breath escaped him and stars burst before his eyes as she fell against him.

"Stay . . . here," he ordered, too furious to raise his voice.

"I will not," she panted.

"You will bloody well do as I say." He grasped her upper arms, turned and plopped her into the mud puddle, bottom first. "Do . . . not . . . move . . ."

She stared up at him wide-eyed and nodded as she held out the rake, miraculously still in her hand. "Here, take this."

He grabbed the rake and didn't bother to see if she obeyed as he lunged into the kitchen and took the back stairs, his lips pressed together in a tight line of agony.

His sister wasn't in her room.

"Gwyneth!" he shouted, his chest heaving, every breath another stab of the knife in his side.

"You needn't shout," a voice said from behind him. "I am right here. Heavens, the way you and Priss were stumbling all over one another one would think you were running toward a fire."

"You're all right," he said flatly as he leaned on the rake. "No one—"

"Oh is that what you thought? That someone meant me harm? Nothing of the sort, though I vow William will come to harm the moment I see him again." Her hand grasped his elbow. "Really, Gavan, your ribs might only be bruised, but you must take care," she admonished as she led him down the hall and pushed him down to sit on the stairs. "Now catch your breath. Where is Priss? I know I saw her dashing across the yard."

Oh hell.

Using the newel post for leverage, he pulled to his feet and descended the steps, halting in the middle of the kitchen.

Miss Whitmore sat in the puddle outside, still staring wide-eyed at the door.

"Miss Whitmore, you may move now," he called, then collapsed into the nearest chair, leaning forward, his forehead against the handle of the rake.

Miss Whitmore ran inside, her smock streaked with muddy water, her hair a riot of curls down her back and around her face, her gaze darting from Gwyneth to Gavan. "You're all right, Gwyneth? What happened?"

"William," Gwyneth said in high dudgeon.

"Ah," Miss Whitmore said, as if clarity had been achieved.

"Where the bloody hell is Whitmore?" Gavan asked, though he knew. He had briefly discussed possibilities with Whitmore before they'd each retired to their bedchambers. The idiot must have decided right then to manage the problem on his own. Except that Whitmore was not an idiot. He was a seasoned fighter and adventurer, more than capable of taking care of himself. What was idiotic was that he'd decided to take care of all of them when he could have Gavan's help. The attack on his coach earlier that day and Owan's murder were St. Aldan business. For that matter the book was St. Aldan business since it was found on his property and was purportedly written by his so-called ancestor.

"God save me from bloody misplaced nobility," he muttered.

"Mind your mouth, Gavan," Gwyneth said.

"I'll bloody well mind my mouth when you tell me what in blazes is going on," he roared.

Miss Whitmore turned her gaze toward him, bemused and seemingly fascinated by his temper.

"Take that thing off," he barked as he gestured toward her wet smock.

"Yes, do Priss before you catch your death," Gwyneth said as she waved a mangled sheet of foolscap in front of Gavan.

Gavan didn't bother to try to read the note as Gwyneth waved it about. She would no doubt recite it to him chapter and verse.

"He had to leave," Miss Whitmore said as she contorted her body to reach the buttons at the back of her garment.

Without thinking, he grasped Miss Whitmore's hand and tugged her toward him, then began slipping buttons free. "So he spoke with you before haring off to save us all," he said flatly.

"He only told me why." Firelight shimmered through the masses of hair cascading down her back as she stood passively under his ministrations, as if she were accustomed to allowing a man to aid her with her clothing, though it was only a smock.

Gavan's mouth tightened as he wondered about the cowardly George and how many other men who might have been familiar with her. The thought fluttered away, as if his instincts at least had better sense than to entertain anything that was none of his business.

It infuriated him that he'd thought it was his business, even for a moment.

"Willie said the note would explain," Miss Whitmore offered.

"It explains why women should be running the world," Gwyneth exclaimed. "It explains that he is hoping to divert the villains who are certain to attack us again." She gnawed on her lip as she averted her gaze and paced the room. "Really, I should have known something like this would happen. Men are ever determined to play hero whether it is warranted or not."

Suspicion curled in Gavan's gut that Gwyneth was up to something he knew he wouldn't like. "And why is it not warranted? What have you done?"

Gwyneth whirled around, the very picture of outrage. "I have done nothing . . . nothing at all. I simply do not feel that we will be attacked here. You and William beat the miscreants once; surely they would not make the same mistake again."

Only Gwyneth would believe such tripe. "If they dared enough to attack an earl and his party once, they would dare to do it again. And at the moment, I could not beat a dead snake," he gritted out, as the graceful curve of Miss Whitmore's back was revealed between the edges of her smock. A smooth back clothed in a well-fitting muslin gown, tapering to a small waist and flaring out into wide hips.

Voluptuous . . . inviting a man's hand to separate the fastenings of her gown as well . . . to trace the line of her spine . . . to—

He jerked the shoulders of the smock down over her arms, then wrenched his hands away and turned partway in the chair to avoid the sight of her.

A sight indeed as from the corner of his eye, he saw the smock fall into a soggy pool on the floor, saw her turn and favor him with the full reality of her lush body so primly covered from neck to toes, saw her suddenly shiver, as if she realized he stared at her with lascivious interest.

He wanted badly to kick the damned smock into the fire blazing in the inglenook. It was a crime to cover any part of that body. A crime to want it so badly . . . so completely.

"Well it serves you right," Gwyneth said. "No one asked you to come charging in when I called."

"You shrieked," Miss Whitmore stated. "We thought you were in danger."

"I distinctly remember calling your names."

"You shrieked first," Gavan said patiently, only because he hadn't the energy to turn his sister over his knee and fight his awareness of Miss Whitmore at the same time.

"Oh, well, I was quite overset at finding William's note under my door."

"I think perhaps you should save your shrieks for something more dire," Miss Whitmore counseled.

Unbelievably, she picked up her preparations for tea as if she'd never been diverted by a sudden need for mint leaves, a kiss that had shaken his world, and the fear of Gwyneth's being murdered in her bed.

A crime that she could be so calm when he was suffering the slow torture of remembering her in his arms, remembering her sighs as he kissed her, remembering the strawberry-wine intoxication of her response.

Obviously the kiss had left her world quite balanced . . . if anything about the situation could be termed as such.

"Let me see the note," he said quietly, knowing that if he raised his voice to a normal tone, it would continue rising until he shouted loudly enough to crack the walls.

Gwyneth smoothed out the paper and held it in front of his face, again retaining her hold. "He thinks that someone overheard him tell Owan that he'd copied a portion of the book and that they will want that since he doesn't believe they found the book—or if they have, they will still want to destroy any evidence that it was ever in William's possession." She turned the sheet over to scan the contents. "He believes that they will either want to claim credit—and any fortune to be had—for finding it themselves, or they will want it destroyed, depending upon their motives. He has left to lure them to him rather than to us. He says that the only way to catch them is to set a trap."

"He had copies?" Gavan asked and stifled a savage curse.

"I don't believe Willie wanted your brother to know about that, Gwyneth," Priss said.

"No, he didn't, but it hardly seems fair for Gavan to be left behind to protect us when he doesn't know all the details." She pulled down cups from a cupboard. "Besides, Gavan can't destroy the copies if William has carried them miles away." She set the mugs on the table and leaned over to inhale the aroma of brewing tea, then turned to glare at him. "Really, Gavan, you do not deserve my consideration and should appreciate the gesture rather than sitting there growling under your breath. You've complicated matters considerably by threatening to destroy the book. We've had to protect it from you as well as the criminals."

Gavan sighed and eased back in the chair, silently conceding the point. He might hate the book and all it stood for, but he also understood Gwyneth's and Whitmore's desire to protect it. If it weren't for the harm old legends and prophecies had caused his father, and consequently himself and Gwyneth, he might well have wanted to preserve the book for its historical value alone.

But the harm had been done and no amount

of reason would change his mind. The book had to be found, and it had to be destroyed. History would continue to be made quite nicely without it.

"William has asked that you remain here," Miss Whitmore said quickly and cast him a sidelong glance, as if she feared an eruption of temper from him. "He feels that you can control the situation easier here than in the city."

Easier? The episode in the greenhouse had proved that nothing could possibly be easy with Miss Whitmore except a passion that rose too swiftly to be controlled. "Miss Whitmore—"

"We have moved beyond such formality . . ." she said vaguely, then caught the corner of her lower lip between her teeth.

Gavan fixed her with a glower, resenting her reminder of what had taken place between them in the greenhouse, resenting, too, his attraction to her in spite of his dislike of everything about her.

A strong word—dislike. Impatience with her vagueness and hesitant manner perhaps. Incomprehension of the way she lived and still seemed to be happy, more than likely. Anger for the way she turned him into a savage ruled by lust rather than reason most definitely. But dislike? He wished it were so.

"I mean . . . we . . . since you are to remain my guests . . ." She gave a short, impatient sigh. "You may call me Priss."

Priss. The name suited her. With her high-necked gown and voluminous smock, she appeared quite prim and prissy . . . until she opened her mouth. He clamped his mouth shut on the courtesy of telling her that she could call him by his given name. Encouraging more "informality" between them was the last thing he should do.

"We are not staying here," he said firmly, avoiding the subject of names altogether.

"*We* may not be remaining here, but I most certainly am," Gwyneth stated. "Unless Priss tells me where William has gone, in which case, I will follow immediately."

"Willie didn't tell me for that very reason," Priss said with an apologetic smile. "He knew both you and I would follow him and get in his way. Willie is very methodical, you know. I hate to admit that we most likely would hinder his efforts, as neither you nor I have his orderliness of thought."

"Amen," Gavan said under his breath. Still, it surprised him that Miss . . . Priss would recognize such a shortcoming in herself, much less acknowledge it.

"Men!" Gwyneth exclaimed. "They really are such misguided creatures. Still, I suppose it would damage William's pride if we were to help him. I do not understand such pride. Do you, Priss?"

"I have learned to live with it," Priss said. "And in Willie's case I have learned to trust that he is quite sensible and cautious. He has fought savages in America, you know," she added, as if the information actually related to their current situation.

Gavan rubbed his temples to ward off a headache and the uninvited thought that the best way to prevent Miss Whitmore from speaking in spirals was to keep his mouth firmly planted over hers . . .

"We are not staying here," Gavan said to drown out the demands of his libido.

"As I said before, Gavan, you may do as you wish but I am remaining. Since Priss has agreed and William wishes it—"

"Well, I don't think I did agree," Priss said as she poured tea into three cups. "I really haven't had the opportunity to think about it, since Lord St. Aldan appeared in my workroom right after Willie left." Snapping her mouth shut, she frowned down at the cakes she was tossing onto a plate. "But, of course, you must remain. I think Willie is right in his assessment of the situation, and he would be most displeased if you and your brother were put in unnecessary danger because of him."

"Miss . . . Priss," Gavan said tightly, fighting the alarm racing through his mind. "Whitmore is not right, and we will not strain your hospitality any further."

Gwyneth rolled her eyes. "Really, Gavan, give me one good reason why William is not right."

"I needn't explain myself to you, Gwyneth," he said with an edge of desperation. The problem was that Whitmore *was* right. They were in danger as long as he and his damned copied pages from the book were near them. Worse, Gavan suspected that Whitmore had somehow retrieved the book from the cushions in the coach without anyone the wiser and kept his possession a secret to protect them all. He hadn't shared his theory with Gwyneth and

Priss, not wanting to add to their anxiety over Whitmore's safety. In any case, he was certain Whitmore would put out word that he did possess the book, whether he did or not, in order to draw off the villains.

Much as he hated to admit it, Whitmore's thinking was sound and it made perfect sense to remain here until light could be shed on the criminals involved. Here, with Priss's property fenced and insulated in the country, a better watch could be kept. There was no population to get in the way and confuse what one saw and heard. And if he didn't miss his guess, Whitmore feared that Priss might be in some danger as well and required protection.

The only flaw in the plan was that Whitmore was protecting sheets of paper that neither argued nor plagued, while Gavan was saddled with protecting two women who did both. Whitmore was provoking and enjoying action while he had to rusticate in a place called Butterfly Lane with two women who were doing their best to drive him mad.

He mentally cursed Whitmore for not sharing his plans and not giving Gavan the opportunity to take action by invoking his rank. He hated inactivity. It would have been nice to know that Whitmore had copied those pages, thus compounding the danger, before they'd set out on their journey to London. It would be nice if they knew what they were up against and why. Something in his gut insisted that there was more to this than simple greed for a valuable find, though he couldn't imagine who would pay a high price for such a book.

Still Gavan chafed at sitting about taking tea while waiting for someone else to implement justice.

"I cannot fathom why I should listen to you when it is obvious you haven't any clue as to why we shouldn't enjoy Priss's company," Gwyneth huffed, then turned to Priss. "We will have a lovely time, Priss. Perhaps I can help you with some of the more routine tasks of assembling your hats. I would love to learn a new skill."

Because he feared he might again try to enjoy more than Priss's company, though he couldn't admit such a thing to his sister. "Miss . . . Priss's livelihood depends upon the success of her creations, Gwyneth," he said dryly.

"Well, I have a lively imagination," Gwyneth said brightly, completely missing his point.

"There is that," he agreed as he accepted the cup Priss offered him and took a deep draught, then squeezed his eyes shut as it scorched his tongue and throat on the way down.

Priss immediately poured cool water from a pitcher into a glass and handed it to him. "Gwyneth, please do remind me tomorrow to alert Jenny that you will be our guests. Fortunately, she lives in a small cottage behind the stables."

"Really?" Gwyneth said. "Why with the quarters above the stables and Jenny's cottage and your greenhouse, you have a veritable village of your own. How marvelous."

Priss shrugged. "I did not want Jenny traveling back and forth from her attic flat in the city so I had them erected—"

"You have more than Jenny's cottage? Goodness. I am impressed."

So was Gavan, though he wouldn't admit it when logic dictated that a property this large and this diverse was hardly practical for a woman who could not even keep her workroom in order.

But then he was having difficulty keeping his sister in order. "Have either of you considered the impropriety of our being here day and night?"

Priss paused in sipping her tea, her eyes narrowed on him. "Here, I am mistress of all I survey, and no one questions what I do or why. Society hardly cares what their pet milliner does as long as their hats are delivered on time."

"You are grasping at straws, Gavan," Gwyneth said with hands on hips. "I am a proper chaperone . . . and it isn't as if you are threatening Priss's virtue."

Gavan rose abruptly, paid the price, and turned his back to hide his grimace of pain and flush of embarrassment. "We will speak of it in the morning," he said tersely.

"I think you must consider the matter settled if you have any regard for my brother," Priss snapped. "He is courting danger to protect you."

Gavan turned slowly to face her. "I have become quite impervious to applied guilt, Miss . . .

Priss—a case of my sister wielding it once too often." He heard his voice—cold and distant and felt a moment's regret as her gaze fell before his. "I understand what your brother is doing and why." He sighed in defeat, unable to bear his own arrogance. "And I reluctantly admit that I also believe he is right. We will remain, for a few days at least, so that I may conduct my own investigations." *And to protect you*, he added silently, resigned to how much her safety had come to matter in the few hours of their acquaintance.

"What investigations?" Priss asked. "Surely, Willie is doing all that can be done."

"That is a point I will not concede," he said flatly. "England is not the American wilderness replete with ferocious natives. We have Bow Street Runners, who are trained to ferret out information, as well as people. And though I do admit his plan is sound, I also must point out that there are other possibilities we could have explored should he have seen fit to remain until morning." He held up a hand to stay the protest Gwyneth had opened her mouth to utter, impatient with the need to speak with forced formality and restraint when all he wanted to do was snap out orders for them to trust him and go about the business of being helpless females.

To hell with it. They *were* helpless females, whether they accepted it or not, and he was bloody tired of arguing. The idea of planting his mouth on hers to silence her gained appeal—a sure sign that he was addled with the combined effects of brandy, tea, and Miss

Priss. Gathering his dignity securely around him, he stared down his nose at her instead. "If I do not find the answers I seek, or if Whitmore has not returned in a reasonable length of time, Gwyneth will return to St. Aldan for the obvious reasons. Since your brother has placed you in my charge, you will accompany her—under guard if necessary—and I will take a room in the city while searching for your brother."

"The reasons why I should go home are not at all obvious to me," Gwyneth huffed.

"Then I trust that pondering the mystery will keep you well occupied," he replied.

"I most certainly will not accompany her to Wales," Priss stated. "And contrary to your assumptions, sir, Willie did not place me in your charge. He knows that I can take care of myself."

"As you took care of yourself earlier?" he asked silkily. "I was quite certain you would collect more than one injury in your perilous journey from greenhouse to kitchen door." He glanced pointedly at her muddied smock, then the rake, and afforded her a smug smile at the embarrassment staining her face.

Satisfied that he had made his point, he decided to leave well enough alone and repair to his bedchamber before another round of arguments began, tempting him to confine his sister and his hostess to their rooms for the duration.

"I am not in your charge," Priss repeated. "And I fail to see how any injuries I might sustain in my haste to protect *my* home and *my* guests are your concern."

"Ah, but it is my concern," he said with his last ounce of indulgence. "Should you be harmed in any way because of me and mine, I would be prostate with guilt that I had not prevented it."

"With lofty pride, you mean," she snapped, then clamped her mouth shut as he gave her the cocked-brow look of haughty authority perfected by generations of St. Aldan males.

He was almost tempted to heap arrogance upon patronization just for the pleasure of seeing her at a loss for words. But prudence counseled that he should not press his luck. Thankful that she had been impressed enough to silence herself before he did it for her in a most unconventional but pleasurable way, and forsaking a formal bow in favor of a less painful nod of his head, he bestowed on Priss a gracious smile. "We are most grateful for your hospitality, and will endeavor to keep out of your way."

"I do hope you are sleeping in a chair," Priss said apropos of nothing, as if he had never issued orders to her and she hadn't defied him with the most preposterous statements he'd ever heard.

Still, he had the uneasy feeling that she was the one doing the ignoring—of his intentions and his edicts. Perhaps it was a female trait, for Gwyneth had the nasty habit of doing the same when he said something she didn't like.

Damn Whitmore for leaving him in this coil. He'd be in far less peril fighting criminals than trying to decipher the feminine mind.

"No, I am not sleeping in a chair," he replied as he recalled the misery he'd suffered in his bed. "There is no chair in my bedchamber," he said.

"Are you quite certain?"

"Quite. Didn't you know?" he asked, unable to resist.

She shook her head and pressed her fingertips to her forehead, her hair falling in a wild curtain around her face. "The only time I go into the rooms upstairs is to gather materials I've stored in some of the rooms . . ."

"And since you haven't worked your way as far as my bedchamber, you have not been in there and can't recall how it is furnished," he finished for her.

He was beginning to understand her—a frightening thought.

She frowned more deeply. "I suppose you should use one of the chairs in the parlor," she said as if each word choked her.

"The parlor," he mused. "The room that was once a dining room and that is situated directly across from your workroom . . . and bedchamber." The taunt circled him and attacked him with more visions of the enticing Miss Whitmore . . . in her night rail . . . out of her night rail . . . kissing him . . . offering—

He cleared his throat and took pity on her as well as himself. Tipping up her chin with his forefinger, he forced her to look at him— a mistake of cosmic proportions. Her lips were parted, her eyes wide and soft, her breath a shudder in the air.

He released her and stepped back. "Never fear, Priss," he whispered. "I will not compromise your virtue."

"You won't?" she asked breathlessly. "Why not?"

Why not? Anger rose swiftly as he wondered if she were inviting him to do just that. As if perhaps her reasons for living beyond the watchful eye of society had more to do with her baser instincts. The memory of a man cowering in the corner while brandishing a fireplace poker presented a distasteful image. He backed away from her, yet unsavory speculations followed. "Because, I am not in the habit of indulging my baser instincts with any woman who asks that particular question," he said coldly.

"Really?" she shot back, taking him by surprise. "Then perhaps I should have asked that question before you followed me out to the greenhouse."

He lowered his head to hide the sudden twitch of his mouth. Audacious chit. And as sharp as a blade concealed in the shaft of a boot, striking when it was least expected. Raising his gaze to her, he studied her shuttered expression, seeing no anger or remorse or anything at all beyond a warning flash in her eyes. She was being cautious again, a state he did not like. She was far more interesting when her mind and her tongue were unguarded.

"Touché," he said and saluted her with an open, appreciative smile. "Shall we cry *pax*?"

She smiled back—a brilliant thing that flashed dimples in her cheeks and brought sunshine into her eyes. An enticing thing that he wanted to trace with his tongue.

"Pax," she agreed, and turned to the table, her hands flying as she tidied up the remains of their tea.

Obviously, he had been dismissed.

Thankfully, he had been dismissed before he could share smiles with her in a most intimate way.

Yet as he trudged up the stairs, he was reluctant to seek his own counsel, to remember the feeling he'd had in the greenhouse that something beyond lust had driven him to take Priss into his arms, that the experience had been more profound than momentary pleasure, that the need increasing by the minute was less easily explained. He hadn't felt such uncontrollable lust in his life—a circumstance he'd attributed to an emotionally cold nature. Other men would think it unnatural. He considered it a blessing which saved him from the messy alliances and often stupid behavior of others of his sex. He'd always prided himself on his ability to keep his brain above his neck . . . until today.

He told himself that a monk would react in the same way if confronted with the voluptuous Miss Whitmore.

Gwyneth would insist that his reaction to their hostess was magic. He knew better. Magic could not be explained and, therefore, could not exist.

One way or another, he would find a rational, acceptable explanation for the intoxicating effect of strawberry scent on his senses, the feeling of floating above the earth while holding her in his arms, the sudden and overwhelming need for her that rose with little more than a look . . .

The warmth and pleasure he'd experienced just by being on the receiving end of her smile.

His smile. It lingered in the air like warm summer mist as Priss mindlessly cleaned up the kitchen and scrubbed the table over and over again. Never had she seen such an incredible smile as the widening of his lips and dimpling of one cheek and crinkling of the skin at the corners of his eyes. It opened his face like a door inviting one into warmth. It brightened his vivid blue eyes like light shining from the windows of an otherwise dark house.

She'd been able to do nothing but smile in return—and in thanks. She'd wanted only to look at the man she had thought to be forbidding and rather too full of himself. He might well be both of those things, but his smile was full of mischief and his voice rich with droll humor and irreverence.

It had been quite naughty, that smile. He had been quite naughty in the greenhouse. So had she. Certainly, she'd never felt such a racing of blood in her veins, such an explosion of sensation, at a simple kiss. With George, she hadn't even been able to feel mild pleasure.

Magic . . . his most overbearing lordship's smile had looked like magic. His kiss had felt like magic. His touch had created magic within her.

She hadn't thought it possible. Yet within hours of the earl's arrival, he had robbed her of all that she had worked for—her caution and composure, her common sense and ability to separate dream from reality, her carefully thought-out concepts of what kind of man could bring magic into her life.

Not an emotionless man who took more than he should in stride. Not a man who had "predator" stamped into every feature. Certainly not an earl. It would have been one thing to marry George, who was not yet titled, and quite another to fall under the spell of a man whose title seemed as much a part of him as his hawk's nose and assured bearing.

An intrepid man, unafraid to take what he wanted when he wanted it and devil take the consequences.

A man who fit her ideals to perfection. A strong, confident man with an intriguing air and a hint of mystery and danger about him.

Apparently she had yet to learn that ideals were well and good in the imagination but seldom fitted into the molds into which life cast her. One would think that at her age and with the experiences she had gained through her own misconceptions, she would have known better than to reach again for the unattainable.

Yet she had not reached for anything at all. It had reached for her and held her in thrall, numbing her to all but the embrace, the sensation, the magic.

This evening she had learned for certain that

magic was real. But she had never before considered that it might control her rather than the other way around, or that it could be capricious and cruel to those who fell too easily under its spell.

Ideals had no place in the real world. Certainly they didn't fit into her life. To have an ideal, she suspected one would have to *be* an ideal, and she fell far short of the mark. Once a suitor had told her that she would be perfect if she were mute and given to languishing in a chair embroidering baby gowns.

While she had no objection to baby gowns, especially if they were for her baby, she possessed too much energy and imagination to be content portraying a languid picture of domesticity. Her version of being domestic was to engage in daylong whims of cooking and baking while worrying an idea for a hat into submission. And today had proved that she could not be mute even when she tried. More than once, she had tossed inappropriate and silly comments at Lord St. Aldan.

An earl . . . what had she been thinking?

She hadn't been thinking at all.

She stared down at the smock still lying in a puddle of soiled cotton on the floor. She'd allowed him to free the buttons down the back as naturally as she would have turned and asked Willie to do it. But Willie was her brother. Lord St. Aldan was a man.

An ideal man with a naughty smile who made her forget to mind her tongue.

Chapter 9

‹‹**I**'m certain that your most impressive glower keeps your tenants hopping to do your bidding, but I am not your tenant. It is rather the other way around at the moment,'' Priss said, wondering where the words had come from and how she'd acquired the courage to loose them. She knew better. She knew how easily her runaway tongue and instinctive whims could cause trouble, yet she couldn't seem to stop herself. The earl had only taken yesterday to rest his ribs and for some reason his pain mattered to her greatly. She had the strangest compulsion to protect him.

Very strange since he was clearly the predator.

Yesterday had been quite nice and uneventful. She'd managed to avoid the earl, seeing him only at a distance as he'd prowled about her property as if he were searching for something. She didn't care what he did as long as it was at a distance from her. She'd even managed to complete three hats yesterday while enjoying discourse with Gwyneth, and had ended the day reassured that all was well and her behavior of the night before was simply an aberration . . . or so she'd told herself as she'd watched him through the window and spun dreams that could not possibly come true.

Today the earl appeared in her workroom just after dawn, filling the space with his presence as he restlessly paced in and out of her vision, disturbing her with his tall form clothed in snug doeskins, riding jacket, and high leather boots, demanding the use of a horse.

Gwyneth trailed in a few moments later, fully dressed and bright-eyed. Obviously the St. Aldan's kept country hours, rising with the sun to take full advantage of every day.

Priss would have liked to have an hour or so to sip her tea and fortify herself for another day of unaccustomed company.

She was tempted to give the earl the dratted beast just to get him out of her way. She needed to complete another dozen hats by the end of the week and she couldn't concentrate when he was nearby. She probably would have agreed to his use of one of her horses if there weren't complications with her stock.

"It is the coach or nothing, Gavan. I must insist," Gwyneth said from the chair in Priss's workroom.

He fixed a stare on them that would freeze flame. "I am quite capable of assessing my abilities." He pinned Priss with his attention. "A horse, if you please."

"I will not provide you with a horse, sir," Priss said as firmly as she could under his hard stare. "You have no business riding in your condition."

"I have bruised ribs, Miss . . . Priss. Please do not make it sound as if I am increasing."

She bit back a grin at the image. "Was there ever a man who did not think himself invincible?" she said to no one in particular.

"Never," Gwyneth said with a delicate snort.

"They believe that the world will stop altogether if they are not dashing about brandishing swords and principles and flexing their muscles," Priss blurted and tried to swallow the last of it too late. Why had she felt compelled to mention muscles? She needed no reminders of the chest with which she'd come into intimate contact two days before, or the strength of the earl's arms as he'd held her and kissed her later that night. She certainly didn't need her gaze instinctively sailing to the chest in question now.

A most imposing chest garbed in a perfectly tailored coat that left not an inch of his broad shoulders to the imagination.

Precious chose that moment to saunter into the room and wind his body around the earl's leg. She would not look at his long legs. She would not look at any part of him.

She kept her resolution until Precious began to purr. Precious never purred except when he was perched on Priss's shoulders or curled against her in bed.

Her gaze found the cat in the earl's arms, its

front paws on his shoulders as it rubbed its cheek against the earl's.

Traitorous beast.

Gwyneth cleared her throat and nodded toward Priss's feet, where Daisy sat, paw lifted in anxious entreaty. Smugly, Priss scratched behind the dog's ears and fed her a bit of biscuit from the supply she kept beneath her table.

"My!" Gwyneth exclaimed in delight. "How interesting that your respective pets seem to have traded loyalties. I'm certain it must mean something."

"It means that they are fickle and will go to whoever will give them what they want," the earl said with a note of disgust as he unceremoniously set the cat on Gwyneth's lap.

"No, that's not it," Gwyneth said.

With a roll of his eyes, the earl strode from the room.

"He's going to the stables," Gwyneth said on a sigh, "with all confidence that your groom will not deny his command."

"He won't . . . oh dear!" Priss tossed her work down, lunged from her chair, and ran through the kitchen and out the rear door.

Sure enough the earl was entering the stable. Fortunately, her groom would be in the pen at the other end of the building at this time of day.

"Burns," she called in a loud whisper as she ran up to the fence.

"Yes, miss?" The groom removed his cap as he approached her, a yearling on a lead in his hand.

"Lord St. Aldan will be requesting a mount to go into the city."

"Oh mum—"

"Yes, I know it is a problem, but I fear he will not take no for an answer, and he will never believe the truth. Go ahead and saddle the twins, but slowly, Burns. I require a quarter hour."

Burns grinned. "Yes, mum. 'Twon't be a problem at all. The twins is feeding right now anyway."

With a grateful smile, Priss dashed back inside and into her bedchamber with a distracted smile at Gwyneth.

The earl's sister gave her a wicked smile and continued to stroke Precious. "I will be quite content to remain in for the day, Priss."

Priss didn't have time to ponder Gwyneth's knowing look or her sudden acceptance that the earl would likely be taking to a saddle despite her protests.

The girl was distinctly odd. For that matter, so was Priss's habit of thinking of Gwyneth as a girl when she was several years older than she.

Clothing flew as Priss searched out what she needed and quickly changed, with anticipation propelling her movements and speeding the flow of blood through her veins. She felt invigorated, all thoughts of caution and restraint subdued by a rare sense of excitement.

She recognized the feeling. She ought to be full of dread.

But she couldn't seem to stop rushing

through her toilette, with visions of new worlds of sensation frolicking in her head.

Gavan chafed at the incessant delays. He should have known that Priss would employ either misfits or people as dotty as she was. Burns was both.

For the better part of half an hour the man had regaled Gavan with the history of his employment at Butterfly Lane, the full and rather gory details of the birth of twin horses, and how Miss Priss—as everyone seemed to call her—had insisted on building a stable and the larger of the cottages strung around her property like scattered beads for the benefit of her employees.

Mistress of all she surveyed indeed.

He didn't want to know any more about her oddities. He would rather risk a ride into the city than spend another minute trying not to look at her, seeing so vividly in his memories what lay beneath her ever-present smock. Never had a woman so unraveled him.

Finally, Burns had a mount saddled—actually he had two mounts saddled. "Burns, you will not be accompanying me into London," he stated.

"No, my lord, I won't."

"You may inform my coachman and postilions that they will not be going either."

"They're out in the field exercising your team, sir." He nodded toward a large fenced meadow across the lane from the forest in which Priss's home was situated.

Gavan eyed the two horses and entertained

a suspicion as large as a cannonball. He turned slowly, his glare fixed firmly in place. "Gwyneth, you will remain here—"

"She plans to," Priss said as she strode into the stable. "I gave her a hat form and the trimmings. She will be busy playing with them for hours."

Gavan had been looking at Priss for a day and a night in one way or another, but he had never seen her like this—regal, in a well-made riding habit of rich brown wool trimmed in velvet, provocative, in the way the fabric molded to every curve and dip in her figure, and quite saucy, with a hat sporting a peacock feather with tiny delicate gold butterflies perched in the fronds over her brow.

Butterflies . . . she'd used one on the hat she'd fashioned the night he'd arrived. Perhaps it was her trademark. What better to represent her?

"It doesn't match, does it?" she asked ruefully. "But I must deliver it to the shop, and I haven't a box large enough to keep it from being crushed."

Fascinated, he watched the butterflies waver and sway with her every movement, as if they were indeed fluttering in the air. Leaning forward, he studied the contraption, wondering how she had contrived such an effect.

He refused to ask.

"I am going into the city alone," he said, employing every ounce of the St. Aldan arrogance.

"You can try," she said.

What the blazes does that mean? he wondered.

He refused to ask as he nodded curtly, mounted the nearest horse, and urged it forward.

"His name is Tweedledum," Priss offered.

"Of course it is," he said without surprise, as the chestnut gelding walked out of the stable with a smooth light gait. He breathed a sigh of relief as they emerged into the sunlight, free at last. Yet suspicion remained with him, a weight that would not be shed. Freedom had come too easily after all the protests, after Priss had gone to the trouble of rigging herself out for a ride.

For seduction was more like it. No wonder she practically lived in her voluminous smocks. A body like hers should be hidden to all but the man to whom it belonged.

Did it belong to the twit who had been at her home the day they'd arrived? What a crime if it were true. An idiot like him wouldn't have the slightest notion of what to do with it.

He listened for the telltale creak of leather and the swish of skirts that would alert him that Priss was mounting up and heard nothing. For some reason, he was not reassured.

A few feet out into the yard, he heard the sound of hooves approaching at a trot. Turning, he prepared to unleash the full force of his displeasure.

A riderless horse was gaining on him. Burns and Priss stood in the wide doorway of the stable, watching without expression. Gwyneth peeked out from the bow window of the workroom.

Cursing, he continued on toward the lane that would eventually turn onto the main road to London.

A bark sounded as Daisy ran up and fell in beside him, prancing with aristocratic elegance.

"Not today, Daisy," he said regretfully. "The city is no place for you. We'll have a run later."

Daisy whined and sat where she stood, fixing him with a typically feminine, pathetically beseeching look.

Gavan gave her an order in Welsh and watched the greyhound obediently trot off toward the house. At least one female in his life knew her place.

He urged his horse on, refusing to call it by its name. Hooves again clopped behind him. He halted. The other horse—Tweedledee, he assumed—halted also. A few steps forward, and the blasted creature followed.

At the turn onto the lane, he halted and turned his mount partway, his gaze traveling from the twin that stopped so close at his side there was barely an inch between them to the pair standing in the doorway.

He didn't want to ask.

"I suppose that the horse will trot along to hell and back if that is where I take his twin."

"I'm sorry," Priss said.

She looked sorry. In fact, she looked miserable, as if she didn't at all relish accompanying him, but felt she must. She looked as if she'd rather muck out the stables.

"Then by all means, do join me," he said

straight-faced. How much trouble could he get into on horseback? And once they reached the city he would leave Miss Priss and her damned eccentric horses at her shop and hire a hack to take him to Tatt's, where he would find a properly dignified mount.

The butterflies on her hat quivered and bobbed as she mounted the other horse and took up the reins. As her thigh brushed his, he thought he might be better off mucking out the stables than spending the day in the company of the mad hatter and her clinging twins.

Priss heard him mutter—how could she not when Tweedledee insisted on trotting abreast of his brother? The mad hatter was she? And she couldn't take kindly to his insult to her horses either. "I think it's rather sweet," she said. "You adore your sister and wouldn't allow her to come here without you."

"It is my understanding that adoring one's sister is what one does."

"Exactly. Why shouldn't twin horses be as close as human siblings?"

He raised his gaze to the sky. "I cannot imagine."

Insensitive wretch. She could not imagine how she had ever found him attractive. Without thinking further, Priss spurred her horse into a gallop.

Tweedledum immediately followed suit. If the earl's curse was anything to go by, he had not been prepared. It served him right.

But then she remembered his ribs and suffered a vision of him lying broken in the middle of the road.

Tweedledum pulled up alongside, keeping perfect pace with his twin. From the corner of her eye, she saw a tense thigh covered in doeskin perilously close to her hip. She looked higher and saw a mouth drawn into a grimace. Conceding defeat to her better nature, she reined in, telling herself that she would not, under any circumstances, apologize. The man deserved some discomfort for turning her life topsy-turvy, making fun of her animals—and her hats!—and insisting on riding ten miles while injured.

She stared straight ahead, completely unconvinced and riddled with guilt over her hasty actions. How could she have done such a thing? "Are you all right?"

"How would you like me to answer that?" he asked stiffly. "I wouldn't want to say the wrong thing and have you leave me draped over a tree."

She caught her breath at the anger in his voice, all the more daunting for its restraint. Such control was frightening in the strength it revealed. Yet she didn't feel at all frightened. She felt rather cocky that she had inspired something in him other than mockery or desire.

She didn't want to think about desire. Not when it had no other emotion to bind it. For some reason that thought inspired her own anger.

"Then perhaps, my lord, it would be best to say nothing at all." Nudging her mount, she resumed the journey, knowing the earl would be beside her whether she liked it or not. "If I must waste an entire day to satisfy your demands, then I should at least have the quiet I need to work out designs in my head." Swallowing down only God knew what else she might say, she settled Tweedledee into a sedate trot as they turned onto the main road.

Really, the man brought out the very worst in her.

"I comprehend the names for the twins," the earl said after a mile of silence. "But what possessed you to name a black male cat the size of a small pony Precious?"

"Because he *was* precious when he was born. I did not know he would grow so large."

Silence.

"Do you do nothing but work?" he asked.

She closed her eyes briefly, wishing he would be quiet so she could pretend that she was alone. "I ride every day."

"Nothing else?"

"What else is there?"

"I have no idea."

Was that a note of bleakness she heard in his voice? Surely not. She pulled ahead and shot an annoyed glance at Tweedledum as he kept pace. Another crime on the earl's head. If not for him, she would still think the twins' closeness was sweet.

But his last statement plagued her, like a ringing in her ears. He had no idea what else there was besides work? She remembered the firmness and power of his body and the tan on his chest—both signs of physical labor out of doors. And she thought of his eyes—how they had often become distant while conversation drifted around him, as if his mind was working on one problem or another.

"Do you do nothing but work?" she asked.

"I ride every day."

Sadness fell around her like a dark, heavy blanket at the thought of him living such a sterile life. She knew from Gwyneth that he had never married, though there had been what Gwyneth termed "a near thing." Had he been hurt? Or had the woman in question been frightened away by his manner? She couldn't imagine it after seeing how tender and indulgent he was with his sister. Surely he would be the same with a woman he loved.

The pall of sadness tightened about her as she realized in that moment that she was lonely. That something vital was missing from her life. That contentment was the poor relation of happiness.

She'd thought she was happy. The sudden doubt frightened her as the earl's anger did not.

"I suppose I deserved it."

His voice startled her. His words puzzled her. "What?"

"I can only make such an admission once and still maintain a modicum of pride."

She sighed heavily, trying to shake off her sudden melancholy. She could tell him that she was sorry for causing him pain. She could tell him that every time she acted on a whim, she inevitably caused trouble. But she didn't want him to know that about her. It was difficult enough admitting it to herself.

"No one deserves to be hurt," she said. "I didn't know he was a male," she added quickly before she spilled words better left contained.

"What? Who?"

"Precious. I didn't know he was a male when I named him. Girls aren't supposed to know such things."

"Gavan," he said.

She nodded, not knowing how to respond.

His hand appeared and took hold of her reins, halting both horses. Her knee bent over the sidesaddle brushed his thigh. His finger crooked under her chin, lifting her face to his gaze.

"Call me Gavan."

Her mouth dried and her pulse quickened. "I can't. It wouldn't be proper."

" 'Society hardly cares what their pet milliner does as long as their hats are delivered on time,' " he quoted. "Say it. Say my name." He stared at her with a bemused expression, as if he didn't know the reason why he insisted on such a familiar address.

"Gavan," she said hoarsely, suddenly unable to catch her breath.

He smiled. Deep dimples elongated on either side of his mouth. His eyes gleamed with what appeared to be pleasure and something else. Something slumberous, seductive, dangerous.

His thumb skimmed her lips, then he abruptly removed his hand and turned his gaze back to the road ahead.

Shaken, she allowed Tweedledee to follow without guidance from her trembling limbs. He'd looked as if he meant to kiss her again. Heaven help her, she'd wanted him to kiss her . . . and more. So much more that she flushed with heat at the thought of it, of what it would be like.

It would be quite as extraordinary as the kiss in the greenhouse.

Banishing the thought, she took firm control of the reins of both her horse and her wayward emotions. She had no idea if it would be extraordinary or not. And she wouldn't be finding out—not with the earl. Perhaps not with anyone. Not now that she remembered all too clearly how anticipation and need felt. How *special* and inexplicably magical they felt. How could one be satisfied with anything less?

Another mile passed in silence as Priss focused on the buildings of the city peaking and dipping on the horizon. It would be a relief to reach her shop, to find refuge in the chatter of patrons coming and going with gossip and outrageous demands for their hats. Usually she hated that part of her work, but not today. Today, she needed to be reminded that extraordinary things might come along once in a great while but they always gave way to routine and normality. She needed to remember that magic was a trick of the imagination. Perhaps it was a trick of loneliness as well.

Chapter 10

They weren't alone, Gavan sensed as he helped Priss dismount in front of her shop. Yet at such an early hour, there were few people in the streets other than merchants hurrying to their shops to complete chores before opening to the public.

He glanced around and found nothing out of the ordinary. He took his time affixing the twins' reins to the hitching post while continuing to search for the source of his discomfort from the corners of his eyes.

Priss walked to the door of her establishment—Miss Priscilla Whitmore: Milliner, the discreet sign read—and unlocked the door. She'd told him that she never opened before noon unless a patron had made a private appointment. Members of the ton were not in the habit of rising early, much less attending the shops before noon.

He stopped and stared at the interior, stunned. Shelves were neatly arranged with completed hats and elegant boxes. A sitting area in an alcove would do the royal palace proud. No lint or bits of ribbon and lace and feathers littered the rich oriental carpet. He strolled toward the back, studying the details in the muted light from the candles Priss was lighting as she made her way to the back ahead of him. Even the storeroom was neat, with bolts of fabrics, flowers fashioned from fine silks, spools of ribbons and threads, lengths of lace, the ever-present feathers, and rows of hat molds all arranged in logical order.

"Are we in the wrong place?" he asked.

"No, this is the right one," she replied as she opened a door off the storeroom and stepped inside.

He followed and raised his brows. "*This* is your room, I take it."

"Yes, my office."

It certainly was. Here was the chaos to which he'd become accustomed to seeing her. Papers were stacked on the desk along with a tea service, one battered hatbox full of whatnots, another with the biscuits and candies she idly munched on as she worked. Every chair held periodicals or fashion dolls or smocks. The mantel above the fireplace held a jumbled row of hats that looked as if she'd picked them up from the gutters.

"My first attempts," she said, waving a hand at the mantel and frowning down at the desk. "Someone has been here." She leaned over and rifled through the paraphernalia. "They've been through my papers."

"How can you possibly tell?" he asked, as he took in the mess.

"Because the invoices were over in that chair and now they're on the desk. And the bill of lading for my last shipment of Belgian lace was under my biscuits and now it is in the drawer." Her head jerked up as her gaze found his. "I keep the door locked; only I ever come in here."

"Your mother?" he asked, recalling that her mother ran the business and lived in an apartment above the shop.

She shook her head. "She refuses to come in here. Besides, Mummy is on the Continent."

He could understand why but refrained from saying so. "An employee?" he suggested, though he had a fair idea of the answer.

"No. Only I have the key for the office. We have three employees, one of whom is my old nanny and the other two came with us from the plantation after Daddy died. They won't come in here either."

"What of William?" he asked, thinking it perfectly reasonable since there had been no indications of break-in or anything else untoward that he could see when they'd entered the shop. Of course all it would take was an expert in lock-picking to gain entrance without leaving any visible signs of intrusion.

"Hm, yes he has a key but . . ." Her voice faded as she stared at a stack of papers.

"Is anything missing?" he ventured tongue-in-cheek. It would take weeks—months—to search everything to discern if it was all there, even if she could remember all that should be there, which he doubted.

"Not that I can see."

Little wonder. "When were you last here?"

"Last week . . . someone *was* here when no one should have been." She rifled through her papers and sat down hard on her chair as she picked one up, glancing from it to another on the desk.

"That's a blank sheet," he said nodding toward the one on the desk and thought she might be as blank as the parchment.

"Yes, it is," she said absently as she foraged for something . . . a piece of charcoal, and rubbed it lightly over the blank sheet. "And it wasn't Willie. He would have no need to search for my direction." She held up the paper. "Someone copied it from this letter I received from Mummy last week. I brought it to the shop to share with the employees."

He took it from her hand and saw the imprint of writing through the haze of charcoal and amended his latest assessment of her. She was not a blank sheet at all, but quite clever—

Butterfly Lane . . . Gwyneth— He stared harder at the paper as horror dawned. "Lock up," he rapped out.

"The cottage . . . Gwyneth," she said, echoing his thought. "Dear heaven." She hastily unpinned the hat on her head and tossed it onto the desk, then pulled open a drawer, produced a box and threw open the lid. Inside lay a brace of pistols, powder and ball. "Willie gave these to me," she explained. "I never thought I would have to use them."

Clever and prepared, he thought grimly as he wordlessly plucked a weapon from its velvet bed and proceeded to load and prime it. Priss did the same with the other.

Dumbfounded, he paused to watch as she measured out powder in the palm of her hand, seeming to count under her breath. Pouring the powder from a small flask down the barrel, she loaded patch and ball, then opened the frizzen and added powder from another flask.

"Don't you know how to load a pistol?" she asked as she draped the flask crosswise over her shoulder and the pouch of balls around her neck like a necklace. Quickly, she donned a wide leather belt and secured the pistol at her waist. "Here, let me."

"I can manage." He resumed loading his pistol. "One wonders why you can manage such a thing and in a way I've not seen before." He felt clumsy and slow compared to her skill, a fact that bit viciously at his pride.

Later, he would nurse it.

"Willie learned it from the mountain men in America and taught me. He thought it wise since I often go back and forth unaccompanied. Mummy is better at it though. I'm a bit slow." She handed him another belt—the twin to hers. "It is risky carrying the pistols loaded this way but I daresay we might not have the opportunity to load once we reach home. But these are the finest of weapons and I'm certain all will be well." Her gaze darted toward his waist and below, then scurried away as she fluttered her hands. "Just point yours away from your . . . self."

A small comfort, he thought as he put on the belt, gathered his share of the munitions, and slid the pistol into the belt well away from his "self." "We'll have to ride hard," he said, and ushered her into the front room, making sure the office door was securely locked.

Priss had disappeared. He looked out the window and saw her removing the saddle from her horse. It sailed into the shop and landed at his feet.

He didn't need to ask. Priss stood on the mounting block, gathered up her skirts, center back to front and tucked the hem in her belt, fashioning pantaloons that allowed her to mount astride the horse.

Knowing what Tweedledum would do the moment she spurred his brother, he leaped into his saddle and led the way through the streets at a fast clip.

Every pound of the horse's hooves beneath him drove a spike of fear into his gut and a sharp pain into his side. Someone had managed to get into Priss's office for the sole reason of finding her direction. Since no one had been to her cottage before now, he could only surmise that whoever had broken into Priss's shop had done so very recently, and would likely be on their way there now. His men weren't armed, except for the musket kept in the driver's box of the coach, which would probably be as useless to them as it had been when they'd been on the ground, too far away from it during the attack on the road to do them any good. Burns would be little help other than he might try to talk the villains to death.

Gwyneth was alone. Vulnerable.

The twins were fleet of foot and kept pace with the drumming of Gavan's heart. He should have made Priss remain behind in safety, he thought belatedly. It hadn't occurred to him as he'd watched her loading the pistol. At that moment, she'd been an ally rather than a woman.

He was a fool. He never should have insisted on riding into the city, but his ribs had settled to a dull ache and he'd been going mad cooling his heels at the cottage, listening to the chatter of the women.

Gwyneth had no knowledge of or experience with the nastier aspects of life. She was helpless against ugliness in any form. His only hope was that she would cower in fear . . . in a cupboard or under the bed where no one would see her. . . .

After what seemed to be hours, the crooked sign pointing to the turn onto Butterfly Lane appeared. Gavan reached out and grasped Priss's reins, stopping both horses. "You are not going any farther. Give me your pistol."

"This is hardly the time for heroics, sir," she said. "It is my home and my guest, and I have the right to defend both."

"Your house be damned. You are under my protection and will remain here out of harm's way."

She kicked her horse and sped away. His horse followed with no help from him.

Later, he would throttle the impossible woman.

For the second time, he caught her, then brought Tweedledum to an abrupt rearing halt halfway down the Lane. "Listen very carefully," he said with controlled fury. "You will circle around to the back and summon my men. I will see to Gwyneth . . . and if you disobey me in this, I will—"

"You needn't threaten me, sir. All you need do is ask. Your plan is a sensible one, so I will comply." She pulled her pistol from her belt. "Here, you might need a second shot."

"Someone save me from this," he muttered as he dismounted and allowed Tweedledum to follow Priss.

Using the stealth he'd learned from years of hunting game, he approached the house, keeping to the trees and bushes for cover.

His blood ran cold at the outside door to Priss's workroom swinging open on one hinge.

Nothing stirred. The yard was empty, the house silent.

Energy surged, strength doubled in the numbness of fear for his sister. The world around him seemed to be clearer, brighter, every detail magnified as he made it to the side of the door and pressed his back to the wall, listening, fighting the need to charge inside, and peering in the window instead.

Nothing.

He slipped inside and cautiously looked into the parlor and Priss's bedchamber.

Empty.

He heard a low growl.

Daisy.

Someone screamed.

A man.

Gavan charged into the kitchen, both pistols drawn.

The greyhound stood alert, her hackles standing on end as she snarled at something under the huge plank table. She stepped back at the sight of Gavan, allowing him to see her prize. A man rolled on the floor moaning and covering his head as Precious stood on top of him, clawing at anything he could find. From the look of it, the cat had found a good deal of flesh.

"Precious," he shouted above the feline's throaty snarls.

The cat stilled and glanced at him and jumped gracefully from his quarry.

Gavan caught him by the scruff of the neck in two long strides, dodging as the man shoved his elbows backward. The man wrested free and whirled, aiming his fist at the same time.

Gavan snarled and planted his fist in the man's face, sending him flying backward through the kitchen door to land flat on his back in the yard.

"Daisy, stay," he ordered and hurried out to the yard.

A tall, thin man stood pressed flat against the wall, seeming to be trying to become a part of it as the tines of a pitchfork pressed gently against his groin. Priss stood at the other end of the weapon. "Do not rattle me, sir," Priss warned her captive, "lest my hold slip an inch. An inch should do it, don't you think, my lord?"

"Where is Gwyneth?" he asked with a low growl of his own.

"Standing guard." She nodded toward the side of the house and grinned. "Go see."

Gavan closed the distance, afraid to think or feel until he saw his sister safe.

She sat calmly on the back of a man lying facedown in the dirt, an iron skillet in her hand poised above his head. "Gavan! Thank God. I've been so afraid he would regain consciousness and I would have to hit him again."

"Where are my men?" he demanded, fearing that if he did not take action of some kind, he would break down and weep in relief.

"Untying one another. They took quite a beating, Gavan, so please do not shout at them."

"Get . . . me . . . some . . . rope," he ordered, measuring out the remnants of calm he still possessed. "In . . . the . . . stable."

Eyeing him cautiously, Gwyneth rose and dashed for the building.

He heard a whoosh above him. Stars exploded behind his eyes as something landed on him from the window above, bringing him to ground. He gasped for air and fought the pain in his side, his back, his head. Something inside him snapped and released sheer fury. Numbing fury as he bucked and rolled just as a fist flew toward his face, landing in the dirt instead. Cold fury as he aimed his fist and struck bone, receiving the satisfying feel of a nose breaking. Calculating fury as his attacker aimed another blow and he took advantage of the opening, taking the strike and not feeling it, driving his fist into the vulnerable softness just beneath the breastbone and then again in the face, rendering his assailant unconscious.

Burns ran out on his scrawny bowed legs and tossed a length of rope at him, then headed for the back of the house. His men straggled out, battered and bruised and looking for blood.

Breathing hard, Gavan struggled to his feet and barked out orders, knowing that the felons would collect a few more bruises while being trussed up for the constables.

Gwyneth ran up to him and fell into his arms. "I'm certain these are the same men who accosted us on the road to London, Gavan. They took our men by surprise, attacked them from behind. Daisy's barking alerted me; I was in the kitchen and grabbed the skillet. If the criminals hadn't split up to search the house, I fear what the outcome might have been. And Precious attacked the moment one of the men raised his fist to Daisy; it was quite amazing."

An attack cat, he thought inconsequentially, unable to string anything more coherent into a whole thought.

Gwyneth was safe. For just one moment, he didn't want to think of anything else as he held her and tried to soothe her trembles and his own. She was safe and whole ... and barely mussed.

Priss rounded the corner, her hair half-up and half-down in a riot of curls. Her sleeve was ripped at the seam and a smudge of dirt marked her cheek. Her skirts were still fashioned into bloomers. Her right eye was bruised and swelling.

Fury returned at the sight, yet instinct cautioned him not to react just yet. In spite of her courage and sensible actions, her face was pale and her eyes too wide and glazed. She'd been terrified, yet she'd taken events one at a time, dispensing with each as it struck. She'd struck back. Remarkable. She was remarkable.

Gwyneth was remarkable. His hand shook as he realized what could have happened if Gwyneth hadn't kept her head—a thing he'd not thought possible—and if Priss hadn't remained calm and methodical.

The men responsible for violating the world within a world Priss had created for herself and marring Priss's beautiful face would pay. They would all pay for the attack on Whitmore in the village and later, the coach, as they'd traveled to London. And they would pay for daring to accost his sister, for introducing her to the world of evil and fear at home where she should have felt safe and secure.

Yet Gwyneth's reactions suggested that perhaps she was not as naive as he'd thought.

Who would have thought it of either of the women who plagued his life of late?

"I've sent Burns for the authorities," Priss said briskly, though he detected a slight waver in her voice. "He is the least battered of the men. It will take some time—"

"Good," he said. "It will afford me the opportunity to question them myself."

Priss yanked the hem of her skirt from her

belt, smoothed her bodice, and nodded. "I'll get my pitchfork," she said, and turned back the way she had come.

"Priss," he called, stopping her before she disappeared around the corner of the house. "I don't suppose you have another brace of pistols here, do you?"

"Of course I do—two in fact. William insisted upon my having weapons readily at hand should the need for them arise." She grinned, stunning him with her resilience.

"Where?"

"One in the kitchen and the other in my bedchamber."

"I will retrieve the ones from kitchen if you will please fetch the others for me."

"All right," she said, looking at him as if she thought him mad.

He followed close behind her with a firm grip on Gwyneth's elbow, not stopping in the kitchen but following Priss to the threshold of her bedroom. Good, there was a key in the lock. Without ceremony, he pushed his sister into the room, slammed the door, and turned the key.

He'd be damned if he'd allow either of the women anywhere near the villains again. Whether it was for the safety of Gwyneth and Priss, or the safety of the men, he hadn't decided. All he knew for certain was that he was in a mood to do whatever necessary to get answers from their captives.

Chapter 11

❧❦❧

"**W**e are prisoners," Gwyneth said in dramatic disbelief. "How could he do such a thing to us?"

Priss stared blankly at the wall of her bed-chamber, unaware of how much time passed, barely aware that Gwyneth sat beside her, heaping curses on her brother's head for imprisoning them in so cavalier a fashion.

Priss was glad that Gavan had removed them from the scene. Sudden weakness had smothered her as she'd stood outside watching him hold his sister, stark fear in his eyes, not for what had happened but for what might have happened. She'd trembled so hard by the time she'd crossed the threshold into the cottage, she could barely stand. Her eye and cheek throbbed.

She wrapped her arms around her waist as her teeth began to chatter.

Arms swept around her and held her, rocking her back and forth. "It's over, Priss," Gwyneth soothed. "Gavan will not let it happen again. We are safe."

164

Safe. Safe. Safe. ... She repeated it like a chant, trying to feel it, trying to find the strength and the determination that had guided her through the ride back to the cottage and the capture of the men who'd invaded her shop and then her home. If she had been alone, she still would have tried to defend herself, but would never have succeeded. She was accustomed to taking care of herself, yet today, she'd realized that it wasn't enough. She hadn't even been able to bring herself to use her pistol, resorting to a pitchfork instead.

She'd realized just how very alone she was.

Nothing felt so lonely and empty as helplessness.

It had felt good to know she wasn't alone, that her panic and fear had been shared with someone, that she didn't have to fight alone. How easy it was to surrender her autonomy over her property to a man who had been born and raised to protect—his land, his name, his family, and all that he surveyed.

She felt a rush of air and shivered. The arms holding her retreated. Another pair of arms, stronger and harder gathered her close. A hand smoothed her hair over and over again.

"They violated my world," she croaked. "They robbed my sense of safety ... my peace."

He muttered something in Welsh, musical and lilting in cadence, harsh in tone.

She looked up and saw Gavan, his face close to hers, his expression tight and angry, his eyes seeming bleak with helplessness.

Helplessness. She choked on a near-hysterical giggle and angled away from him, determined to summon a semblance of normality to her thoughts. She didn't want him to see her trembling with belated fright, cold and shivering in shock. Not when he'd favored her with a look that suggested admiration after the nightmare had ended. Could one have a nightmare and not know it until it was over? she wondered.

It didn't matter. They were all secure and relatively unharmed. She could not have seen helplessness in his eyes. He wouldn't know the meaning of the word.

She pushed away from him and studied his every feature from hair to booted feet. "You're hurt."

His mouth curved, half grimace, half smile. "Only my pride."

"Why are you here?" she asked, remembering that he'd wanted to question the men, that it was the reason he'd locked her and Gwyneth the room, to keep them out of his way. He'd been so angry in the yard. No, he'd been furious, a dragon seeking vengeance for the violation of his den. "The men—"

"The men are taken care of," he said softly, his voice conveying no satisfaction, no triumph.

"You learned nothing," she stated, as disappointment burned behind her eyes and clogged her throat. "But, we must know who. I must know why—"

"The book," Gwyneth said baldly, with a strange twist of her face as she quickly averted her gaze.

"Yes," he said on a sigh. "The men who attacked us on the road did not find it." He glanced at his sister with an odd, assessing look. "Gwyneth, you appear quite well."

"Of course I am well. The experience was quite enlightening, though I am appalled that I enjoyed bashing that man in the head rather too much." Gwyneth spoke quickly, as if she were nervous. She suddenly looked as if she were near tears. "Oh drat! How does one know when one is doing the right thing?" she all but wailed.

He tilted his head and fixed Gwyneth with a penetrating stare. "You always seem to do the right thing and the rest of us muddle through. I would counsel you to continue in that vein for all the rest of your days."

Gwyneth hesitated, still holding her brother's gaze, then nodded and turned away.

Priss studied brother and sister, feeling as if they were holding a conversation without precisely saying what they really meant and yet still understanding one another. She and Willie had done the same on occasion—a sort of abbreviated language peculiar to people close to one another. As curious as she was and as badly as she wanted to ask for a translation, she held her tongue, respecting the unique familiarity shared by siblings. Besides, Gwyneth was undoubtedly referring to her recently discovered ability to commit violence in the name of survival.

Priss shuddered as she wondered if she could have used her pistol if the pitchfork hadn't worked. Could she have shot a man?

She hoped she would never have to find out.

"Will you make tea, Gwyneth," he asked, still quietly, as if he were measuring his words carefully, "and see that cold water is drawn from the well for Priss's eye?"

"Oh! Of course." Gwyneth rushed from the room as if she could not escape fast enough.

"Can you stand, Priss?"

Priss inhaled deeply and tried her legs. "Yes, I'm all right . . . really," she added at his narrow-eyed scrutiny.

"Is there a place where we can all sit without displacing your"—he swiped a hand across the back of his neck—"system of organization?"

She almost smiled at his attempt to be tactful. It hadn't escaped her that he viewed her clutter with distaste. The realization warmed her just as his comfort had a few moments ago. "We can go into the sitting room. There is no clutter there."

Within a quarter hour, Priss was situated in a chair with a lap robe draped over her knees and a soothing cup of tea laced with honey and brandy in her hands, determined to display calm even if it was a disguise for lingering fear. With the memory of Gavan's admiration so vivid in her mind, she could do no less. When had any man ever looked at her in such a way? George had always treated her with amused tolerance, as if she were a foolish child. Others had favored her with various measures of exasperation and annoyance and disapproval. It hadn't taken her long to realize that the society of the *ton* was not for her.

Gavan was taking care of her, but not as Willie ever had, not out of brotherly habit. His hand had lingered too long as he'd applied the cold cloth to her eye. His gaze continued even now to study her, as if searching for what was not readily apparent.

"Did they tell you nothing?" she asked to keep another giggle from escaping at the half-hysterical thought that this imposing man might think her a woman of mystery, even for a moment.

Gavan sprawled in the chair across from her, legs outstretched to their full impressive length, his hands holding a mug of brandy on his midsection. "They were hired to find both the book and your medallion, which they assume to be still with the book. If they learn it is not and that it is in your possession, you will be in even greater danger. At the moment, the only reason they came here was because they think that your brother is still here. I doubt he has yet had time to make it known that he is . . . elsewhere."

Panic struck out at her again as her hand raised to her throat and pulled the medallion out from beneath her jabot. Her fingers clutched the pendant hanging from a ribbon, feeling the reassuring shape of an incomplete circle of trees rooted by an inner circle representing the sun. She couldn't bear to lose the charm. Not after the intent way Gavan had studied it that night in the greenhouse. Not when a sense of it being a part of her had followed his discovery of it around her neck.

"They cannot have it," she said far more bravely than she felt.

Silly . . . at times she was incredibly silly.

"Of course they cannot have it. 'Tis yours," Gwyneth said from her seat on the sofa, her legs tucked under her skirts, her expression seeming inaccountably smug. "Did the men reveal who hired them?" she asked Gavan.

"They said that they came from the Marches—miners who did not want to die underground, so they met with a man who concealed his features with a broad hat and a scarf around his face, and took money to do his dirty work. They had no more information to offer." His mouth crooked as he favored Priss with a wry look. "I even took a page from Priss's book and threatened their . . . reproductive capabilities with her pitchfork. They were too frightened to lie."

"Priss, you did that?" Gwyneth asked with excitement. "Really?"

"She did that," Gavan confirmed. "Really." Again the gleam in his eye, amusement rather than mockery, respect rather than exasperation.

"I never would have thought of it. How did you?"

Priss shrugged. "Willie and his partner taught me how to defend myself with weapons, and how to improvise with anything at hand." She squirmed under the earl's stare, her face flaming as she tore her gaze away from him. "Willie and Drew told me that one could threaten a man's life and he might still contrive to bluff or escape. Threaten a man's . . .

reproductive capabilities, and he will barely contrive to breathe."

"William's partner? Surely you don't mean Drew, Baron Cassidy," Gwyneth said. "I met him and his wife, the Countess Saxon during my Season. *He* taught you how to defend yourself? My that must have been great fun. He is so dashing and so wonderfully open in displaying his love for his wife." She smiled wistfully and tucked her hem more securely under her feet. "But of course you mean him. William regaled Gavan and me with tales of his adventures with the baron. He just didn't mention a name."

Gavan's gaze shot to Priss, compelling her to meet it.

She refused, forcing herself to sip her tea calmly, though she shrank inside with the humiliation that never failed to awaken at any thought or mention of the man she had once loved with thoughtless and destructive ambition.

Drew and his wife, Harriet, had been the first friends she'd ever had, forgiving her for the disasters she'd visited upon them, but like a nightmare, memories of her transgressions refused to retreat.

She'd often wondered why the happier memories she had of time spent with Drew and Harriet since her sixteenth year had not the power to banish her shame.

"Well, in any case," Gwyneth said, thankfully interrupting Priss's thoughts, "I shall remember about pitchforks and how to threaten a man. It could prove useful the next time—"

"There will be no next time," Gavan said gruffly, as he rose to his feet, then stood perfectly still, his face twisted in a grimace. "At first light, we will—" The mug fell from his hold and splashed brandy onto the carpet. "We will return—" He shook his head and sucked in a slow, deep breath. "Bloody damn," he choked out and swayed, then fell to the floor, unconscious.

Gavan awakened to a dark room and an unfamiliar bed beneath him. As he reached out his hand collided with a soft barrier that felt like velvet. The sofa back. He groped with his other hand and found another barrier—wood ... carved wood. He breathed deeply and focused on shadows in the room. He was still in the sitting room. It appeared that someone had placed the straight-backed chairs from the kitchen against the edge of the sofa.

He started to rise and groaned in pain. Falling back, he squeezed his eyes shut until the worst of it passed. He remembered now. All of it including the man jumping onto him from the second-floor window. His ribs. His head. The pain had struck suddenly as he'd been speaking with Gwyneth and Priss. In the heat and anger of the day's events, he'd been aware of pain, yet it had not seemed as significant as protecting the women and questioning the felons. As calm returned to the house on Butterfly Lane, he'd been dimly aware that he was hurt, but had thought to ignore it until he was alone.

He'd collapsed like a bellows riddled with

holes. What a charming picture that must have made. It would have been nice if Priss hadn't been present to witness his fall. He'd rather liked holding her in comfort, feeling her cling to him as if his strength were the only thing keeping her together. He'd felt pleasure when she'd asked if he'd been hurt, her face paling and her eyes stricken and full of concern, as if it mattered a great deal to her.

Why the hell hadn't he told her that his head felt like a burst melon, that his vision had begun to blur?

Pride, his mind replied. Stupid male vanity.

His vanity would not have suffered so much disgrace if he'd simply told Priss that he was hurt. The only time a man should fall at a woman's feet was in fealty to his queen or in honor of his God.

Priss was no queen—not in any obscure nook of the imagination. She was a waif—a very proud waif who knew how to survive. How could he have ever thought her scatter-brained and deceitful?

And how in bloody hell had he come to be lying on the damned sofa, ringed in like a damned infant in his cradle?

He had to get up. Had to know how much time had passed. The men who had attacked them were no longer a threat, but he had no illusions that whoever had hired them would hire more men. If he was still in the Marches of Wales, they would have a week's—perhaps more—reprieve while word reached him and he gathered more accomplices. If he was closer, they might have only a few days.

Cautiously reaching out, he tried to push away a chair. It wouldn't budge. Odd, the chairs didn't weigh that much, and he wasn't that weak. He turned his head as he groped the seat of the chair nearest his hand . . . and felt softness . . . the softness of a hip too full to be Gwyneth's.

Wonderful, now Miss Priss was playing nanny to his infant.

Amazingly, he felt his face burn in embarrassment and wondered why. If it were Gwyneth watching over him, he wouldn't mind. If it were a servant, he would take it for granted. He minded greatly that Priss saw him at anything but his best. He wanted to watch over her, not the other way around. He wanted her to cling to him as she had that afternoon—whether for comfort or passion, it didn't matter.

Comfort meant a degree of caring. He didn't like the sound of that, not when undertones of lust kept creeping into what he wanted to believe was simply the duty of a man to take care of a woman—any woman—in his charge.

And not only lust. Pleasure hummed in his mind when he watched her work or ride or make tea, or when he listened to her often disjointed end of a conversation and picked up the threads with no confusion. Curiosity thrummed a steady beat, prodding him to learn all there was to know about her, to understand her.

Until two days ago he'd had no desire to spend his time understanding any female other than his sister.

Yet he understood that Priss was sleeping on a bed made of chairs to care for him. How many women would do such a thing when there were servants about to do the nursing?

None that he'd ever known, other than his sister. He responded to the thought with a sense of pleasure in knowing someone cared enough to suffer discomfort for him. The last woman who had touched his life had taken great satisfaction in shattering his finer emotions into fragments on the floor. He'd never bothered to put them back together again.

He'd met Priss two days ago, he reminded himself. Not enough time for any sliver of his finer emotions to be reclaimed. Not enough time to summon any response but lust. He had to remember that.

Lust. Only that.

"Are you in need?"

Priss's whisper in the darkness rolled over him with a frisson of awareness that she was close . . . too close. That he could touch her, trace the contours of her body, feel her flesh.

Was he in need? His own body spoke volumes in reply. His ribs weren't all that pained him, a fact that he couldn't explain. A man in his condition shouldn't be in . . . this condition.

"No," he said, not trusting himself to say more. He squinted down the length of his body, afraid of what he would see. Nothing rose beneath the blanket covering his nether regions. Yet he wanted her with the same force he'd felt every time she was near.

A frightening thought that he could want a woman with something other than his body.

"Please do not attempt to rise," she continued to whisper. "The physician says that you are concussed and must rest."

That explained the feeling that his head was trapped beneath a boulder. "Where is Gwyneth?" he asked. It was important to know why Priss was here instead of his sister. Important to understand though he couldn't form his thoughts beyond that.

"She was vibrating like a tightly strung bow. I gave her some tea and sent her to bed. I was afraid she would want to talk your ear off if she didn't calm down first."

Nervous babbling, Gavan thought. *Priss is nervous.* "Gwyneth is energetic," he said. "She does not deflate unless one punctures her."

"Like you," Priss replied. "I have never seen such restless individuals. You were unconscious, yet we had to hold you down for the physician." Her shadow rose and a chair slid out of the way. Then another and then the third. She perched on the edge of the sofa, careful not to jar him, her hands skimming lightly over his midsection, adjusting the bandages.

Bandages. His chest was bare. She had bound his ribs again without his knowing it. Perhaps she had removed his shirt. Upside down, he thought. Everything was upside down. It was he who should be undressing her.

Her fingers brushed his nipples as she followed the line of the linen wrappings around to his other side.

Instinctively, he captured her hand, meaning to move it away from him, but holding it still in the center of his chest, feeling her touch, wanting more. "Your eye—how is it?" He squinted, trying to see if it was as bruised as he remembered. "I can't see it."

"It looks like the design on a peacock feather, but it doesn't hurt." Her fingers curled and opened, as if she were uncertain whether to touch him or leave him. Her breath shuddered as he lifted his other hand and stroked her cheek and searched for a strand of hair. For the first time not a tendril fell over her face in disarray. He slid his hand around her neck and felt a braid, sorry that her chaotic curls were restrained. He didn't like anything about her being held back—

As if a decision had been made without his knowledge, he cupped the back of her neck and urged her head down, needing her for reasons he couldn't explain.

Her mouth met his, unresisting, yet tentative. Last time he'd kissed her fully, deeply, aware of nothing but the kiss itself, the depths of her mouth, the texture. Now he wanted only the shape of her lips, the learning of softness.

The taste and scent of strawberries. The sweetness of discovery.

Metal brushed his chest, warm, seeming alive. The medallion, symbol of sorcery and all things impossible. He deepened the kiss, his tongue parting her lips and seeking her sweet intoxication, denying everything but what he could see and touch and hold.

She pulled away and jerked to her feet,

backing a step at a time from the room, her hands covering her mouth, her head shaking. "I cannot do this. It cannot be ... real." Her voice snagged. "I *will not* believe it is real."

He watched her go, wanting to call her back, yet he didn't—couldn't—because she was right. It was all illusion, all beguilement. Only the physical responses were to be trusted.

He watched light appear in the room across the hall and knew that Priss was escaping into her work. He always did the same. Work distracted the mind from thinking too much about oneself, about what one had and did not have. It provided innocence from the truths of the world, if only for a little while.

He'd found his solitude at Castell Eryri, the abode of eagles, thinking he could be like the magnificent birds who soared so far above the world separated from man's folly.

He'd forgotten that the world would have its way no matter how high one built one's nest.

Chapter 12

More failure. And some success.

He sighed and paced the aisle of the church, admiring the stained-glass window above the altar and the cushions on the hard wooden pews. How had three hardy men accustomed to laboring in the mines been bested by one man and two women? He'd taken such care in choosing them, even going so far as to travel to the Marches, where men escaping the hardships of the mines could be found before they crossed into England in search of better fortune.

At least the fourth man had had the sense to stand guard while the others did their work. When he'd seen that there would be no success that day, he'd escaped and returned here to report their failure.

He'd been careful to chose reasonably moral men who were desperate enough to commit trespass for money but who would not abandon human decency to the extent of maiming or killing. That, at least, had rewarded him, with a man honest enough to report back to him.

In his secret mind, he admitted that he wouldn't have minded if Lady Gwyneth were disposed of . . . by accident of course. It was she who posed the greatest threat with her knowledge of the old ways and her inability to reason out their danger to mankind. Why, she was so flighty she had to chase her thoughts with a butterfly net to form a coherent sentence. Yet she had rendered a strong man unconscious. And the other woman—a hatmaker—had threatened another of his men with emasculation by pitchfork.

He shuddered at the image it conjured. A most unseemly image, though not surprising given that Miss Whitmore's brother wandered about the country like a gypsy when he could be reaping the pleasures of the wealth he'd amassed. But then his mother kept a shop and his sister lived alone and made hats. The whole Whitmore family lacked breeding. At least his agents had managed to follow Whitmore to Cambridge, where he was conferring with a scholar who had long since abandoned his native Wales for the lofty universities of England.

If his sources were to be believed, Whitmore had the book in his possession all along and was finding success in having it translated. He grimaced at the knot of tension in the back of his neck. Was it true, or was it a ruse to draw attention away from his lordship and the women under his protection? It didn't really matter. Whitmore for certain had copied the first few pages of Myrddin's book. He didn't dare leave even those intact, for Whitmore would surely use them to publish a monograph at the very least. Word would reach the district of St. Aldan, and all his efforts would be for naught.

Amazing how one as educated and intelligent as Whitmore cared so little for the consequences of his actions. Only his lordship seemed to care about the welfare of his people, though some of his notions were incomprehensible. How could planting trees and establishing all the craftsmen in his domain in small enterprises of their own compare to the wealth and overall good the mining industry could bring? Certainly the talents and crafts that had been handed down from one generation to the next should be preserved, but to depend upon them for an independent economy displayed peculiarities that could destroy them all in the end.

The whole St. Aldan clan was peculiar— again, hardly surprising, given the history they'd been spoon-fed with their morning porridge. Myrddin's ancestors indeed. They'd even named their family and their land after the sorcerer's mother, which struck him as being pretentious to say the least. And then an early ancestor had thought to add the St. to their name in an effort to prove their loyalty to the Church.

Blasphemy! They should have changed their name altogether and forbidden the telling of their shameful history.

A history that might be proven true if the

book were to fall into the wrong hands.

He sagged into a pew in his beloved church and stared up at the circular stained-glass window above the altar. What to do now? He should go to London. It was too difficult to direct matters from Wales, and it took days for word to reach him from the men he'd hired. Four days past they had attacked, and only today had he received word of their failure.

It was obvious he could not trust others to aid him. They did not understand enough or care enough to make necessary sacrifices. He had to do it himself . . . somehow.

If only the earl and his sister were at home where they belonged, it would be so much easier. There were some in the district who felt as he did and who might aid him in his worthy cause. But with them so far away, he had no choice but to trust hirelings. He couldn't abandon his flock. Not when the earl had already done so to pursue a relic that could only bring evil to them all.

Sunlight blazed through the stained glass, seeming to set fire to the aisle with blazes of brilliant color.

He smiled and bowed his head in thanks as an idea, fully formed, struck him like the sunlight striking the brass plates set on the end of each pew.

Yes! He knew what to do now. He knew how to bring the earl back.

And with the earl, the cursed book.

Gavan sat in the chair in Priss's workroom, his legs stretched out, his ankles crossed, his face an arresting study in light and shadow in the dancing glow cast by the fire in the hearth. After that first night in the parlor four days before, he had sought her out, often just sitting in the chair and dozing, other times simply watching her work, and yet others, initiating conversation. Regardless of how they passed the time, it seemed too intimate, too natural, as if they had always shared events of the day and the isolation of night in such companionship.

During each day, she dreaded his appearance in her doorway, his hair tousled and his eyes slumberous, and convinced herself that she was counting the hours until her guests would leave. Each night, she awaited his arrival, knowing that she'd been counting the seconds until she would be near him again.

Nothing seemed the same any longer—neither within herself nor within the boundaries of her home. She felt as if there were no boundaries and if she did not measure each step very carefully, she would fall into a void.

"A silk rose," he said lazily. "And tip up the brim on one side."

Priss frowned and stared at her reflection in the mirror, studying the hat she wanted to complete before morning. Reluctantly, she plucked a silk rose from a pile on the table and positioned it left of center and held the brim curled up behind it. It was not quite right with all the detail on only one side. Defiantly, she tipped up the other side of the brim and turned her head this way and that. It was just right, exactly the jaunty touch she wanted for the otherwise elegant hat.

"Splendid," he said.

Removing the hat she began to stitch furiously as she told herself that she wanted Gavan to go away. She had managed very nicely without his counsel on the proper construction of ladies' hats before he had arrived and interfered in even that aspect of her life. And he was never entirely right, always missing one detail or another, like the brim.

Unfortunately, her designs had been decidedly lackluster for the past five days. Gavan had an amazingly good eye for color and balance even when only half-right. *What self-respecting man would openly employ that eye for the construction of ladies' millinery?* she asked herself in disgust.

Gavan, Earl of St. Aldan, replied a taunting voice in her head. A man who possessed so much self-respect that he did not bother with propriety in any form unless it suited his purpose. A man who did not plan his kisses or ask for them, but simply took them from her, as if they were his due.

And why not? Through her own actions he couldn't help but believe she was willing.

Mindless was more like it.

Yet he had not touched her since that night in the parlor. Not physically.

"Put the butterfly on the outermost petal of the rose," he advised.

She removed the hat and slammed it down on the table, then plucked one of the small, golden butterflies that she affixed to every hat she made, and attached it to the edge of the molded crown.

"You're right. That works nicely," he drawled. "Has Gwyneth mentioned to you that she is not sleeping well?" he asked abruptly.

She frowned as she veered her thoughts onto a different path. "No. With Gwyneth's high energy it is difficult to tell, though I've noticed that she is sleeping a bit later each day."

"She is usually up with the roosters," he said. "I've noticed light under her door each night when I've come down here."

"A strange house and strange bed can cause uneasy sleep. Since you and she do not venture from your mountain very often, I can see why the different surroundings might disorient her. I imagine the attacks, as well as worry over Willie's safety, would add to her restiveness." She reached for a brush and wielded it lightly over the fur felt of the hat. "You aren't sleeping either," she reminded him.

"Point taken," he said thoughtfully as if he wasn't entirely satisfied with her explanation.

Holding up the finished hat, she examined it from every angle.

"Perfect," he said in a purr to rival the throaty sounds of contentment Precious made every time Gavan came near. The wretched animal was even now curled up on the arm of Gavan's chair, rubbing the side of his face along Gavan's hand.

But then Daisy had developed a preference

for sleeping on top of her feet, Priss thought smugly.

"You're very well connected," Gavan said abruptly, as if it were a part of their current discourse. They were always doing that it seemed—establishing unrelated threads of conversation in the midst of others.

She shrugged, not wanting to acknowledge that she knew what he meant and certainly not wanting to discuss her connections with him.

"Sinclair and his wife, the Countess Saxon, who were favored by Brummell before he disappeared, who was also very close to Lord and Lady Dane, who are related to the Marquess of Wyndham. One wonders why you are serving the *ton* rather than joining in its play. I trust you had a Season."

"Yes," she replied shortly, wanting anything but to follow this particular path with him.

"And you no doubt received a number of proposals," he continued.

"Dozens," she snapped.

"You cook, you ride, you sew—everything and more a woman needs to acquire a husband and conduct a marriage. Your family is landed gentry, and your brother is a wealthy man . . ." His voice trailed off on a speculative note. "Scandal or disinclination?" he asked.

"A horrible scandal," she said on a forced sigh. "I was ostracized, never to be forgiven." She should have known he would get around to the discussion that seemed inevitable no matter the company.

"Liar," he said softly. "You are too careful for that."

"Perhaps that is why I am careful . . . now." Amazing what was coming out of her mouth, yet Gavan was staring at her so attentively that she couldn't seem to help herself.

"Ah, everyone wants to know why a woman over twenty is not married, and if she is but does not have children, the question of whether she is barren is tossed about for months. It annoys you."

She lowered her work to her lap and glanced at him—a glance only, before diverting her attention to the fireplace at his side. "This is not a subject to be tossed about between a man and a woman who have only just met."

"Naturally," he continued, as if she hadn't spoken, "you resent the questions and speculation as it implies that a woman's usefulness is limited to—"

"Yes!" she nearly shouted. "I resent it no matter the source. Since Gwyneth is older than I and also unmarried, I must assume your intuition regarding this matter stems from her frustration."

"It is a weighty decision to defy convention and engage in trade rather than accept a life of ease. What, I wonder, was the source of your disinclination?"

"Why, a lack of men like you, my lord," she said sarcastically. Really, was there nothing he would not discuss with a woman?

Probably not, she answered herself. He and Gwyneth were remarkably close and therefore remarkably frank with one another. She and Willie were equally candid in their confidences.

Expecting one of his naughty smiles that melted her knees, she could not resist a peek at him from beneath her lashes. Her body flushed from head to toes at the brooding intensity of his gaze, searing her with an anger that seemed old and tattered and curled at the edges.

"Well, then," he said in a dangerously soft voice, part challenge, part threat, "a man like me is sitting only feet away from you. Why do you not unsheathe your wiles and trap me? It would be quite easy, you know, to transform disinclination into scandal."

Her flush became a conflagration at the reminder of just how easy. He'd kissed her twice and neither of them had seemed the least bit interested in observing decorum.

"Because men like you are far more attainable in concept than in actuality," she said thankful that her voice was steady, that somehow she'd managed a note of nonchalance.

"So, I've heard." He leaned forward and rose, the movement only slightly stiff, assuring her that he was well on the mend. His tight expression assured her that she had once again given voice to thoughts better left behind her teeth. "I have disturbed your work enough for one night."

She nodded and wondered exactly what had happened. She had said something she shouldn't, but she'd thought it a compliment.

Puzzled, she watched him cross the hall and

climb the stairs to the bedchamber he occupied. Why on earth would a man not be pleased to hear a woman imply that he was too good to be true?

What the hell had she meant by that? Gavan wondered as he slumped in the chair that had appeared in his bedchamber and shifted to avoid a mischievous spring.

He never should have sought Priss out when sleep eluded him. He found too much pleasure in watching her work, too much peace in the silences they'd shared, too much need for her companionship. Sunshine, he thought. She was like sunshine.

And she considered him the equivalent of a dark cloud.

Impatiently, he swiped a hand over the back of his neck. He'd all but invited her to take him on, isolated mountains, ancient castle, and all. What had possessed him? He still didn't know why he'd held his breath for her response or why disappointment had ripped through him with more viciousness than a dull sword.

She thought him difficult to take in actuality? His long-ago fiancée had said much the same thing. Obviously his taste in women was faulty to the extreme.

Yet, Priss had not said he was difficult to take . . . precisely.

How else could he interpret it given the sarcasm with which she'd replied to him regarding her past? He understood sarcasm and employed it regularly to prevent anyone from getting too close.

Exactly what Priss had been doing.

Dozens of men, she'd said. And scandal? In a pig's eye. If he didn't miss his guess, she was terrified of men. Or of herself.

Now there was an intriguing thought.

Ordinarily, his curiosity did not extend to people and definitely not to their private lives. How could he expect to be left alone if he probed into the lives of others? "Do unto others" had always struck him as being the ultimate in common sense. In any case, he'd rarely met anyone who piqued his interest enough to expend the energy to ask more than: What do you want? But Priss had baited his inquisitive nature from the moment they'd met. Curiosity had somehow become compulsion. He damned well needed to know what secrets she kept about herself.

Why would a pretty and socially accomplished woman like her be afraid of herself? Or of men? So afraid that she'd developed sarcasm to an art form to hide the fear? She wasn't the least skittish about touching a man, so he doubted she'd been abused in any way.

But she was definitely skittish about something. Namely about speaking and acting freely. He couldn't miss the hesitation she'd employed in her speech, as if she were considering each word before giving it voice.

She'd tried. As the days had passed she'd become increasingly candid with him . . .

With him. Another intriguing thought.

And then she'd looked away or bit her lip

or immediately found something to fuss with—preparing tea or gathering materials or mangling a hat.

Her hands had been a blur of movement tonight when he'd introduced the subject of her connections . . . and the subject of marriage. Her words had been hung with icicles when she'd made that blasted remark about men like him.

She didn't know a thing about men like him. He was beginning to think that he didn't know a thing about men like himself either.

He had deliberately suggested that she try to trap him into marriage. The delivery had been sophisticated enough, but the motives were purely adolescent. He craved her. Beneath him, above him, wrapped around him and only him.

And why not? He'd toyed with the idea of finding a suitable woman and marrying her before she saw the isolation and backwardly provincial atmosphere of his home. Miss Priscilla Whitmore eliminated the need for subterfuge. She had retreated to the country long before meeting him. She liked solitude. She was too busy being busy to seek constant rounds of entertainment. Her lack of organization suggested an equal lack of social ambition.

He could give her an entire wing of Castell Eryri to fill with clutter. If she needed more room, he would give her another wing. He had several, not to mention towers everywhere one looked. He even had a few caves and tunnels. She could fill them all with whatnots as long as she left his private quarters alone.

At least then the caves would serve a practical purpose rather than a harmful one.

He'd been admirably practical in his motives even if he hadn't realized it at the time. As a wife, she would suit very well. They would each be so immersed in their individual pursuits that the only time they would see one another was in the bedchamber.

Now *that* was an intriguing thought. Lust was far more practical and much less confining than the illusion of love.

An illusion he'd drifted in only once, and that had burst quickly enough with words tossed at him like stones as the object of his fantasies had left him standing in the courtyard, watching her direct the arrangement of her trunks in the coach that would take her back to "civilization and refined men."

You were too good to be true, Gavan. I should have known you couldn't live up to the image I had of you. Next time, I will choose a man more wisely. The words reached out across eleven years, sounding pathetically similar to . . . *far more attainable in concept than in actuality.*

He shook his head and glared at the window, willing the sun to rise. The darkness was too empty, too silent, and encouraged introspections better left under a rock.

Chapter 13

Priss stitched fur trim onto a hat as she tried to ignore the argument taking place between Gavan and his sister in the sitting room. Her nerves felt as raw as the splintered handle on her pitchfork. With the earl chafing at enforced inactivity and his sister chattering on about Myrddin and spells and family legacies, the minutes seemed twice as long, the hours agonizingly slow, the edges of reality seeming to blur more with the passing of each day.

Gavan had not appeared for a late-night chat since he'd left her two nights ago. She was relieved. And she was disappointed.

Unable to concentrate on her latest creation, she stared at the open portal to the sitting room, watching Gavan pace restlessly, his body moving only a little stiffly. He'd not been still since the Bow Street Runner he'd engaged the day after the intrusion at the cottage had arrived this morning to report that neither Willie nor any clues as to who had instigated the attacks had yet been found. The moment

the Runner had left, Gavan had mentioned
that they would return home and search for
the villain where it had all begun.

Pray it would be soon, before she fell too
deeply under his spell to save herself.

While Gavan had been closeted with the
Runner, she had received a note from Willie
assuring her that he was unharmed. She knew
that could change at any moment. Years of
waiting for Willie to complete his travels and
even hearing once that he had died in the
American wilderness had not lessened the degree of her anxiety when he was gone. This
time it seemed worse.

"Gavan, the book cannot be lost to us or to
our people," Gwyneth cried. "Why can you
not see that?"

"I see that our family and our people have
survived and prospered for fourteen centuries
or more without the book. I daresay they get
more pleasure from the legend and the incessant speculations it breeds than they would
from whatever knowledge it might impart."

Priss had stopped caring about the book.
Nothing was worth the trouble it had brought
them all. Gavan was right—the speculation
was more satisfying than the truth, just as
dreams were safer when they remained in the
imagination. Who could live up to a dream?

Gavan St. Aldan could.

She winced as her scissors slipped and
punctured her finger. Gavan might well live
up to her dreams, but she knew that she could
never live up to his . . . if he had any.

Listening to him debate with his sister the

past few days, Priss had learned that Gavan believed in nothing so frivolous as dreams and illusions. Having pared down his life to work and more work, he knew nothing of frivolity. He concentrated on the present problems until he found a practical way to solve them and prevent them from continuing into the future.

"Priss, you know how important the book is," Gwyneth said as she sailed into the workroom. "Please explain it to Gavan."

Priss stared blindly at her finger, unwilling to look up and see the earl. Hearing him stride into her sanctuary was enough to trip her breath and stall her heartbeat. "I cannot," she said. "The book has brought harm and promises more. I fail to see how finding it can change that for the better."

"I cannot believe you feel that way," Gwyneth said with an edge of desperation that puzzled Priss. "The book is a link to the past. Myrddin's name will become a part of history rather than legend—"

"What will it change for the better?" Priss countered, still focusing on the work in front of her.

"It's truth!" Gwyneth argued. "It will prove that magic does exist."

"And then what?" Priss blurted, angry at being drawn into the conversation. Angry at having to voice the conclusions that had saddened and disappointed her. "Do we learn that it is not such a wonderful thing after all? We learn that it, like everything else in life, can harm as well as help? That it can be evil as well as good? That knowing the truth takes all the pleasure out of wondering and wishing? What will people dream of then, Gwyneth, when they know that magic, like any power, is only wielded by a few and often to the detriment of all?" Becoming more agitated with every word she uttered, Priss jerked to her feet and rounded the table. "I, for one, know too much truth and have no desire for more."

Gwyneth backed away a step and plopped into the chair behind her, her expression stricken. "I thought you believed," she whispered. "You *must* believe . . . and you *must understand*. I do not speak of magic wands and potions—"

"I wanted to believe—doesn't everyone?" Priss said flatly. "But at what cost, Gwyneth? Your brother could have been killed and even Myrddin's magic would not be able to bring him back to life. Willie is in danger even now. Do you really believe a spell can be conjured to protect him?" She fumbled in the pocket of her smock and pulled out a folded sheet of parchment. "Having proof that sorcerers existed centuries ago would be small comfort if you had only your truth as a companion for the rest of your life."

Her gaze collided with Gavan's and held, captured by the same gleam in his eye she'd seen before . . . of bemusement mixed with admiration.

She wanted to scream in frustration. Why couldn't she have seen such a gleam in George's eye or any one of the men who had sought her favor over the years? If she had, she might have been less critical of them and more willing to become as attracted to one of them as she was to Gavan. She might have been happily married by now. But no, they had all been pompous and patronizing, and she had coldly analyzed them until no attraction had been possible.

She was not in the least cold with Gavan.

In Gavan, her critical eye saw strengths in every flaw and her heart seemed to be completely blind, and stupid as well. There was no such thing as an ideal except in the imagination, which appeared to be disturbingly vulnerable to influence from the body and the senses.

Hadn't it always? She'd once before loved a man who was larger than life. She'd failed to consider that he loved a woman who was his equal. Not in her wildest dreams could she have been that woman.

She clenched her fists and heard the crackle of paper. Ripping her gaze away from his, she opened the folds and held up the letter. "I received this in the post this morning—delivered by a messenger I imagine. It's from Willie. He says—" Her throat seemed to close around the words, denying them escape. She swallowed and forced them to come forward, knowing it was best.

She would not question for whom it was best.

"He has freely spread the word that he has had the book all along and is . . . gratified that his loose tongue has elicited the response he wished for. He is even now being followed and watched, and his room was ransacked."

She glanced up at Gwyneth's gasp. "Willie is a seasoned fighter, Gwyneth, and I expect that by now the Runners have also located him. We can rest easy that they will look after him," she added, though she didn't quite believe it. Willie knew how to elude when he wished and she doubted he would want the criminals to know that Bow Street Runners were watching out for him. Realizing that her earlier angry remarks would negate the comfort she attempted now, she continued without offering more platitudes. "He adds that he has help and is not alone, but had not specified who is aiding him. He has obtained a translation of the pages he copied from the book and has found them to be disappointing from a scholarly aspect, though he is certain you will be pleased with what they reveal . . . he does not explain why."

"The legend," Gwyneth breathed. "It must speak of the spell Myrddin cast to ensure that the love he and his lady shared will be claimed by two others."

"Blast it, Gwyneth," Gavan nearly shouted, then lowered his voice, "I cannot tolerate your belief that you require a magic spell before you will find love."

"What?" Gwyneth said. "Me? Gavan, you never do pay attention. *I* am not lost. The spell is meant for two who are *lost*. Do you not see?"

Anxious to divert the conversation before Gwyneth revealed exactly who she believed was lost and therefore the heirs to Myrddin's supposed legacy, Priss took a fortifying breath and plunged into the first lie she'd told in eight years. "Willie says that we are no longer in danger and you should return to Wales to await his arrival in the near future. That all has been quiet here for the past week confirms that. If you will let me know when you plan to leave, Jenny and I will prepare some food-stuffs for your journey."

Her eyes burned, and she felt suddenly hollow inside. Since that night in the parlor, she had suffered bouts of weeping and melancholy without warning. That was unsettling enough without Gavan witnessing her distress. "I am going to rest for a while now," she said in a small voice. "I . . . was up all night completing an order. . . ."

Before she could seek Gavan's gaze, as she seemed to do without a will of her own, she fled to her bedchamber and firmly shut the door.

The key fell from her grasp and she stumbled backward as the door was pushed open. Gavan's hand shot out to steady her as he stepped inside, shut the door, and leaned against it. "You are up every night, yet I have never seen you nap this early in the day."

She turned her back to surreptitiously swipe at the tear rolling down her cheek. "Shouldn't you be preparing to leave?"

"Shouldn't you?"

She whirled on him—a mistake. Every sight of him tempted her to reach out to him. "I am going nowhere but into the city to deliver hats to the shop." That was it—she would leave the house and not come back until they had gone.

She did not want to see Gavan disappear from her life.

She might even stay in the flat above the shop for a while to keep from coming home to a cottage that would hold nothing but memories of a time when she had almost believed in magic.

"You will accompany us to St. Aldan," he said harshly, as if he found the idea distasteful. "You lie badly, Priss, and do not believe the danger has passed any more than I."

"Then I will stay in the city, in Mummy's flat. The men you hired to watch the shop for intruders will—"

"I will not trust your welfare to strangers," he said.

"I will visit Harriet and Drew—"

"And possibly visit danger on them as well? They have several children, do they not?"

Her shoulders sagged, and she straightened with a jerk. "The moment you leave here, I will no longer be part of all that you survey, and therefore my welfare will not be your concern."

"Very well," he said in that deep-soft voice that seemed to reverberate inside her, "we shall remain here until your brother returns, so I may survey you at all times."

She blinked at the sound of the door opening and shutting, stunned by what he had said. Stunned that he had not given her the opportunity to reply. He was beyond arrogant, thinking that he could settle into her home and take everything over, including her.

Walking stiffly to her bed, she sank onto the

mattress and curled around a pillow.

Gavan would remain. To protect her. As if he cared about more than stolen kisses in the moonlight.

The moon had set early, leaving the night a bottomless pit of loneliness and silence. Gavan prowled the workroom, opening cupboards, poking through piles of fripperies, and watching the horizon for signs of dawn . . . for Priss and her sun gold hair and sky-blue eyes.

She had not emerged from her room since that morning. And it was not yet midnight—hours until sunrise.

He hated this. The inactivity, the aura of threat hanging over all their heads, the woman who had turned him inside out in less than a fortnight.

What had he been thinking to make such overbearing pronouncements to her? And how was he going to stand by his word? Remain there indeed. Survey her at all times, indeed. Every time he glanced at her his body awakened, prepared for action.

It had been the very devil keeping his hands off of her.

Indeed, he was an idiot.

A man's shadow appeared in the drive, a musket in his hand as he ran toward the house.

Gavan reached for a pistol, never far from reach, pulled shut the door between workroom and corridor leading to the kitchen, and snuffed the candle burning on the mantel. His own men, whom he'd armed well with Priss's weapons and a few more he'd had delivered from London, kept watch, as did he, through the night. He had hired Runners to keep watch during the day. He had more Runners watching Priss's shop should the criminals return there threatening mayhem or taking hostages to gain their ends. And he had Runners seeking William, though as Priss had predicted, they had found him and promptly lost him again when he'd escaped their surveillance. At the moment, though it seemed he had employed the whole of the private police force, it didn't seem enough. Since the original attackers had been thwarted he fully expected that the mastermind behind the criminals would increase the number of men sent to take the book. He might be able to fight and to protect his own but he was not so foolhardy as to think he could do it singlehandedly.

His eyes adjusted to the darkness by the time the form reached the yard. Recognizing the man as the postilion he'd assigned to guard the front of the property at night, Gavan opened the door.

"My lord," Dafydd panted. "A messenger from St. Aldan just brought this. He was a Welshman, but I didn't recognize him, so I wouldn't let him turn off the lane."

"Thank you, Dafydd. Keep a watch until full light, then break your fast and get some sleep."

"Yes, my lord. Thank you, my lord." Dafydd turned and returned to his post at a rapid lope.

Cold dread froze Gavan as he opened the

missive and scanned the contents. Crumpling the paper, he strode to the door, called Dafydd back, and met him halfway.

"Sir," the postilion panted as he almost ran into Gavan.

"You and the other men may leave your posts and get some rest—three hours, no more. Summon Jenny on your way back to your quarters and ask her to come at once." He tersely explained the contents of the letter and issued orders for their departure.

Striding to the stairs, he took them two at a time and entered Gwyneth's room.

She sat at a small desk, her head in her arms over several sheets of paper, sound asleep.

"Gwyneth," he said, with a hand on her shoulder.

She raised her head and blinked up at him, then stared at him as if he had three heads. "Oh! Gavan. What is it?" Immediately she stacked the papers neatly and folded them. "I was writing letters," she said quickly.

To whom? he almost asked, but let it pass. Now was not the time for the confession he suspected Gwyneth would make. "Pack immediately; we must leave before first light."

"But—"

He sliced his hand through the air. "No buts, Gwyneth. We have no choice."

Her gaze fell to the paper still in his hand.

He glanced down at it and sighed, a rough sound that wrenched him from the inside out. "We have to go," he said baldly. "According to this, the village of St. Aldan South has burned to the ground. Someone set the fire."

*   *   *

Everything was done. Gavan had sent the men into their quarters for a few hours sleep though the order had stuck in his throat as he thought of the delay. The Runners had arrived for their scheduled watch and were preparing to accompany the coach for the journey. Burns was feeding and watering his team of horses and making the coach ready. Jenny bustled in the kitchen, preparing enough food to keep them from having to stop for more than a change of cattle for the first half of their journey.

Gavan paced, impatient to be on his way. Though he doubted the veracity of the letter, he could not be certain until he saw for himself. St. Aldan had four villages, as well as numerous farms, all dependent upon him for their protection and aid in times of disaster. He could not leave to chance any possibility that his people needed him. And if this were a ruse meant to bring him home as he suspected, the perpetrator would pay doubly for using the village and its innocent citizens as an instrument of his iniquity.

Priss had not emerged from her room, in spite of the hushed activity throughout the house and the yards. No doubt she thought he had changed his mind and was waiting for them to leave.

He had decided to let well enough alone for the moment. If she were to argue with him in his present state of mind, he would likely roll her in a carpet and stow her on top of his coach. Fortunately, Priss's dressing room had a door at each end—one leading into her bed-chamber and the other into the back hallway leading to the kitchen. Jenny was taking care of what had to be done with a conspiratorial grin that grated on his nerves.

At least Gwyneth was properly subdued, her paleness and uncharacteristic silence plainly showing her own anxiety for the people in the smallest of four St. Aldan villages.

He heard his men enter the kitchen and speak quietly with Jenny and Gwyneth as they wolfed down their meal. They hadn't taken the full three hours' sleep, which didn't surprise him. At least none of them had come from St. Aldan South. He was in a rush to return home, but he didn't need his driver taking the road with reckless speed either.

A dozen questions tramped through his mind, none of which he could entertain at the moment. It didn't matter whether something about this situation didn't make sense. He had to see for himself. He had to be there to take care of his people if it were true.

He plowed his fingers through his hair and stared blindly out the window as if he could see across the distance, see his beloved home rising out of a crag in the mountain, see the villages intact and bustling with people going about their lives.

But he couldn't see. He could only pray that no one was hurt.

Loosing a string of Welsh curses, he vowed that if his people had come to harm over that damned book, he would personally tear apart every reminder of Myrddin in his domain and forbid the speaking of every legend spawned by the mythical sorcerer until none remembered or cared.

"We are ready, my lord," Dafydd said from the doorway.

Gavan pivoted from the window. "All is loaded on the coach?"

"Yes, my lord. My lady Gwyneth is already inside. Jenny and Burns will follow."

With a short nod, Gavan grimly strode toward Priss's bedchamber, hoping he wouldn't have to break down the door.

Chapter 14

Gavan knocked, softly at first, then with a hard rap. No answer. He tried the door. It wasn't locked, but it wouldn't open.

Resigned to playing the heavy-handed villain on all counts, he put his shoulder against the wood and braced his legs. All he needed was to fly across her room and land at her feet . . . again.

Priss snapped awake and sat bolt upright, a pistol held in both hands as he burst through the door. She rubbed her eyes and blinked up at him, her face bleached with fear. "What is it?"

He leaned against the doorjamb, arrested by the childlike gesture, by how innocent and young she appeared upon first waking, with her two long braids hanging down either side of her face. Strands of hair fuzzed out from the coils catching the dawn glow just beginning to peer through the window, giving her a golden aura that added to the illusion. The braids fell over breasts that were definitely not childlike. "I did knock," he said.

Lowering her hand, she dropped the pistol into her lap and eyed the door hanging off one hinge. "Did you have to break my door?"

"You didn't answer," he said, barely able to maintain a voice of reason.

"What is so important that you must barge into my bedchamber unannounced?" she asked warily.

"We are leaving," he stated.

If anything, her face seemed to pale even more. "I see. Well, if you will leave me, I'll get dressed and see you off." She swung her legs over the side of the bed away from him, rose, then headed toward her dressing room.

He couldn't allow that. "Only if you can dress quickly. Gwyneth is already in the coach." He picked up a velvet dressing gown draped over the back of a chair and judged it both concealing enough and warm enough. "This will do." Holding it open, he slanted a smile at her, inviting her to step into it. "Your night rail covers you quite as much as any gown," he said.

Damn, but he hated tricking her.

She approached him cautiously and turned to slide her arms into the sleeves, then stepped away quickly and whirled on him. "You are too impatient. You're trying to trick me."

How the hell had she known? he wondered in consternation. His request had seemed quite reasonable and straightforward. He didn't have time to ask. "I'm not trying to trick you," he said as he grasped her hand and tugged her out of the room. "I already have."

Determined to get the thing over with before his conscience attacked him in earnest, he strode swiftly through the workroom, hoping to keep her moving too fast to have the breath left to argue.

"Where are my things? What have you done to my hats?" she cried.

Intent on getting her into the coach and getting it moving before she could escape, he refused to answer as he pulled her through the kitchen.

"Jenny," she squeaked, "stop him."

"No, mum. It's for your own good."

Gavan nodded in thanks to the servant as he hauled Priss out into the yard.

She skipped and hopped in an effort to keep up. "Gavan, I am not going—"

The coach door swung open and Gwyneth reached out to take Priss's arms. "Priss, it's for your own good, trust me in this." With surprising strength, Gwyneth tugged Priss up as Gavan lifted her.

Pain shot up his side. Obviously he wasn't completely healed.

Priss resisted, digging her bare heels into the dirt.

Shoes—he'd forgotten her slippers.

Priss's elbow jerked backward and almost caught him in the stomach. "You have no right. Drat you, let go!"

Cursing under his breath, he pushed her up into the coach with his hands on her bottom.

She landed in a heap on the floor and struggled to right herself.

"Go," he shouted to his driver as he climbed up into the coach and swung into the seat with a grunt. The door banged shut as the coach lurched ahead.

Priss glared up at him from the floor, steadying herself by bracing a hand on each seat. "This is not for my own good," she grated. "I will not go."

"Come along, Priss," Gwyneth said. "Get up on the seat beside me and we will talk."

"We will do nothing of the sort," Priss said, hauling herself up and toppling onto Gavan as the coach turned onto Butterfly Lane.

He steeled himself against the second jab of pain and wrapped his arms firmly around her to keep her from inflicting any more damage on him.

She glared up at him, a waif with schoolgirl braids in her hair and murder in her eye. "You cannot kidnap me."

"I just did," he murmured, breathing in her scent. Now he knew what strawberries smelled like when touched by morning dew. They smelled just like Priss.

"I cannot go to Wales in my nightgown and robe," she said breathlessly, her lips parted as she stared up at him. "I have no shoes."

"We will stop when we are too far away for you to consider walking home, and you may change," he said, his mind filling in every movement she would make, removing her robe, her gown, her body prickling from the chill, her nipples puckered at the kiss of air . . .

"And into what should I change?"

"Jane packed for you . . . even shoes," he replied, devilishly offering only what information she sought, enjoying the diversion. Now that they were finally on their way, he had relaxed, knowing that continual worry would accomplish nothing. Only speed would serve them well. That and discovering the truth.

"So that is why you didn't want me to go into my dressing room. I would have known."

"I would not have liked to order my men to carry you out of your home," he said softly. "Now if I were capable of carrying you myself..." His voice trailed off at the image. It would have been quite satisfying to carry her, holding her against his chest, except that he likely would have dropped her as his ribs protested.

Her face flamed, fascinating him. "You look like strawberries." He stroked her heated cheek, which matched the crimson velvet of her robe.

She trembled against him, awakening his body with a start. Her eyes widened and she shifted, trying to escape the arousal growing beneath her bottom and succeeding only in encouraging his interest.

"Please let me go," she said. "Please... Gavan. I can't—"

"Yes you can," he murmured, uncertain as to what she referred.

"Come sit by me," Gwyneth said, patting the seat. "We will get this all sorted out and you will see—"

Gavan released Priss. Gwyneth. He'd forgotten that she was present, observing the entire show with bright eyes. Gritting his teeth as Priss slid off his lap, he scowled at his sister, wondering why she had not spoken up sooner.

"Turn the coach around this minute," Priss ordered as she plopped onto the seat facing him and crossed her arms.

"I cannot take the time," he said as he shifted his position to hide his erection.

"Then stop and let me off here. It's not far to my cottage."

"No."

"Why?"

"Because your clothing is in a trunk at the bottom of the boot."

"I'll manage. I can borrow from Jenny— from Burns if I must."

The vision of Priss wearing breeches threatened to undo him completely. "You can't."

She sighed with a roll of her eyes.

"By the time you reached your cottage, Jenny and her mother and Burns will have left in a second coach with all your supplies. They will arrive at Castell Eryri a few days behind us."

Her eyes narrowed on him as she proceeded to fasten the black frog closures marching up the front of her robe. Below the neck, she looked incredibly exotic. Above the neck, her braids and rosy cheeks added an interesting contrast. "And did you perchance also think to arrange care for my animals?"

He nodded, his attention diverted by the way the dressing gown hugged her waist and molded to her breasts. "Precious became quite annoyed that we should separate him from

Daisy, so he is in a cage in the driver's box with her for the moment."

"You ... you are moving my entire household?" she sputtered. "Just how long have you decided to keep me?"

He didn't dare answer truthfully, so he gave her a lazy smile instead. "The twins and your mount are following with Burns."

"Gavan is very organized," Gwyneth said. "He's thought of everything but to tell you why you have been brought along in so awkward a fashion."

"She hasn't asked," he said with a lift of brow. "I can only deduce that she isn't interested in why."

Priss adjusted her arms, folding them tighter across her midsection in an enticing frame for her breasts, and pressed her lips together. Such lips, beautifully formed with twin peaks on the upper and a full curve below. He had a sudden need to pry them apart with his tongue, to taste the sweetness within.

"Get some rest, both of you," he said roughly as he angled his body into the corner of the seat, stretched his legs along its length, and closed his eyes.

With the rock of the coach lulling the anxiety lurking in the back of his mind, he sighed and drifted almost immediately into the ether of exhaustion. All was under control. Gwyneth and Priss were safe under his protection. Whitmore was unharmed for the moment. If anyone again trespassed on the property at Butterfly Lane, they would find nothing. He was going home where he belonged. Home ...

"Why?"

Her voice reached into his slumber, dragging him up. She was a diabolical wench, waiting until he had found the rest that had eluded him for over a week. "What?" he murmured thickly.

"Why have you done this? Why must you insist upon hauling me and my entire household along with you?" Priss asked. "I cannot appreciate it. There were any number of alternatives that—"

He met her gaze, holding it. "Because the village of St. Aldan South has reportedly burned to the ground."

Her face crumpled. "Oh . . . oh no. How ghastly . . . but why am *I* here, other than to pander to your overprotective instincts?"

Her quick recovery from sympathy irritated him. "Because your misguided sense of independence is less important than the welfare of over two hundred displaced souls, and I bloody well didn't have time to make arrangements for you," he said with a growl.

"Oh," she said weakly, then seemed to recover her indignation as she again crossed her arms. "You had but to say so, sir. Under the circumstances I would have understood your overbearing manner." At his skeptical look she smoothed the fitted bodice of her robe and gave him a defiant glance.

"But you still would have fought me," he added.

"I most certainly would. I am not in the habit of allowing anyone to take care of me but myself."

"Become accustomed," he snapped.

"It would seem that I have no choice," she said. "I daresay that by the time this is over, you will regret your presumption regarding my protection. I warn you, I will not be a contented or cooperative guest."

He couldn't summon the control required to make a civilized reply, so he shut his eyes and ignored her, then mentally groaned at her aggrieved sigh followed by the rustle of velvet.

Opening one eye to a slit, he watched her settle sideways into the corner of the seat and lay her head on the back.

"There!" Gwyneth said happily. "Everything will work out just as it should."

Gavan shuddered to think what she meant by that. For several days he'd been nagged by a suspicion that Gwyneth was keeping a secret regarding the book that affected them all. Her behavior after the trespass on Priss's property had convinced him that more than a general point regarding right and wrong plagued her conscience. Since their argument the day before, he'd refused to allow himself to consider it. To do so would mean he would have to take action—a thing he did not want to do until the whole bloody mess was settled. The harm had been done and nothing would be gained at this juncture by confronting her just now.

Hell, he was too flummoxed by the implications to want to consider it.

Chapter 15

❝**I** suppose William told you,❞ Gwyneth whispered as the coach rumbled on toward Wales, ❝about the legend and your part in it?❞

Gavan dimly heard the words from the middle reaches of sleep, but he registered them immediately. Hastily, he reached for his scattered thoughts and set them in a row, keeping his eyes shut as he listened with unbridled fascination.

❝Yes,❞ Priss whispered back. ❝And I don't wish to discuss it.❞

❝But, Priss, we must. Especially with you and Gavan so caught up in one another. It proves that Myrddin's legacy will at last be claimed.❞

Oh hell, he thought. Leave it to Gwyneth to initiate the subject he least wanted to hear.

❝Lord St. Aldan and I are not 'caught up' in anything much less one another.❞

You've been calling me Gavan for days, he replied silently.

❝Really, Priss, I am neither blind nor stupid.

I have observed you and Gavan together. I vow you fogged the glass in your greenhouse that night—"

Gavan made a mental note to keep his amorous pursuits out of glass houses. His sister was entirely too observant. Still, the conversation had possibilities. He might learn something that would further his plans to convince Priss to marry him. He had seen no reason to uproot the idea, given the practicalities of it . . . and the potential. *Do go on, Gwyneth.*

"You were watching?" Priss squeaked.

"Priss, the building is all glass, and you had candles burning. I wasn't sleeping well and awakened at the sound of the kitchen door opening and closing. Of course I looked out to see if anything was amiss"—she shrugged—"and then I found William's note. You do understand that I must know what is going on if I am to help you and Gavan fulfill your shared destiny."

Priss made an angry sound in her throat. "The greenhouse and the sitting room have nothing at all to do with your dratted spell," Priss snapped.

"The sitting room? Oh, I missed that one," Gwyneth said. "I suppose you will tell me that it is merely a severe case of lust."

Of course.

"It could be nothing else," Priss said. "Your brother and I are recluses who seek fulfillment in work."

Seek . . . she said seek rather than find—a telling distinction. Or was he reaching for encouragement—any encouragement?

"It is not surprising that he might respond to my . . . attributes, and I to his, given that neither of us gets about much."

Attributes are good. In your case better than good.

"I'm certain your brother would say the same," Priss added.

I might. And you might sound cold, Priss, if your voice weren't faltering.

"Deprivation, is that it?" Gwyneth huffed. "You're both deluding yourselves. I would expect it from a man, but not from you."

What do you know of men, Gwyneth?

"It is more than lust," Gwyneth stated. "You are each quite enchanted with the other."

"With our bodies, perhaps," Priss acknowledged. "But it is a natural response rather than anything mystical."

It feels rather uncommon to me. The thought gave Gavan a turn. Lust was not at all uncommon. Any other explanations for what he felt for Priss were unacceptable.

"How blunt you are, Priss," Gwyneth said, with admiration in her voice.

Delightfully blunt.

"I am a spinster, Gwyneth, but I am also a grown woman with a brother. We lived on a West Indies plantation and had a less sheltered upbringing than you had here in England."

"I allow Gavan to think I am sheltered," Gwyneth confided, lowering her voice even more. "But it is impossible to nurse sick tenants and visit the farms in our district and remain unaware. And the older I get, the less careful the tenants' wives are in their conversation with me."

How unaware are you, sister? Never mind. I will have more peace of mind if I do not know.

"I am in love with William, you know."

"Yes, I know," Priss said with a wistful sigh. "I'm very happy for you both."

I'll be happy for you if you are still deluded about love in ten years.

"I have no attributes, you know. My chest is flat and my face quite plain and William is very dashing and handsome . . . so how do you explain the attraction between us?"

The question gave Gavan pause, applied as it was to physical versus emotional response. How *did* one explain it?

"Lord Dane plainly adores his wife, and she is six feet tall and rather abundant in form. He says that beauty is in the eyes of the beholder," Priss explained. "If everyone's ideas of what is appealing were the same, we would all have to look the same or go lonely for the rest of our lives."

Well, that makes sense, if one doesn't look into it too deeply.

"You are falling in love with Gavan."

"Don't be ridiculous."

Ridiculous. Absurd. Impossible, Gavan agreed, yet the imp that had so recently taken up residence in his mind seemed to shake a chiding finger at him.

"Try to fool me if you must, Priss, but do not fool yourself."

"Better to fool myself, than to *be* a fool," Priss said.

What the hell does that mean? he wondered, his own spirits sagging at the note of sadness in her voice.

"Aha!" Gwyneth's whisper rose in volume. "I knew it. It is more than lust. You would not be concerned with being a fool if it was not."

"Pray tell me why," Priss said wearily.

Yes, pray tell us why.

"Because lust does not require emotions. It only requires gratification."

How the hell would you know? Gavan made a mental note to have a discussion with Whitmore.

"It involves vanity," Priss argued. "No one wishes to appear the fool. And no one wishes to use or be used."

"Have you ever used or been used?" Gwyneth asked, obviously fascinated.

Yes, Priss, have you?

"I have happily avoided bringing such humiliation upon myself," Priss said primly.

He bit the inside of his cheek to keep from smiling.

"Then you *are* waiting for love," Gwyneth stated smugly.

"I have stopped nurturing such illusions. I have concluded that searching for a man with a like mind who will offer companionship is a more reasonable pursuit."

Good girl.

"And if your man with a like mind provides you with enough excitement to ignite the air between you, all the better."

"That would be a requirement," Priss admitted.

Indeed it would.

"Then I see no reason at all why you and Gavan should not suit. He said himself that it was time to again seek a wife. You are attracted to him. You are certainly of like minds—in some rather distressing ways, I might add—"

"Gwyneth, why is it that anyone who fancies herself in love thinks it her personal duty to see that all around her are also?"

Touché.

"You believe in love!" Gwyneth crowed, then lowered her voice back down to a whisper. "I knew it!"

"I believe in it. But I stopped believing in schoolgirl dreams a long time ago. No dashing prince is going to awaken me with a kiss or sweep me off my feet."

No starry eyes here, thank God. He had no patience for lovesick declarations and long, yearning looks that inspired nothing but guilt.

"We'll see," Gwyneth said slyly. "And when you see our home, you will change your mind. The spell will become stronger there."

"What is it like?" Priss changed the subject on a note of exasperation. "Tell me about your home."

Damn. He'd really hoped for one or two revelations as to how Priss had come to her way of thinking. But, then he had learned more than he'd expected. Priss was indeed the ideal woman for him to marry. She had no illusions whatsoever. No dreams of love everlasting and as little patience as he with Gwyneth's certainty that Myrddin's legacy would come to pass through—God forbid—himself and Priss. Of course, Priss's lack of illusions might make it more difficult for him to convince her to marry him, but he would manage with the unexpected aid of the practical streak that overruled her eccentricities and female notions of love. In any case, his sister had given him more than enough practice in dealing with eccentricities.

"Oh, it is wonderful there, Priss—"

"It is mountains—the highest in England," Gavan said as he opened his eyes and favored the women with an ingenuous smile.

Gwyneth raised her brows, as if she was not surprised that he had been listening.

Priss's eyes widened in realization, then narrowed in an accusing glare. Her face was an interesting shade, achieved, no doubt, by the mixture of embarrassment and anger.

"It is," he continued, amused at the way she skewered him with her gaze, "Castell Eryri, the abode of eagles, overlooking a lake folded into the palm of the mountains. Mist rises there and from a distance, the castle appears to be floating above the water, its outline one of power against the luminous streaks of dawn. And it is solitude and silence, with only four villages, some farms, and nature itself." He stared at Priss, willing her to understand, to see what he saw, to appreciate the wild beauty. "There is no society beyond the simple folk. No cities. No opera or theater or assemblies at Almack's. In the winter, snow glistens everywhere. The roads are narrow and primitive and often closed depending on the elements. One can look out and see the world as fresh and pure and ruled by the eagles soaring overhead rather than by man. One forgets that there is any world but ours.''

''And one doesn't care,'' Priss said in a soft voice, as soft as the glow in her eyes, the musing smile on her face, all traces of anger gone . . . for the moment.

She didn't nurse her anger into a grudge. He liked that. Such things were a waste of time.

''He has a passion for the land,'' Gwyneth confided.

''If it is all that he says, I can see why.''

''It is,'' Gavan said, his gaze on Priss, holding her in the only way he could. She understood the words. It would remain to be seen if she understood the place.

Priss could not wait to see it. To take in the primitive, silent land Gavan had spoken of. A land that sounded like heaven to her. The passion and reverence in his voice as he'd described his home two days before had touched her deeply, making her feel the snow beneath her feet and the sharp bite of a mountain wind, making her hear the cry of eagles and the creak of a farmer's wagon over rutted roads, making her see the harsh crags of granite mountains and the play of wavelets on a mountain lake.

How could he have left it?

On the other hand, she didn't seem to regret leaving her home at all. She felt no anxiety to return, no lingering outrage that she had been forced to leave. The journey had been amazingly pleasant given the cramped quarters, hastily devoured meals, and the need to travel both day and night with Gavan's men taking turns sleeping and driving.

She'd always wanted to go on an adventure.

She sat quietly at her side of the coach, her feet propped on the seat opposite alongside Gavan's sleeping form. Gwyneth's position was the same on her side. Gavan's legs were stretched out, his feet situated between her and his sister.

They had gone beyond formalities and proprieties in the last few days of enforced closeness, Gavan's strict schedule for the journey forcing them to contrive the best way to find comfort both day and night as they traveled on, drawing ever closer to the place that inspired Gavan to poetry. It had caught her so by surprise at first that she had completely lost her anger at his eavesdropping in favor of fascination at the images he conjured with his words, the lilting Welsh accent that became softer and more musical as he spoke of home. A man like Gavan given to poetic ramblings was rather bemusing. Yet on further introspection not surprising at all. He could see and touch his land. He knew it existed.

He was a homebody—a rather odd word to apply to a man of heroic stature and temperament. A man content to remain within his boundaries and work alongside his people. That, too, had taken her by surprise when Gwyneth had spoken of a normal day in the mountain domain. Few aristocrats could put on their own shirts without the aid of a valet, much less roll up their sleeves to help rebuild a collapsed dwelling or to help save a crop. Few nobles would actually concern themselves with the commerce of their people beyond collecting the rents.

But then Gavan was like no other man she had ever known. She was learning not to be surprised by anything she discovered about him. It was more difficult to keep her attraction to him from growing in equal measure with each revelation of his character.

That, too, seemed larger than life.

She held the curtain away from the window and peered out at the countryside. A large manor house set off the road loomed into view.

An idea sprang into her mind—an impulse really. "Stop!" she called, and rapped on the roof.

The coach lurched to a stop. Gavan pitched forward and opened his eyes, his gaze immediately skidding to the window in search of trouble. "What is it?"

"You wanted to breed Daisy," she said, eyeing him warily. What a silly thing to do, yet the idea had taken hold before she could think about it.

"What?"

"What happened?" Gwyneth said as she straightened in her seat. "Are we under attack? Are you ill, Priss?"

"What the hell are you about?" Gavan snarled.

"Daisy. A mate for Daisy. That is Winter-haven, Lorelie's—Lady Dane's—estate. I told you that she has greyhounds, among other breeds. She is always happy to place her orphans in good hands."

Gavan swiped his hand down his face. "I haven't time for this. We are in a rush. That is why we have been in the coach night and day . . . remember?"

"I remember, but surely a quarter hour or so won't make a difference, and when will you leave your eagle's nest again? Poor Daisy will end up an old maid."

"Daisy *is* lonely, Gavan, since we lost her sister. A few minutes won't hurt, and I have a dire need to stretch my limbs. We have been in this coach so long I fear the seat has grown to my . . . person and will have to be removed by a surgeon."

He yanked the curtains all the way back and glanced at the manor. "There is no banner; Lady Dane is not in residence."

"Her servants know me. I have come here before. Her stablemaster—who isn't really a stablemaster but he refuses to be called a pet master—helped me pick out Precious."

Muttering unintelligible Welsh phrases under his breath, Gavan fixed Priss with a glare that promised retribution. "Very well. If the house steward doesn't mind, we will eat the sandwiches we obtained at our last stop beneath the trees at the side of the stables." He leaned over her to give instructions to the driver, his thigh pressing against her calves. Heat radiated from her feet upward. Her skin tingled even after he resumed his seat and the coach turned onto the drive leading to Winterhaven.

"Oh, Jenkins won't mind at all," she said belatedly, averting her gaze from the thigh in question. "And when she hears of it, Lady Dane will be thrilled that some of her animals have been taken into a good home."

"Are you going to try to escape?" Gavan asked suspiciously.

"I hadn't thought about it until you mentioned it."

"Really, Gavan," Gwyneth said. "Priss is quite intelligent enough to know that she would cost us valuable time by doing so. She knows that you would chase her down . . . you would, wouldn't you?"

"I would. I hardly think that a house steward and a gaggle of parlormaids could offer adequate protection."

"I would not think of placing that burden on Lady Dane," Priss said.

"And you are looking forward to tormenting me while under my care," he said with a twitch of his lips that annoyed her.

"I am. It is no less than you deserve." She crossed her arms, unwilling to tell him that the farther they'd traveled, the less she'd wanted to return home. The thought of being alone in the country with only a maid and an aging groom terrified her, though she would never admit it to Gavan. And Gwyneth was right; she would never think of causing them delay or trouble when the tragedy of a burned village awaited him. Under the circumstances, it

would have been churlish to admit that the
spirit of adventure had taken hold of her as
he'd described his land to her or that it felt
rather good to be so reckless as to hare off
without plans or careful thought. She had been
so careful about everything for so long.

The coach pulled to a halt outside the stables Lady Dane used to house orphaned dogs,
cats, and the odd exotic bird.

Gavan continued to watch her, no doubt
waiting for a direct answer.

"I won't try to escape," she said on a sigh.
"I wouldn't wish to cause you or Gwyneth
more trouble than you already have."

He looked at her suspiciously, then oddly,
down at her limbs, still stretched out to the
side of him. "Then we can go see Lady Dane's
menagerie and take lunch . . . if you would be
so kind as to allow me to leave the coach."

Embarrassed, she scrambled to remove her
feet from his seat and grope for her shoes. She
didn't even remember taking them off.

He held them up hooked on two fingers. He
had removed them from her feet while she
dozed.

He'd touched her and she'd missed it, drat
it all.

She snatched the shoes from his hold and
hurriedly slipped them on.

Choosing greyhounds had become an adventure in itself as Gavan looked over Lady
Dane's six adult hounds and the litter of four
squirming pups playing about his feet. He'd
wisely left Daisy with his driver.

He crouched down and played with the pups, checking one then the other for flaws or signs of illness. Through it all, he continued to hold the runt, carrying it about in the crook of his arm while inspecting the adult male dogs.

Gwyneth flitted from one pen to another, petting each animal and proclaiming that she must have "this one . . . no that one."

Priss silently pondered the wisdom of taking the puppies Gavan did not choose.

"I'll take the male, if Daisy likes him," Gavan said, indicating a handsome male greyhound slightly larger than Daisy.

If Daisy likes him? Priss smiled. His most overbearing lordship had some rather endearing soft spots.

"And I will take this one as well." Keeping a hold on the runt, he stared at the frolicking pups doing their best to become tangled in his feet. "I will arrange to send someone to fetch them to St. Aldan."

"No need, my lord," the stablemaster said. "Lady Dane employs a man to deliver the beasties to their new homes and make sure they will be well cared for."

"Do I perceive a subtle threat?" Gavan asked.

"Well, sir, if Johns doesn't like the look of things, he will bring the beasties back . . . but in your case, he won't." He nodded at the runt in Gavan's arms. "I c'n see you have a right touch with animals, sir. And Miss Priss already vouched for you."

"The pup is weaned," Priss said hastily. "Why do you not take this one now? It appears he has formed an attachment for you."

"She," Gavan corrected absently as he again stared at the other three pups. He was almost as bad as Gwyneth, wanting every animal he saw.

The runt remained in the crook of Gavan's elbow while they took their meal beneath the trees. Watching Gavan feed bits of meat to the creature, Priss thought that learning all the layers in Gavan's nature could be an adventure in itself.

Chapter 16

Gavan stroked the little mite of a puppy in his lap and watched Priss from the corner of his eye as they rounded the last turn in the mountain road. Looming at the turn was an ancient crumbling tower constructed during the turbulent days of continual invasions and warfare. A man waved from the top of the outpost. Madog's family had been keeping watch for centuries, a matter of pride that had become tradition. On the slope sheep grazed—Madog's second vocation.

Ahead lay a sweeping vista of home.

Priss sat forward in her seat, staring at the panorama of mountain slopes layered as far as the eye could see. In the distance, a lake glistened deep blue, capped by wavelets agitated by the wind. Castell Eryri rose over the water, its foundations swathed in morning mist, its shadow lying gently over the slope like a loving and possessive hand.

He said nothing, wanting—needing—to know Priss's impressions.

"It looks . . . it seems almost . . ." She shook

her head as if she were at a loss for words.

"Enchanted?" Gwyneth offered quietly. "Mystical?"

"That, too," Priss breathed. "One could become lost here and never care if she were found."

She? Surely a good sign, Gavan thought. Pleased beyond comprehension at her response, he leaned forward and pointed to a high peak already blanketed in blue-white snow. "Yr Wddfa," he said. "Mount Snowdon. She greets us in the morning and watches over us through the night."

"I cannot imagine anyone needing a guardian here," Priss said.

"Even here," he said tightly, as his gaze sought the road to St. Aldan South. "Make no mistake, our history is rife with war and unrest. That is why so many castles have been built in Wales."

"If something does not happen soon, *our* history will end within this century," Gwyneth said. "So much of what is Wales is being absorbed by England—our traditions and beliefs, our language."

"It's such a beautiful language, like music," Priss said. "Even the spellings invite the imagination to wander down ancient paths." She turned to Gavan. "How can you bear to leave here?"

"I can't," he said, allowing her to see all the emotion he felt for this place, his home.

She stared at him, unwavering, her eyes shining with a light that seemed to reach the darkest reaches of his soul with understanding. "Yes," she said softly, "I can see why."

"I don't understand," Gwyneth said as the coach rumbled over the cobbled streets of the village. "It isn't burned at all. Every house is standing. The people—"

"—were used as a reason to summon us home," Gavan said as if he were not at all surprised.

"You suspected as much?" Priss asked.

"The message was delivered by a Welshman but not one from our holdings. It made no sense."

"We were tricked!" Gwyneth said in outrage. "How cruel."

"Did you never wonder why the men who attacked us on the road carried no weapons? Neither did the men who trespassed on Priss's property," he said grimly. "Whoever is responsible for the attacks and the message is taking care not to cause extreme harm,"

"Someone we know?" Gwyneth breathed.

"Perhaps. There are those who feel as I do about bringing back the ancient ways, Gwyneth. They may believe they are protecting rather than terrorizing."

"Then they believe wrongly," Gwyneth said, bristling with indignation. "Have you any idea as to who it might be?"

"Not at present," he said. "I suspect it is some misguided fool who sees no way but his own and seeks to impose it on us. It could be someone determined to bring mining here— an outsider. Or it could be someone who fears the old ways will bring more harm than good."

"Or it could be someone who wants the proof of the old ways in his possession so that he might gain power over all the people who would believe," Priss offered.

"Yes." Gavan replied, again feeling unexpected admiration for the working of Priss's mind. They might often seem absent and a bit balmy, but she was sharp as a rapier when the situation demanded. In fact, the less she thought about her speech and actions, the less balmy they seemed. An interesting concept that bore further investigation—

"Then you perceived that there really was no danger to us beyond the odd beating or two," Priss continued thoughtfully. "And you suspected that the village stood unharmed."

He nodded shortly, wishing that she wasn't quite so quick. He'd counted on at least a day or two before she caught on.

"And you forced me to come along, even though you suspected I would come to no personal harm." She inhaled sharply and sat stiffly against the squabs. "Why?"

Because I have decided to marry you. Because I needed to know how you would respond to my home. Because I have to make certain you would be happy here. He could voice none of the reasons. He could barely admit the importance of those reasons to himself. Until Priss, he had thought that if a woman could bear living here and be reasonably content, it would be satisfactory. He hadn't thought in terms of outright happiness. It hadn't seemed a reasonable thing to expect.

He met her accusing stare, examining the nearly healed bruise surrounding her eye. Reaching out, he gently stroked the delicate skin, tracing the faint stain of blue and green. "Because even this is too much harm," he said softly.

Her tremble gratified him. Her glare did not.

"That is not good enough," she said. "Why?"

Sitting back, he smoothed his expression. "Because it suited me," he said tersely, and turned his attention to the road leading to Castell Eryri.

It was as imposing as its master, and as grim, Priss thought as she stared upward at the solid stone and crenellated towers of Gavan's "nest." Situated above the lake and overlooking what seemed to be all of creation, it did indeed deserve its name. High above the mountain peak, an eagle soared, as if it were the true master and merely allowed man to believe in his own sovereignty.

She stepped down from the coach, deliberately avoiding Gavan's hand outstretched to support her. She could not be civil to him at the moment. Perhaps not ever.

"I'll show you around," Gwyneth said, apparently ignoring the tension between Priss and Gavan.

"No, thank you, Gwyneth. I am weary and must rest if I am to secure transport back to London tomorrow." She met Gavan's gaze squarely. "Or will you lock me in your dungeon?"

"You are free to roam as you wish... within reason," he bit out.

"Priss, you will find no transport unless Gavan grants approval," Gwyneth said with frightening calm. "I admit that I agree with him. You are here now. Why not enjoy it? I daresay you have not taken a holiday in years."

"I have never felt the need," Priss said, struggling to keep her voice even. "I do not feel the need now." As tears threatened, her composure splintered and fell apart. She rounded on Gavan and poked a finger at his chest. "Unlike you, sir, who are no better than a petty tyrant, I will lose all I have worked for if I am away too long. You have no right to take me from it."

He stood his ground, staring down at her with eyes as cold as the icy peak in the distance, unheeding of the servants who gaped from every corner of the outer courtyard.

She didn't give a fig if she was causing a scene. "You deceived me and took control of my life without good reason. You dragged me across the country and—"

He grasped her wrist and held it to his chest as his other arm swept around her and hauled her into his arms. "Enough, Priss," he said as his mouth swooped down on hers.

Caught off-balance, she gripped his arm to keep from falling into him as his tongue delved into her mouth, taking possession of her body and her wits. She responded with a sigh as desire quickened in the pit of her belly. It had been so long since his last kiss. Too long. . . .

Forever.

The thought hit her like a splash of cold water. Forever meant commitment and love—both of which meant danger where Gavan was concerned. She'd aspired to forever once before with the wrong man and had almost destroyed herself. Never was a man more wrong for her than Gavan.

During the journey she'd almost forgotten that he was an earl and she little more than a shopkeeper. It didn't matter that her father had been landed gentry—albeit in the West Indies—or that she had connections. All society saw was a milliner. The soaring stone walls of his castle and the way he kissed her in full view of his people provided a forceful reminder.

She flattened her palms on his chest and pushed hard as she tore her mouth away from his. "I believe we are several centuries beyond *droit du seigneur*," she said with forced coldness.

He released her with an odd look on his face, as if he were stunned by what he'd done, as if it surprised him as much as it had surprised her.

"You insult me, sir," she said, her chest heaving. "And you insult yourself if you think that is the only effective method open to you to get your way." With that, she whirled around and pushed past Gwyneth and the servants, who suddenly scattered in every direction.

"Oh my stars," Gwyneth said as she ran to catch up with her. "No one has ever spoken to Gavan like that. For that matter, Gavan has never kissed a woman like that."

Priss raised her hand to her lips, still stinging from his kiss. An incredible kiss. A possessive kiss.

And if her thoughts hadn't gotten in the way, she would have continued to enjoy being possessed no matter who watched. "I doubt Gavan makes a habit of making you privy to his kisses," she replied absently.

"I saw him kiss his fiancée eleven years ago. It was all very sweet and chaste and rather pathetic since he was supposed to be in love with her. Now that I think of it, she was the last person to speak to Gavan as you did just now, only she was far more cruel."

That nearly stopped Priss. Nearly. She didn't care whom Gavan had kissed or who had spoken to him in such a way. She *couldn't* care.

"Imagine a woman coming here to marry Gavan and then telling him he was as desolate as his land," Gwyneth continued. "She was a wretched creature."

Priss stopped in the great hall and gave in, telling herself it was simple curiosity. "She came to marry him and then left him before the wedding?"

Gwyneth nodded. "He met her during the Season and fell in love with her. She fell in love with the idea of our wealth and the idea

of marrying a man who had the closest thing
to a kingdom without being a king, though we
are descended from princes. But then Wales always has a prince around every corner or near
enough. She said she could not bear marriage
to a man who insisted on rusticating year-
round in what was little more than a rock pile
when there were entertainments to be enjoyed
in more civilized parts of the world."

"Gwyneth, please, where is my room?"
Priss decided she didn't want to hear more after all. It created a sympathy for Gavan she
did not want to feel. And it fostered an understanding that couldn't matter to her. Understanding of why Gavan had spoken so
offhandedly about acquiring a wife. His for-
mer fiancée had diminished his love for her to
beneath the status of a social occasion.

She wouldn't wish such disillusionment on
anyone, even his most overbearing lordship.

"Oh, yes, your rooms . . . this way." Gwyneth passed her and led the way to an immense staircase that branched off in two
directions. Above, a long gallery overlooked
the hall hung with tapestries and portraits and
beautifully maintained armor.

"It's a bit like Camelot, don't you think?"
Gwyneth said. "I used to pretend it was,
though I never could decide whether I wished
to be the Lady of the Lake or simply a lady
who stole all the men's hearts. I could imagine
Myrddin walking these halls with his robes
flowing and his voice booming like thun-
der . . ."

Priss tried to shut out Gwyneth's chatter as

she followed her a fourth of the way around the gallery to a spiral staircase enclosed by walls. *A tower*, she thought a bit hysterically. They were putting her into a tower.

How fitting. She supposed it was better than a dungeon.

"Up there is the original ladies' solar. I am in the process of refurbishing it. Perhaps you would offer some suggestions." Gwyneth breezed past the tower entrance and down a corridor with doors lined up on both sides.

"I doubt I will be here that long," Priss said, unaccountably disappointed that she would not be in a tower.

Gwyneth opened a door and stood aside for Priss to enter. "Would it be so horrible to live here?"

No, not horrible at all, Priss thought wistfully. "It does not signify, Gwyneth."

"It will. Wait and see. The prophecy is being fulfilled with amazing precision."

At the end of her tether, Priss rounded on her. "Gwyneth, the prophecy *is not* being fulfilled. At best it is a result of an overfertile imagination or perhaps an inebriated mind. At worst it is the product of the senile ramblings of an old and lonely man. I *am not*, nor will I ever be the woman to fulfill Gavan's dreams."

"Gavan has no dreams," Gwyneth said blithely, apparently unperturbed by Priss's outburst. "At least none he is aware of. But he soon will be aware, and you will soon stop protesting too much to be convincing." With that Gwyneth pulled the door shut, leaving Priss alone in the bedchamber assigned her.

Praying for strength and patience, Priss glared at the door and vowed that if she heard one more word about Gwyneth's legend or Myrddin or his legacy, she would personally find the blasted book and tear it into shreds page by page.

Turning, she took several steps into the room, halted, and stared at a bedchamber the likes of which she had never seen before. The walls were stone, great blocks of it, covered with tapestries faded by time to a soft sheen. At one end an alcove was partially shielded by an oriental lacquered screen inlaid with various colors of jade and mother-of-pearl. A sofa and chairs were arranged in a cozy grouping around a fireplace with a carved wood surround and a long window pouring sunlight over the area. At the other end of the enormous room was a high tester bed with ornate carvings and rich lace and velvet hangings and yet another fireplace as if the one large room had once been two. A dressing table, two old ironbound coffers, a chinoisserie desk and high armoire filled in the spaces. Thick wool carpet covered the floor nearly from end to end.

It was like entering a different world. Gavan's world—elegant with old and new merging seamlessly and, like Gavan, larger than life.

Bemused, she walked through an arched doorway into a bathing chamber as large as her workroom at home. A huge cauldron sat on a grill in the fireplace steaming over a hearty blaze. Set on a dais in the middle of the room, a square, marble tub large enough for two invited her to shed her clothes and sink into the first bath she'd had in what seemed like years.

She didn't hesitate, but checked for towels and found an ample supply stacked on a table. She studied the array of bottles arranged on one corner of the bath, pulling out stoppers and sniffing each one. Oils. Wonderfully luxurious oils. In a dish she found fine milled soap.

All the comforts of home on a more lavish scale. Old and new artfully blended for comfort and aesthetic appeal. She had expected rushes on the floors and bare, handhewn furnishings.

She needed no urging to use the water in the cauldron to fill the tub with hot water. Dashing into the bedchamber, she rummaged through the armoire, finding no clothing, but several sheets were folded neatly in the bottom. Snatching one, she shook it out as she ran into the bathing chamber and laid it over a rack in front of the fireplace to warm. Her clothing lay where she dropped it in puddles of cloth across the floor.

Precious strolled in and leaped to the edge of the bath as she sank into the water. "I was wondering where you were," Priss said as she stroked his black silky coat. "I thought you'd deserted me for good in favor of Daisy."

Lying back against the sloped end of the bath, she closed her eyes and felt like echoing the cat's loud purr as it began to swipe at the water with one paw.

"One of these days you will fall in doing that, Precious. My feet are farther down than you think." She scooted down, submerging her head, then rose, her hair drenched.

Sitting up, she reached for the soap and lathered her hair, her eyes squeezed shut.

She popped them open as another arched door opened at the opposite end of the chamber.

Imposing in simple white shirt only partially buttoned, his doeskins molded to his powerful legs, his feet bare, Gavan stopped short at the sight of her.

Drawing her knees up to her chest, she huddled within the marble walls of the tub and tried to cover parts of herself with the sponge. Wet hair and lather ran down her face as she stared back at him, unable to utter a sound.

"I can see nothing but your head," he said, his gaze seeming to penetrate the marble.

"Please leave," she choked.

He stepped inside and shut the door behind him. "It occurs to me that this is the perfect time to speak to you," he said with a wolfish grin. "A captive audience, so to speak." Propping a shoulder against the mantel, he crossed his arms. "I have been searching for you and couldn't find Gwyneth to ask where she put you. I should have realized she would become more obvious in her matchmaking attempts."

"What has that to do with my quarters?" she asked suspiciously. "And why am I conversing with you as if we were in the sitting room sipping tea?"

"This is the master suite," he said. "My bedchamber is on the other side of this door. And you are conversing with me because you don't know what else to do with yourself." Pushing away from the mantel, he sat in a Roman-style chair a few feet away from her, looking like Caesar himself.

"I have nothing to say to you." Gasping as soap ran into her eye, she slopped the sponge over her face to rinse it away.

"Need some help?"

"Yes," she snapped. "Go find my trunk so that I may dress and leave this place."

"Shouldn't you rinse your hair first?"

He was playing with her just as Precious was playing with his paw in the water.

Suddenly, she felt awkward and frightened—not of him, but of herself, of the sensations spiraling through her belly and breasts, of the anticipation brought on by Gavan's stare. She should be shrinking in mortification that he sat so casually observing her bath. She should be outraged that he seemed to think it was his right. She should not be wondering what it would be like to share the bath with him, to ply the sponge over his broad back and shoulders, to—

"You didn't know Gwyneth had given me the adjoining room," Priss stated to dispel her wayward thoughts. It wasn't working. Desire quickened everywhere at once. Trembles raced along her body. Her breasts tingled and swelled at the slightest caress of water, as if it were Gavan's hands stroking her.

"I didn't know," he replied. "Though I should have. Gwyneth is determined to see us marry . . . I tend to agree with her."

Chapter 17

❦

Thoroughly rattled by his offhand statement and not knowing what else to do, Priss slid down in the water and remained submerged until she had no air left. She emerged gasping to see Gavan watching her with a smile. *That* smile. The naughty one.

"What did you say?" she asked with as much calm as she could muster. Surely this was more of his droll humor, which drove him to tease her in unconventional ways . . . like advising her on how to construct her hats. He couldn't possibly be serious.

"I said I tend to agree with Gwyneth. We should marry."

He was serious. She heard it in his voice, saw it in his suddenly grave expression. Her heart danced a jig, and her instincts shouted a warning. She had to heed it, right now, before she did something impulsive and stupid, like agreeing with him. "We most certainly *should not*."

"No? Why not?"

"Because . . . because . . . Oh drat, you know why not."

"I can think of any number of reasons you might *think* are valid, though they are not."

"They are."

"It matters not at all that I am an earl and you are a milliner," he said, stating one of her concerns with uncanny accuracy. "Society wouldn't care. In fact it would give them something to gossip about for months. Things have been rather dull in the *ton* since Brummell left England. In any case, your connections are quite acceptable to king, country, and code of all things proper."

"Leave my connections out of this."

"All right," he agreed with a devilish gleam in his eye. "Of course it is only fair that you leave my title out of it also."

"My enterprise—" she said frantically. She was too close to chucking it all and saying yes, too close to giving in to her heart.

But her heart had duped her before.

"Your enterprise can be situated anywhere. Ladies in Wales also require hats. It would fit in nicely with the other industries we have in the district. You could design hats and hire another artisan to make them for your London market."

Artisan. He thought her an artisan? "Did you lie awake nights thinking of all this?" In spite of the rather bizarre situation of holding such a discussion in the bathing chamber, Priss was too intrigued to do what she ought and flounce out of the room, naked or not. The man was as dotty as his sister.

"I lie awake nights thinking that if we do

not do something soon, we will give society more scandalbroth than it can handle."

"They wouldn't know what we do," she blurted, and bit her tongue as she tried to stop herself.

His brows rose and the smile returned, wicked rather than just naughty. "I see you've thought about it as well."

"I have not thought about marriage." Oh mercy, that sounded even worse.

"Then I suggest you do so." His expression smoothed into gravity. "I cannot keep my hands off of you, Priss. Since you have objected little, I am convinced you are in the same coil. There are worse reasons for marriage."

"At least you aren't invoking enchantments and destiny and arguing that we are meant to be together as Gwyneth does."

"*You* are enchanting, like sunshine is enchanting, Priss. And destiny is what we make of it with the situations at hand. There is nothing magical about it." He rose abruptly and scooped a bucket into the cauldron, then brought it to Priss. "Your hair isn't completely rinsed."

She stared at it, wondering how she could reach for the handle without displaying her body to him. As it was he stood over her seeing more bare flesh than he should. "If you will hand me a towel—"

"I think not," he said, with a mocking tilt of his mouth. "I find it refreshing to have you at a disadvantage for a change. Just fold yourself up and I will see nothing more than your back as I pour."

Completely distracted by his remark and wondering what it meant, she hunched over, her arms wrapped around her knees. *Disadvantage . . . for a change . . .* He surely couldn't have meant that she'd had him at a disadvantage. The implications boggled the mind.

Water cascaded over her head. His hand held up her hair, rinsing the soap away as warm silky water sheeted over her back, down her chest. She sensed Gavan still standing over her, staring at her, adding a new kind of heat, a different kind of caress. All she had to do was stand up and reach for him, kiss him, and give him what he wanted from her. Take what she wanted from him.

She gathered her hair in her hands and wrung out the water, then coiled it around her crown and fashioned a knot to hold it in place. Too late, she realized she had just provided Gavan with a full view of her body. Stricken, she stared up at him.

He took a step toward her, his gaze focused on her breasts.

She couldn't move, couldn't raise her knees or her hands to shield herself. She wasn't at all sure she wanted to.

Gavan pivoted on his heel and paced the width of the chamber. "You are easy on my temperament, Priss," he said as if determined to conclude the discussion. "We get along well in silence and in conversation. You like my home—" He plowed his hands through his hair as his gaze again found her and jerked away. "I have to get out of here before I demonstrate how very well we get along." Striding to the door, he yanked it open.

Precious swiped at Priss's foot and lost his balance, falling into the water with a yowl, then shot straight upward, his claws raking Priss's leg as he leaped away from the tub.

Priss cried out as the soapy water stung the scratches.

Gavan turned and reached her in three long strides and cursed at the sight of red marbling through the water. He reached for a towel and lifted her to her feet, wrapping the linen around her.

"It's not deep," she said desperately, feeling more from his touch than from the long scratch on her leg. "It's nothing, really. I am fine."

"Shut up, Priss," he said savagely as he pushed her to sit on the edge of the tub, knelt in front of her, and placed a folded towel over her thigh. "Damned cat. It's a bloody conspiracy."

His anger struck her as funny though she knew she wasn't in the least amused. "You mean Gwyneth is in truth a sorceress and Precious is her familiar?"

His head raised, his gaze skimming her flesh, barely covered by wet linen, on its way to her face, terrifying her, even as her body responded to the hunger of his expression.

"I'm fine, Gavan, really. It doesn't hurt."

"I do," he whispered hoarsely as he framed her face with his hands and took her mouth with his in a hard, hungry kiss.

She opened her mouth allowing him inside, allowing herself to feel without thought, without care, without reservations, forgetting everything but his urgent seduction. His mouth softened and nipped at her lips, skimmed lower to her neck, paused as he pulled the towel away from her, revealing all of her.

"If I believed in magic, I would give it your name," he said as his voice touched her and his hands caressed her and quickened every nerve and muscle in her body to urgent, desperate need.

The words brought sudden tears to her eyes. The break in his voice robbed her of everything but the need to hold and be held by him. The tremble of his hands turned her to hot, flowing liquid.

She had the dim thought that she should feel modesty or shyness or shame for what she was doing, for what Gavan was doing to her. But, she felt only profound sensation, knew nothing but that this was right, that such beauty of feeling should not be denied.

She didn't care about proper, only about Gavan, and herself, and the moment. She wanted this, had wanted this from the first day, wanting it more as she'd learned about this enigmatic man who believed only in what he could see and hear and touch.

She was here. She was real. Maybe it would be enough to be seen and heard and touched by him. Maybe there was nothing more.

His mouth closed over a nipple, his tongue teasing, the pull of his lips driving her mad with a frantic, overwhelming need. She held his head to her, hearing a soft whimper, realizing it was her voice, crying for more.

She sobbed as his mouth traveled lower over her belly and lower still. She clutched at his shoulders as he did more than touch . . . as his hand cupped her and his fingers worked magic on her body, probing inside her, opening her . . . as he tasted and devoured and consumed her.

Sensation blinded and deafened her as she tore at his shirt, needing to feel him, needing to be as close as possible to him.

Sensation lingered and tormented her as he rose, drawing her to stand against him, holding her. "You should be telling me to stop, Priss."

She shook her head, knowing that he was right, yet knowing, too, that the only regret she would have was if she did stop him. "Don't stop." Stepping back, she allowed the towel to fall to the floor between them.

Her hands instinctively moved to cover herself, but his gaze stopped her. A gaze that said she was beautiful and precious and desperately needed. She lowered her hands, accepting what he told her with a look, knowing that at that moment it was true. Knowing that as she looked at him, he, too, knew that he was beautiful and precious and needed.

It was too late for second thoughts. It had been too late from the moment he'd come into her life. Too late when she'd first forgotten to think before speaking and had spoken her mind instead. He knew all that she was . . . and wasn't. He knew that she wanted him. To protest now would be to utter the worst sort of lie.

He took her hand, led her into her bedchamber, lowered her to the mattress, holding her hands above her head and groaning as he began all over again, leaving nothing untouched, unkissed, untasted. He stood and slowly removed his shirt, his doeskins, watching her face as he revealed the measure of his need to her.

She stared at him in awe and thought him more beautiful than any dream.

Sensation renewed and redoubled, expanding inside her as he covered her, entered her, filled her.

It wasn't enough.

She arched her hips, taking more of him, all of him. Taking him until she trembled inside over and over again, until all strength left her and she drifted on some high current of air even eagles couldn't reach. Taking him as he thrust again and shuddered and held her so tightly she didn't know where he ended and she began. Taking all of him as warmth poured into her, a part of him becoming a part of her.

It wasn't enough.

She breathed deeply of his scent, stroked his back and his shoulders and his chest, tasted the salt of his flesh as he rolled to his side, still inside her, still holding her, kissing her as if he could not get enough of her.

Time swept by lazily as his hands explored

her with a slow touch, learning rather than seducing, gentling rather than exciting her.

She loved him. She felt as if she had always loved him. As if every moment in her life had led her to this one, perfect fragment of time. Perfect. Ideal. But not magic. Not when he did not love her. Not when he wanted to marry her because it made sense.

It wasn't enough.

She'd wanted it to be enough, had hoped it would be enough, had tried to make it enough. But having him wasn't the same as holding him for a lifetime.

She eased away from him and rolled to her other side, her back to him. He hooked his arm around her waist and drew her against him. She clung to the moment a while longer, clinging to a small spark of hope as well.

Her hand rose, clutched the medallion still hanging from a soggy grosgrain ribbon around her neck, her fingers stroking the design fashioned in fine gold. A promise. It was supposed to be a promise given by Myrddin to his lady. A promise that would endure wherever love dwelled.

She looked down at Gavan's hand covering her breast, caressing her, his family seal a golden gleam in the late-afternoon light pouring through the window and casting a burnished glow over the bed.

She grasped his hand and lifted it, holding the medallion next to the ring, seeing what she had not seen before. Many men wore signet rings. She'd noticed his family crest on the side of his coach and thought nothing of it, barely registering the design.

Gavan raised up on one elbow and looked over her shoulder as she fit her charm over his ring, frowning as they fit together, completing her circle, adding dimension and texture to his.

"It's part of the legend," Gavan said on a heavy sigh. "Or so Gwyneth believes. More likely, some ancestor lost it while riding. Wales is steeped in symbolic baubles."

The legend. William had said he'd found the medallion recently. "Gwyneth spoke of a circle completed, but she did not mention that it was something tangible."

He lay back down and nuzzled the nape of her neck. "Some nonsense about the heirs to these pieces making the connection themselves. It is supposed to prove that they are the chosen ones."

She released his hand and the medallion popped away from the nest of his ring. Nonsense, she told herself. One had only to look closely at the two pieces to know they were two parts of a whole, no doubt commissioned for a lord and lady of St. Aldan. There was nothing mystical about it.

An odd frisson spiraled up her spine.

Pure, unadulterated nonsense. Simple pieces of gold could not determine destiny. Only love and trust had the power to bring two people together.

"Nonsense," she said in a small voice.

"Hmmm," he said as he nibbled the lobe of

her ear. "Nevertheless, Gwyneth will believe it more than ever after I have the banns posted. We can marry in six weeks."

So practical he was. Practical enough to speak of what must be done and when. If only he had instead uttered words that would seduce her into believing that *why* it should be done was a matter of emotion rather than logic.

"I can't marry you," she whispered, unable to trust her voice not to break.

His hand stilled on her waist and then withdrew as he sat up on the edge of the bed and pulled on his trousers. "You haven't much choice now. Neither of us has a choice. I won't bore you with the obvious reasons why." His voice sounded empty, hollow, without inflection.

She curled into herself and held back her tears. If only she could lay the blame on him. But she couldn't. He'd given her a choice by telling her to stop him. She'd known what she was doing and why.

Because she loved him. And because she loved him, she reached for the only thing she could use against him. "I can't . . . I can't live here, Gavan. Nothing you say would convince me that I could be happy here."

"Of course," he said flatly. The mattress shifted as he stood. "I'll show you to a room elsewhere in the castle, if you wish."

Wish? All she'd done since meeting Gavan was wish. "Since I am leaving tomorrow, I see no need. There are locks on the doors, and we both know how to knock."

"A bit redundant, don't you think?"

She sensed that he stood over her, felt his nearness like a live thing reaching out for her. His hand grasped her shoulder, turned her to her back. She forced herself to look up at him with the same calm he'd employed while telling her they should marry, to stare at his bare chest without the desire to touch him, to not remember how complete she'd felt only moments ago.

"Since you obviously have less trouble taking me than you do my home, perhaps we should enjoy it while we can." He bent one knee beside her on the bed, loomed over her as his fingers deliberately, slowly freed the fastening on his trousers.

Her breath shuddered as her body began to hum in anticipation, wanting him again, needing whatever he could give her.

His mouth slammed down on hers in harsh possession, then gentled into tender seduction. His hand claimed her breast as his body lowered onto her. . . .

And then he was gone, standing above her again, his face like the stone eagles at the gate to his castle. "I am going to keep you here for a while, Priss. If consequences arise from our actions, we will wed."

She turned away, avoiding the pain of looking at what she could not have. "I hadn't thought of . . . consequences." She hadn't had time to think of anything but him.

"If the worst comes to pass, we will marry and then you will be free to go . . . with certain obvious conditions. I would expect to see you and my child often." He stopped speaking abruptly, staring at her, his mouth drawn tightly shut, as if he could no longer bear to speak to her.

But the words he had spoken fell on her like an avalanche from the highest peak of the mountain, burying her in misery and regret for causing him to behave so coldly and so cruelly. Gavan was neither, yet she'd told him that she couldn't be happy here, in this place he loved with all of his being. She'd hurt him, wanting to hurt him as she was hurting now.

If the worst comes to pass . . . the worst . . .

Oh dear heaven but it hurt to hear him speak of a child they might have created as "the worst."

She listened to his muffled footsteps cross the carpet, telling herself to call out to him, to take back everything she'd said. To tell him that she wanted to marry him. That she would marry him. Somewhere in the back of her mind, she'd thought about it and wished for it. She'd even thought she would say yes when he'd discussed it so calmly with her. Calmly, as if he were discussing plans to institute a new crop or breed Daisy. They would suit; she knew that. They would share views of the mountains and the narrow valley with a lake set into it like a jewel. They would make love without sharing love. They would be content.

She had thought that she was too far beyond dreams and illusions to expect or want more. But she was not. She wanted love—his love. She wanted him to believe in her love for him. She wanted him to make her believe in magic.

She wanted Myrddin's legacy. She wanted so badly to believe it was true, to have it be true for her and Gavan.

If I believed in magic I would give it your name.

He'd melted her with those words, banishing all doubts, all thoughts of right or wrong. It had filled her with certainty. It had echoed her feelings for him.

How could she know he didn't love her? He'd sought her out, as if he enjoyed her company. He couldn't keep his hands off her. He'd watched her in the coach so intently, as if her reaction to his home was of paramount importance to him. . . .

Could she deny that her immediate attraction to him was inexplicable, like magic and love were inexplicable? All of the moments she'd shared with him had been instinctive, as if she could do nothing else, as if they were right and natural, as if she'd been compelled by some inner wisdom she hadn't known she possessed.

Magic—the rise of the sun and the glide of the moon across a midnight sky and two people sharing the wonders of living with one another. Magic—not spells or potions or some mystical power, but what one felt rather than touched or saw.

She'd made love with him because of what she'd felt. She'd refused his proposal of marriage because of what she'd feared. If he had said "love" instead of "magic," she wouldn't have refused to marry him. But they were words, only words. Perhaps there was no difference between the two.

Magic—dwelling in the heart, awakening at a smile or word or touch, compelling one to listen to emotion rather than logic. Gavan had been anything but logical when he'd carried her off to his castle, when he'd swept her off her feet in the courtyard, when he'd spoken of marriage in the most unlikely of all places and times.

She had not only lied to Gavan but to herself. Out of fear of herself, of being careless and taking the wrong chance. Of again making a mistake.

Whether Myrddin had existed or not wasn't the point. Love and what was meant to be and how she felt about Gavan was exactly the point. She'd loved once before, but not like this. Not so completely that she wanted to marry him no matter what, against all reason, in spite of doubt and fear.

Leaving Gavan without trying would be the worst of all possible mistakes. Loving Gavan was not.

Myrddin's legacy belonged to anyone who had the courage to love and be loved. It could be hers if she but reached for it, claimed it. If she but had the courage to accept the truth, to tell Gavan the truth, to share with him the magic that dwells in every heart.

Chapter 18

H e didn't believe her. The realization struck Gavan in the middle of the night as he'd dreamed of strawberry patches growing in the sun, of eagles soaring overhead watching over them, protecting them.

Why had she lied? Not because she didn't want him. Not because of her shop in London or because he was an earl and she a milliner. Those were excuses rather than reasons.

And not because she couldn't live in his home. He'd seen the glow in her eyes as she'd taken it all in—the mountains and lake, the great birds of prey soaring overhead, the ancient castle and the village where each person waved and smiled as his coach had rolled over the cobbles. He'd seen her smile as she'd waved back, her gaze darting everywhere at once. And he'd seen her rapt expression as he'd told her of his home long before she had seen it.

She would like it here. He was as certain of that as he was of his own name. So, what had happened? Why had she refused him with a lie?

Daisy voiced a growled protest as he nudged her aside, displaced Precious, and sat up. He swung his legs over the edge of his bed, abandoning his efforts to sleep. Had it been something he'd said? Or something he'd done?

No, nothing he'd done. He'd bet his manhood on that. She'd responded to him fully, openly. She'd found pleasure, fulfillment.

Fulfillment. The word stuck in his mind and wouldn't budge. It was an answer though he couldn't pin his thoughts on how or why or to what.

Lowering his head onto his hands, he wondered why men needed women for . . .

Fulfillment?

No, that couldn't be it. Work was fulfilling. Accomplishment was fulfilling. Even trying one's best was fulfilling. On the other hand, he supposed that dealing with the female mind was work. Comprehending it was certainly an accomplishment.

"You may both have the entire bed for the rest of the night," he said, eyeing the animals. Precious raised his head from Daisy's leg and meowed.

Shaking his head at the animals who had taken over his bedchamber, he rose, shrugged into his robe, and strode from the room before he could change his mind. One way or another he had to comprehend what he would have preferred to remain a mystery. Marrying Priss had become far more important to him than it should. Perhaps it was the challenge. He might think that doing one's best was fulfilling, but he was accustomed to succeeding.

Only once had anyone said no to him. He liked it much less now than he had then. Who could accept failure in something as vital as this?

Vital? A rather strong word. One would almost think that he was falling in love. Or had.

More fool he for even considering that a possibility. He liked Priss. He enjoyed her. She didn't bore him. She enchanted him, drove him to passion and to anger, gave him pleasure in silence and in conversation, strolled through every thought, tempting him to forget everything but her.

Never had he felt like this, even when he'd thought himself in love before.

Confusion followed the realization, sweeping denial and certainty into a pile he would have liked to kick under a rug.

Oh hell. If he wasn't careful, he would become the newest bat in the St. Aldan belfry.

A light shone beneath Gwyneth's door. He wouldn't have minded waking her. After all, none of this would have happened if she and Whitmore had not found that damned book and the cursed medallion Priss wore like a charm to ward off evil.

. . . when the parts of the circle come together, two who are lost will be found and they will discover the joy and completion denied Myrddin and his lady.

A pretty story. Ironic that if he and Priss believed it, their marriage would be a foregone conclusion.

Shaking his head at the peculiar turns his mind was taking, he rapped on the door.

Gwyneth answered, her face flushed, her expression anxious. "Oh! Gavan. I thought perhaps it might be Priss wanting a chat."

"At this hour?" Gavan asked as he strolled into her room.

"It is late," Gwyneth agreed. "I was just about to snuff the candles."

Quite a lot of candles, Gavan noted. "You've been reading?"

"Oh . . . yes. A Gothick. . . . Why on earth are you wandering about?"

"I have little experience with women," he said baldly.

"Quite deliberate on your part," she observed. "You could have had all the experience you wanted if you had not gone sour after *she* left you."

"I did not go sour," he muttered as he sprawled into a chair. "I simply learned from the experience and strove to avoid it in future. I went on."

Tilting her head, Gwyneth regarded him soberly. "Gavan, you can't possibly have come to me for advice."

It was difficult to believe, but here he was. He slanted her a wry smile in reply.

"Oh my stars, you *are* coming to me for advice. How lovely. Please wait just a moment," she said as she ran to her bed, gathered two pillows, and plopped them at his feet. "I want to do this properly. Who knows when the opportunity will again present itself for me to play the wise sister to your befuddled brother." She sat on the pillows, arranged her dressing gown around her, and folded her hands in her lap, the very picture of attentiveness. "Now, I am ready."

He wasn't ready. He wanted to run and take refuge in his very comfortable conceptions of life and how it should be.

"You must have caused a disaster of cosmic proportions to swallow your pride like this," she said. "I daresay you must be choking on it." She gazed up at him expectantly. "Would you like me to begin for you?"

His brows snapped together. He had to tell her something after getting her all aflutter over playing wise sister.

"Priss?" she prompted. "Of course I'm only guessing. It could be any number of things, though I doubt you would come to me for counsel on the administration of the district, not that I wouldn't be able to help in that quarter—"

"I told her we should marry," he blurted, to ward off a round of unrelated chatter.

"Oh really, Gavan—you *told* her?"

His mouth flattened.

"You don't *tell* a woman you *should* marry. It takes all the romance out of the moment."

He averted his gaze. He'd gone a bit beyond romance that afternoon.

"Why, Gavan, I do believe that there is more to this than your simply telling Priss anything. Did you make love to her?"

"That is not a matter for discussion."

"You did! How wonderful. I knew it was right to place Priss in the master suite."

"Gwyneth, you are a maiden. You should not be hatching plans of this nature. In fact you should not be thinking of things of this nature."

"Are all men this naive?" she asked the ceiling. "Being a maiden has nothing to do with it, Gavan. It is a condition, not a separate breed of female. We possess the same needs and . . . urges as men, you know. Though I daresay men prefer to think that passion is all their idea and it is their duty to educate women as to its character. It is instinct, and if we weren't intended to use it, we wouldn't have it in the first place."

Gavan rubbed the bridge of his nose. When had he lost control so completely? His spinster sister was blithely speaking to him about urges and instincts she should know nothing about, and Priss wanted him but wouldn't marry him. He ruled the closest thing to a kingdom here, administering villages and industry and even manipulating nature. He ought to be able to control two eccentric females.

But then he'd been so busy with his little "kingdom" he'd never bothered to concern himself with females other than to protect them when it was required.

Priss didn't need his protection. That afternoon, she had damn near unmanned him without the aid of her pitchfork. Even his fiancée's rejection had not affected him so profoundly.

"Gavan, you must cooperate if I am to advise you. Please attend."

"Then get on with it," he said with an annoyed growl.

"Only if you toss your pride out the door," she said with a sniff. "I cannot manage with it getting in the way every time I offer a word."

"Pride? What pride?" he said in exasperation. "I left mine somewhere in the bathing chamber—" Heat climbed into his face. "I cannot believe I said that," he muttered.

"Your bathing chamber? Really? Gavan, you can't mean you actually committed a spontaneous act?" She leaned forward and regarded him smugly. "This is so marvelous."

"I am so pleased that you are pleased," he said sarcastically.

"Well then," she said as she adjusted the skirt of her dressing gown. "I won't embarrass you by asking for details; I believe I am capable of filling in the blanks in any case. You told Priss you should marry. That is the crux of the matter, is it not?"

He gave her a short nod and a glower.

"And Priss undoubtedly refused you. Little wonder. How do you plant a tree?"

"What?" He shook his head at the non sequitur.

"Let me explain in terms you will understand. You very gently nurture a sapling, do you not? You water it and coax it, and I've even seen you talk to it."

"Priss is not a tree."

"She is a living being. As fragile as a sapling and as strong as a tree. Her emotions are involved, don't you see? And they are fragile. But she has the strength to listen to them and do what is right for her."

Her emotions? He hadn't considered that. It put a whole new complexion on the situation. He hadn't wanted her emotions to be involved. If Priss's emotions were as chaotic as her home, it would take a lifetime just to know where to begin.

Yet he didn't feel disappointment or frustration over the idea. He felt rather . . . satisfied.

"Oh dear, I've said the wrong word, haven't I? Whenever emotions are involved, you go ten miles out of your way to walk around them."

He flinched at the implication that he was a coward and turned his head, his gaze landing on a small mound beneath the sheets. Had Precious wandered in and burrowed beneath Gwyneth's counterpane?

"Yet you are not walking now, are you, Gavan?" she said drawing his attention back to the conversation. "You're listening."

Yes he was. Listening as if his life depended on it.

"This must matter a great deal to you . . . as much as your trees matter at the very least."

Trees again.

"Have you no imagination at all, Gavan? Think of Priss as a sapling. As your wife, she will become a tree, providing shade from the heat of too many problems, and she will cool your anger and frustrations. She will nourish your life in many small ways that will grow into life itself for you. You need her."

"Finally, a point," he muttered. "I need a wife and an heir." Not just any wife. He needed Priss. So complicated yet so simple.

"I'm certain you realize it is not so simple as that. If it were, you would not have come to me like this. Nevertheless, I will not goad you into admitting you need all the things that go with having a wife and an heir, like family closeness and companionship and joy and love."

"Heaven forbid you should mention such things," he said wryly. "Will you please get on with the advice part. All you have done is tell me that Priss is like a tree."

She nodded. "Exactly. Your coax her and nurture her and protect her." She raised her arms like a pastor proclaiming salvation. "You must court Priss. Give her romance and new experiences and love."

She'd had a new experience that afternoon. They both had. Priss was twenty-four, beautiful, and a virgin, as if she'd been waiting for the right man. His experience had been profound, as if it had been the first time . . .

With the right woman.

Oh, God. Shaken to the core, he wiped his hand down his face. The first time . . . because no matter what had come before in his life, it had never been with the right woman. The first time . . . because before Priss, he'd been untouched and with Priss, he was new, different than he'd ever been before. The first time . . .

because Priss had been a virgin beyond the physical. She, too, had been untouched. He had seen it in her eyes, felt it in the completeness of her giving.

Because it all had felt right . . . destined.

"I will not lie to her, Gwyneth," he said, desperately taking a last stand against what he had vowed never to feel, never to want or need.

"You won't be lying, Gavan. If your flummoxed expression is any indication, you already know that. Doubtless, you will insist upon wasting time searching for explanations and understanding. But in time you will accept it without explanation because nothing else will matter."

"Pretty words and flighty concepts to fool the mind into believing it has no control over one's life, Gwyneth. At the moment I almost wish I could be so deluded."

"Well, for a man who scoffs at Myrddin's prophecy, you've done a great deal to see it fulfilled," Gwyneth said smartly.

Fulfilled. In that moment when Priss had refused to stop him, when she had taken him without question or protest, he had felt fulfilled—

"Tell me, have you made the connection between your ring and Priss's medallion yet?"

The memory of seeing the medallion for the first time rose to taunt him with reminders of how he'd viewed it with a sense of inevitability. As Priss had fit the two circles together earlier, he'd felt it again. "There are any number of explanations for that."

Like destiny. The thought sat in his mind, refusing to be dislodged.

"So you have seen how they fit together," she said, ignoring his denial of anything mystical.

"How would you know if they fit?"

"I just know. Some things can't be explained or proved, Gavan. They just are. Like what you feel for Priss." She paused, giving him the opportunity to argue the point.

He couldn't argue. No matter how many ways he twisted and turned it, logic simply wouldn't stick to it.

"Your lack of debate is encouraging, Gavan. Why, before we know it, you will be shouting your love for Priss from the rooftops."

He fixed his sister with a baleful glare, then looked away from her and focused on several sheets of paper peeking out from under her pillow, as if they had been hastily stuffed out of sight.

"I'm keeping a journal," she said quickly, nervously, as she followed his gaze. "An intensely personal undertaking, so don't bother to ask about it."

He always knew when she was lying. Her hands twisted around themselves, and her cheeks were flagged with color. She was lying now. Opening his mouth to confront her, he snapped it shut again. She had a right to her privacy. And if she was, contrary to his suspicions, composing gushy sonnets to Whitmore, he didn't want to know about it. Not when she had spoken so frankly to him about female urges. Only God knew what she might write down.

He was having enough difficulty managing his own life at the moment. And he could hardly lecture his sister on chastity after what he and Priss had done only that afternoon.

Because it seemed, neither of them could do anything else.

Life was changing too fast for him to follow. Somehow he had to catch up. Sighing, he rose to his feet and shuffled to the door, reluctant to return to the solitary confusion of his thoughts.

"Be impulsive, Gavan," Gwyneth said as he stepped into the hall. "Sweep her off her feet."

Sweep her off her feet? He thought he'd done that quite nicely. And quite impulsively.

"Gavan?"

He turned at Gwyneth's call. She still stood in the threshold, smiling at him. "Thank you, for coming to me," she said softly. "You have made me feel quite special."

With a sudden thickness in his throat, he reached out and rubbed the backs of his fingers along her cheek. "You *are* quite special, Gwyneth." He gave her a slanted grin. "A bit misguided, perhaps, but quite extraordinary just the same."

She turned her face into his hand and kissed his fingers. "Misguided, Gavan? You're the one who does not know what to do with love when you find it." She firmly shut the door before he could comment.

For the first time in years, he couldn't comment on the impossibility of love.

All right, he was a reasonable man. He would work it out. It might take some time—one didn't change one's entire way of thinking in one night—but it had to be done. He didn't appear to have a choice in the matter. And when he did work it out, he would accept the results, regardless of how many of his beliefs they upended—a thought that filled him with anticipation rather than bored cynicism.

He hadn't been bored since he'd been thrust into Priss's life.

Priss . . . she required courting and spontaneity. He had no objection. Spontaneity had certainly reaped excellent results that afternoon in the bathing chamber. Impulse did have its benefits.

If he planned it just right, he would again sweep Priss off her feet and keep her there for the rest of their lives.

Chapter 19

~~~~~⌒◯◯⌒~~~~~

He thought he had planned so carefully, yet so much had gone wrong. His men had killed old Owan when they shouldn't have. Then they'd attacked Whitmore while Lady Gwyneth was present. They'd failed to find anything at Miss Whitmore's shop or her home and been caught and turned over to the authorities.

And now this.

The Reverend Price stared down at the pages his man had brought to him only moments ago. Gibberish, nothing but gibberish. Either Whitmore hadn't copied pages from the book or he'd written this tripe to throw his men off the scent.

Still the disappointment had been accompanied by new possibilities and the certainty that one of three people at the castle possessed the book. It troubled him how devious people could be.

"You're certain Whitmore came back here, Morgan?" he asked the man he'd hired to follow Whitmore and get the copied pages. He couldn't blame Morgan for not knowing he'd taken the wrong papers. He should have sent someone who could read.

"Right after I took those papers," Morgan mumbled as he shuffled his feet. "I left off watching him as soon as I found these pages, just like you told me. He followed me here . . . saw him when I reached the village. Lost sight of him then, but he's here right enough. He knows some tricks, he does."

Yes, Whitmore knew some tricks. But he might have outsmarted himself by returning here.

Now everyone was in one place again.

It would be easier to accomplish his mission now. Morgan had done his job well on all counts, no matter that the papers he'd taken from Whitmore's rooms were fake. How could anyone have known that? The important thing was to find the real copies, as well as the book itself.

Opening a drawer in his desk, he pulled out a small bag of coins and paid for services rendered. "Thank you. I will have no further need of your services. Be sure to leave the district tonight."

The man weighed the bag in his hand and grinned. "Thank you kindly, sir. I'm already gone and won't be coming back."

As the door closed, Price sighed in relief and offered a prayer of thanks that he no longer had to rely on hirelings to do his work.

He was convinced that someone at the castle had the book, that Whitmore had tried to divert his attention from the others until the book could be translated and offered to the academic community.

But with Owan dead, who here could translate it? The language was old, archaic, and from what he'd overheard old Owan say, the writing was difficult to read.

It was of no consequence. Better for everyone if the book was not translated. And if it were, he would see that the words turned to ash before seeing the light of day.

Soon. It had to be soon. *Samhain* was tomorrow night, a celebration he abhorred for its pagan origins. His flock might use it to celebrate the harvest and the end of summer and a dozen other seemingly harmless events, but it once had been a time when Druids believed that spirits of the Otherworld mingled with the living. The villagers had already erected a wooden circle on the small plain at the end of the lake for their ritual. He'd been fighting against it since assuming his post here. Soon, he would eliminate it altogether.

At least the pagan festival would provide him with an excuse to visit the castle today. Since he'd left Seminary and assumed his post here four years past, he had regularly presented his arguments against such ceremonies to the earl. They would expect it and wonder if he didn't follow his usual habits.

He stared out the window, making out the Druid wheel across the lake, the Valonia oak standing above it—for hundreds of years it was said.

An abomination.

He turned away from the sight and paused beside the ironbound trunk that had seen seven centuries of Prices in the service of God. His legacy—all that was left to guide him in his vocation. How proud he was to be descended from Crusaders. They had fought for what they believed in to the death. He could do no less.

And he would do it without involving anyone but the two members of his flock who had willingly joined *his* crusade and were even now searching the castle for the book. They were a bit too fanatical for his taste, but they were loyal to the Church and that was all that mattered. That they were employed as servants inside the castle was a sign he could not ignore. A sign that he was doing the right thing.

He'd doubted when matters had gotten out of hand. Owan's death was on his head as it was, though he didn't think he'd be called to task for that. He hadn't committed the deed himself and had expressly stated that no one was to be hurt. He should not have offered an extra bag of coins if the book were found. Greed was ever a corrupter of men. Even so, the old Druid had been a century old and failing in health. He'd been everything that opposed the Church. Reverend Price could not regret that he was gone.

Still, he didn't want to be responsible for anyone else being hurt. The earl and his sister were members of his flock. Whitmore was a scholar, misguided in his belief that all knowledge was truth. The hatmaker—Whitmore's sister—was merely a pawn from what he could see.

He would not harm innocents if he could help it. He didn't want to create any martyrs. People tended to elevate such victims to virtual sainthood.

Unfortunately, the longer the book went missing, the more he feared violence was inevitable.

He would do what he must. He would sacrifice life if necessary, even his own.

Kneeling, he opened the trunk and lifted out a tattered tunic—white yellowed by age, with only a red cross to proclaim the fealty of the wearer. A Knight Templar, sworn to serve God, to fight the lies of infidels with sword and wit and even subterfuge. In the end their Crusades had been lost. His would not.

He would protect and defend his district, and perhaps all of Wales from evil. He would destroy, once and for all, the relics of paganism, and in the doing destroy his flock's romanticizing of evil.

Tucking the precious tunic away, he rose to stare out his window at the castle. Lord St. Aldan would thank him for doing what he had not the foresight to do himself. But then he understood in a way. The earl was being loyal to his family traditions just as he was, by indulging his people in their legends and superstitions and rituals. He could not fault the earl for that.

Reverend Price smiled in pure joy as he saw a man and woman ride into the village, know-

ing that another sign had just been delivered
into his hands.

Priss rode beside Gavan as they entered the
village of St. Aldan North, wishing she had
not come.

Gavan was driving her mad, performing
every little ritual of courtesy from standing
outside her door while delivering his stiff invitation, to handing her up onto a horse and
stopping every few feet to point out one thing
or another as if he were conducting a class.
Other than that he'd said nothing.

Neither had she. A dozen times she'd
thought to talk to him, to tell him the decision
she'd reached the night before, yet courage
failed her as she struggled for the right words,
afraid to say the wrong thing. What had been
so simple and reasonable in thought was like
taking a leap of faith across a chasm in reality.

Now it was too late as his attention focused
on the people and the condition of the shops
and dwellings.

"My lord," a voice called out.

Gavan rolled his eyes, reined in his horse,
and dismounted, then helped Priss down as a
tall, thin man approached them from the direction of the church and vicarage.

A group of women waved the man over to
join their group.

"My lord, you're back." A toothless woman
carrying a basket of herbs and dried flowers
stopped in front of them. "And with a pretty
young lady. Will we be celebrating a wedding?"

"In due time, Maire," he said, and cast Priss a gentle look. A look that weakened her knees and flipped her heart over with the smoldering desire beneath the tenderness. A look so convincing it could be interpreted as loving. She would have given anything to receive such a look from him under any other circumstances. Instead, she fumed at his presumption in announcing a marriage she had not yet agreed to and dug her fingers into his arm.

"What a pretty hat you have, my lady." The old woman raised a gnarled hand to touch one of the golden butterflies nestled in an ostrich feather. With a toothless grin, she backed away. "Pretty hat for a pretty lady."

Impulsively, Priss reached up and removed the hat. "It never quite suited me, Maire"— she placed it on the woman's head and adjusted it to a jaunty angle—"but it is perfect for you."

"Oh, miss, no." Maire's clouded eyes filled with panic even as she touched the hat and grazed her fingers along the soft plume.

Realizing she had created a difficult situation without meaning to, Priss leaned over to inspect Maire's basket. "Is that lavender, Maire? Have you a small bit to spare? I do like to put it under my pillow at night."

If possible, Maire smiled wider than before as she plucked a small bundle of lavender from her basket and held it out to Priss. "Thank you, miss, thank you. I will send more around in a week so's your bed will always be fresh." Suddenly, she peered closely at Priss's jabot, reaching up to poke a finger at the medallion nestled in the folds of lace. "You're the one," she breathed. "You have the token." She looked up at Gavan. "I had a feeling it was you, sprout. Never saw anyone so lost as you."

"Maire," Gavan said warningly, but it was too late to stop her from hobbling across the street to a group of women—to show off her hat and to spread her suppositions to the populace.

"What right have you to announce our marriage like that?" Priss asked furiously.

"The right of a man who knows what he needs and has the sense to hold on to it . . . smile, Priss. We wouldn't want the crones to think we were at odds."

Her breath caught in her throat as he angled his head and favored her with an arched brow. "What you need?"

Nodding, he presented his profile to her. "Later, Priss. This is not the place to speak of my needs or yours. And *smile*. Mrs. Johnson is beginning to look alarmed. A loving expression would not be amiss."

"It will not be forthcoming either," she said indignantly. Recovering her wits enough to smile and nod to the gaggle of gaping women across the street, she silently waged a mighty battle between frustration and outrage and an odd sense of hope. "You are a thorough wretch, Gavan. I cannot find humor in your teasing me about so serious a subject. And does everyone know about my medallion?"

"It's a legend—*the* legend in St. Aldan—passed down from one generation to another for centuries," he said with a rough edge to his voice. "What did you expect when you display the thing so prominently?"

"I didn't think," she snapped. "It appears that I have yet to develop the knack—" Her voice broke off as she glanced across the street.

As Maire spoke and gestured toward her and Gavan with her hands, the man who had first called out to Gavan shot a sharp glance at them from across the road. A glance that appeared both alarmed and threatening as his gaze seemed to fix on the medallion at her neck.

"You've just sealed your fate," Gavan said, with the first humor she'd heard in his voice all day. "The word will have spread throughout the district by nightfall."

"You started it," she said, distracted by the man hurrying across the street. "I can't imagine what possessed you to do such a thing." She might have decided in her own mind to agree to marry Gavan, but she couldn't like him taking it for granted before she'd given her consent.

"It seemed the thing to do at the time," Gavan said.

"The right thing to do is to—"

"My lord," the man said as he halted beside them, giving Priss no chance to further voice her objections.

"Reverend Price," Gavan said cordially.

"My lord, I heard you had returned and was only moments ago readying myself to pay you a visit. How fortuitous that you have come here instead."

"Fortuitous," Gavan said.

"May I invite you and the lady inside for tea while we converse?"

"Miss Priscilla Whitmore, this is Reverend Price."

"Miss Whitmore," the reverend said with a bow, frowning as he straightened. "Whitmore? Are you related to Mr. William Whitmore by any chance?"

"He is my brother," Priss replied, as Gavan slapped his crop on the side of his leg in unconcealed impatience.

"How nice. I thought he mentioned something about a sister. Has he returned to St. Aldan with you? He was quite an interesting conversationalist on the subject of the Roman occupation."

"No, my brother is . . . on one of his excavations. I don't know when we will see him next."

"A pity." He turned toward the vicarage and held out his hand. "Shall we go inside?"

"Another time." Gavan gathered both sets of reins in one hand and offered his other arm to Priss. "I have been away from my work too long as it is."

"Yes, I quite understand," Price said. "I was surprised that you would leave at all, much less remain away for close to a month. Samhain is tomorrow night, you know."

"Yes," Gavan said shortly.

"You must forbid the ceremony."

Priss stifled a gasp that the reverend would issue such an order to Gavan, his voice a boom better suited to a sermon of hellfire and brimstone.

"The people have worked hard through the growing seasons and face a winter of forced idleness," Gavan explained with exaggerated patience. "I see no harm in allowing a festival to celebrate the harvest and culling of the animals for food and breeding."

The reverend clasped his hands behind his back and rocked on his heels as if giving the matter great thought. "It is not harmless, my lord." He nodded toward a circular structure on the opposite shore of the lake. "It is sacrilege of the worst sort and undermines the Church in a way that will mean damnation for us all if allowed to continue."

"That is for each individual to decide for himself," Gavan replied tersely. "They are not slaves, and I am not their keeper. If you will excuse us?"

"In a moment," the Reverend Price said firmly as he stepped into Gavan's path. "There is another matter of concern." His gaze fixed on Priss's medallion. "By nightfall everyone in the district will know about that." He raised his hand to touch it.

Priss backed away a step, the reverend's narrow-eyed frown chilling her to the bone.

"They are already buzzing about Myrddin's prophecy and speculating that Myrddin himself will return for the occasion of your marriage."

"Annoying but harmless," Gavan said unperturbed.

The reverend met Gavan's gaze steadily, defiantly, in a battle of wills that frightened Priss beyond reason.

"I will not allow anyone"—his gaze struck at Priss, then returned to Gavan—"to corrupt my flock, sir. I trust you to recognize and respect my duty to the souls of these people at least as much as you respect their rights to cast their souls into hell."

"My duty," Gavan said in a low, dangerous voice that chilled Priss as much as the reverend's warnings, "is to see to the physical and economic well-being of these people. Their souls are theirs to manage without interference from me."

"Very well, my lord. But I caution you that you are playing a dangerous game with *your* soul and those of your sister and this young woman. I will not intervene on your behalf with divine justice."

"I answer for my own actions, Reverend Price . . . now we really must go." Gavan placed the back of his hand on the cleric's arm and nudged him aside.

The reverend would not budge. "Very well. I am absolved of all responsibility for the consequences of your indulgence and encouragement of pagan practices. Only you will be to blame for what results." Price stepped out of the way with a bow. "Good day, my lord."

Tight-lipped, Gavan steered Priss down the street, their horses plodding along behind them.

"Is he always like that?" Priss asked.

"The villagers sometimes refer to him as Reverend Doom. He delivers a variation on the same message every Sunday in church."

"He is an imposing man. I imagine he could strike fear into a stone."

"We have become accustomed to his fervor," Gavan said. "As you can see, the villagers are not so afraid that they will abandon their ceremony."

Priss glanced at the circle across the lake, very much like the one on Salisbury Plain, only of wood rather than stone. "Samhain?" she asked. "A Druid tradition I take it."

"It began that way and still has the trappings, though the participants no longer pay homage to the Druid deities or offer sacrifices other than food from the harvest." Gavan nodded to passersby and continued his walk through the village at a steady pace, his gaze missing nothing. "Ironically, legend has it that Myrddin retreated from the world in acknowledgement of God's power. Price seems to forget that."

Without another word, he stopped and helped her mount, stiff and silent once more.

Gavan silently recited every curse he knew as they rode back to the castle. Receiving threats and warnings of damnation was not how he'd wanted to acquaint Priss with the largest of the villages under his wing. He'd wanted her to be charmed by both his people and himself.

Instead, he'd shown Priss his impatience, his anger, and his intolerance for the reverend. And he'd blundered magnificently with his announcement of their marriage.

Obviously, he hadn't a knack for charm.

Priss slowed her horse as she craned her neck to see into a woodland and the waterfall beyond.

"The mountain rises just behind the waterfall," he said as he reined in. "And in the mountain, so many caves I haven't seen them all. Gwyneth insists that Myrddin rests in one—an underground cavern with a lake that glows with light." He almost choked on the words as an image rose in his memory of the last time he had seen the cave and its contents, the horror a bitter reminder of illusions lost and trust betrayed.

"How can an underground lake glow?" she asked musingly.

"Phosphorous," he replied. "A simple mineral that can supply light, though it is a bit eerie underground."

"It must be beautiful."

"It's a damp and cold cave with a peculiarity that provides illumination so that one may see nothing but rock."

"You've seen it?"

"I've been there," he said. "But Gwyneth says that I haven't seen it . . . something about seeing rock formations rather than . . ." His voice trailed off as he again saw the memory, as if it were being performed right in front of him. A boy and a man—his father and himself—staring at a rock, each seeing something different. He waited for the hurt and disappointment and sense of betrayal but they didn't come. Only sadness remained.

"Shapes that inspire the imagination?

Beauty that lingers in your mind?" Priss offered.

"Magic?" he said and waited for cynicism to rear its head. But for the first time that he could remember, he felt regret because he had turned his back on all that he'd once believed, forgotten how to experience wonder and awe, as he once had.

He felt as if he'd missed something without knowing what it was. "It is where Gwyneth and your brother unearthed the book and that." He pointed to her medallion.

"But I thought they discovered it in a 'place none but the chosen can see,'" she said as if she believed it.

"As I said Gwyneth will swear that I have seen only the rock walls and formations and the water rather than the place and what it really is." He didn't add that he had spent a great deal of his childhood in that cave, considering it his special place, or that he had seen everything there was to see, including his father, broken and weeping and cursing his son for witnessing his despair.

He'd seen too much at too young an age and it had changed him. Odd that he hadn't realized just how much until now. Odd that mingled with his last, wrenching memory of the cavern, were images of what he'd once viewed with a bright imagination.

"Will you show it to me?" she asked, her eyes twinkling with anticipation. "I've never seen a cavern."

"It's not safe," he said, not wanting her to see it, not wanting to know what she might or might not see. Not wanting anything he shared with her to be dimmed by memories of pain or sadness.

He smiled to soften his refusal, allowing himself to be entranced by her dreamy expression, by the softness of it, by the stars that seemed to glitter in her eyes. He needed it just then, more than he'd needed anything for a long, long time. Needed it because he thought he'd forgotten the moment of his disillusionment—and he had for years on end. Needed it because the memory was a part of the past and there was nothing but today. . . .

Nothing but Priss, inspiring in him wonder at her presence, awe of her sweetness and giving.

He moved his horse nearer to her, his leg brushing hers as he leaned over and slid the medallion onto his fingers, broodingly studying it, and then Priss. She captured both his hand and the medallion in her grasp, spreading her warmth with the simple touch. "There are many things in existence that we cannot see until we first *feel* them, Gavan."

Her words rocked him, shattering something deep inside, as if understanding were trying to break through. He couldn't stop it— the slow descent of his mouth over hers, the skim of his tongue over her lips, the lowering of his hand to her breast as she released her hold and cradled the back of his head. The roar of the waterfall and the cry of an eagle overhead became louder, the smell of autumn leaves on the ground more heady, the taste of her strawberry wine lips more intoxicating.

As if sensing that this moment, like all moments with Priss, were too special for intrusions, their horses moved closer and stood still, as if held by an unseen hand.

Gavan freed the buttons on the jacket to Priss's habit, his fingers slipping inside and stroking her breast through the delicate lawn of her chemise, stroking her nipples, feeling them respond to his touch. Lowering his head he took one in his mouth, drew on it, shaken by Priss's soft whimper. His hand skimmed up the inside of her leg, found her through the opening in her pantalettes, caressed and explored her.

She braced her hands on his shoulders, leaned her head back, shifted to allow him to touch her more deeply.

And still the horses did not move, did not even seem to breathe, as Gavan probed more deeply, driving her to tremble and sob and arch in urgency. She framed his head and leaned forward, taking his mouth as he had taken hers, sharing her cry of completion with him as the final spasms shook her body.

He shuddered and willed himself to control as he ended the kiss slowly, so slowly, gentling himself as well as her, releasing the moment as if it were the most fragile crystal. Leaning his forehead against hers, he fastened her buttons, both of them staring down at the dampness of her chemise, at her nipples swollen beneath the fabric as he slowly closed the edges of her jacket.

"Like this, Gavan," she whispered. "Moments like this can only be felt."

Felt, as he felt a piece inside him fall away, revealing a truth he'd shielded from himself. "I cannot argue the point," he admitted, shaken by what was happening to him, by needing to understand it.

Something else he felt without touching, holding, seeing. Something new and different. Something he wasn't compelled to ignore or mock or forget.

He settled more firmly in his saddle and stared straight ahead. "I will be gone tomorrow, inspecting the preparations for Samhain and keeping Price from interfering. We will talk, Priss, when the festival is over, and I know what to say."

"I would like to go with you, Gavan, to understand more of your home and its people."

His gaze shot to hers, studying her expression, seeing what he could not grasp—an unspoken promise, and a hope he had thought lost to him.

"Not this time, Priss," he said regretfully, not telling her that he had to be alone, away from the distraction of her to sort out the suspicions that had been growing since their meeting with Price. If she were with him, he would be watching her rather than the clergyman.

"Will we go to the ceremony tomorrow night?"

He shook his head as he again turned to look ahead and he nudged his mount forward, knowing that if they lingered here, he would make love to her in the spray of the waterfall. "The St. Aldans always watch from the North tower. It is the people's time, and we do not interfere, once the preparations are approved."

"Gavan?" she said as they approached Castell Eryri at a slow walk. "I . . . it occurs to me that this"—she touched the medallion nested in a froth of lace at her throat—"rightly belongs to your family. William should not have given it to me."

"It is yours, Priss," he said softly. "It can belong to no one else."

Chapter 20

❧

"I belong there, Priss," Gwyneth said as she donned a white togalike garment. "Owan is gone now and has left me to continue on. Maire came this morning with these." She swept her hand over an array of gold jewelry laid out over the bed.

"Maire—an old woman without teeth?"

"Yes, you met her yesterday. She wears the hat you gave her with pride." Gwyneth picked up a large crescent-shaped gorget and fastened it around her neck, then wrapped a twisted torque around each of her upper arms. "She was Owan's sister and too old to do this herself."

"You can't go, Gwyneth," Priss said. "It's too dangerous. You know that Gavan suspects that whoever has been attacking us is from the district. Why else would they contrive to bring you back here? Gavan will not allow you to go; I'm certain of it."

"Gavan is not to know, and the people here love me. I will be surrounded by them." She gave Priss an anxious look. "This is impor-

292

tant, Priss. It is not only to honor Owan, my mentor, but to honor our people. They know he is gone and mourn him and they fear that the tradition of passing our history from generation to generation will end with him. I must reassure them. And though Gavan would never understand it, I do this to honor him most of all." She smiled brightly and turned her head to adjust a fold of cloth at her hip.

Priss watched her, feeling as if Gwyneth were leaving words unsaid. Words that seemed as if each was like a secret she could not tell.

Her imagination was galloping away from her, and she struggled to rein it in, to address immediate concerns . . . for now. "But a Druid ceremony—"

"Is music, the recitation of poetry composed by the villagers, and the telling of old legends," Gwyneth interrupted, displaying an air of clearheaded authority for the first time in their acquaintance. "We speak our language as we should do all the time, no matter how lax we have become in preserving it. We do not worship pagan gods nor offer sacrifices. It's all quite harmless; I'm sure Gavan told you all that."

Yes, and with just as much passion, Priss thought. She wondered if he realized that.

"A festival of the arts," Priss said, refraining from admitting that she, too, would like to go. Yet, yesterday she and Gavan had reached some unspoken agreement to wait until the festival was over before sorting themselves out. She'd also sensed a tension about him, as if something else worried him. She hadn't missed the way he'd continually surveyed the landscape around them as they'd returned to the castle—searching for what? A murderer?

And then he'd focused on nothing but her as he'd kissed her and touched her in ways she'd never imagined.

She could understand why he didn't want her company today. Neither one of them seemed able to see anything but one another when they were together—a realization that kept her from arguing with him about his pronouncement regarding their marriage and his refusal to allow her to accompany him today. It was so easy to forget that danger still lurked in some shadowed corner, that whoever was responsible was likely a resident of the village. So easy to forget when her heart recognized nothing but Gavan.

"Priss?"

She forced herself to descend from the heights of her daydreams and concentrate on Gwyneth. "Yes, Gwyneth."

"You cannot tell Gavan. You know he won't understand. He'll lock me in my room, and I'll be forced to risk my neck climbing out of a window or enlist the aid of servants, which will result in their dismissal." Reaching for a diadem designed with two comma-shaped leaves, like those of mistletoe, meeting in the center, Gwyneth fixed it on her head and added a wreath of oak leaves at its base.

She looked like another person with her dark hair flowing down her back and the large collar and diadem and torques adorning her simple white gown. "You look like an ancient priestess," Priss said, caught in the mystery and fascination of it all.

"Well, I suppose that in ancient times that is exactly what I would have been, but now it is simply a costume worn to honor our history and traditions." Gwyneth turned to study her reflection in a cheval glass. "Traditionally, I would have been bare to the waist, but I fear modesty overrules dedication to accuracy." She stared at Priss's reflection in the glass. "I have already set out the story that I am abed with the ague. You won't tell Gavan the truth?"

Priss sighed, knowing that one way or another Gwyneth would attend the ceremony, and that one way or another Gavan would do what he must to prevent it. "You would never forgive him if he kept you from going, would you? It is that important to you."

"Yes, Priss, it is. Have you never felt so completely right about something that you would move heaven and earth to accomplish it, perhaps even accept risks, as William and I have done because of the book?" She averted her gaze and fussed with her skirt. "Like perhaps loving my brother even though he is too thick-skulled to see what is right in front of his face?" she added quickly, as if anxious to drown out one subject with another.

It had to be her imagination . . . and Gwyneth's penchant for melodrama. "Yes, I know how you feel, Gwyneth," she admitted on a sigh. "But because I love him, I will not lie to him when he asks me where you are." She smiled as Gwyneth's face fell. "I suppose I shall just have to accompany you in order to avoid it."

"Oh! How wonderful! The people are so excited about you, Priss, and will feel honored by your presence. It will truly be a celebration to remember."

"I hope it will not be a celebration to forget," Priss said. "I do have a condition. Please wait here. I will be right back." Turning, she raced down the corridors to Gavan's wing of the castle, dashed into her room to collect a few things from her trunk, and ran back again, careful that no one saw her.

"Here. I will instruct you on its use on the way to the festival." She handed Gwyneth a pistol and held the other. "Drat, I forgot my cloak and I need a deep pocket for this."

"No matter," Gwyneth said happily. "You are to wear this." She unfolded a long white toga similar to hers. "I also have cloaks for us ... with pockets. Now please hurry. We must be off soon." She turned Priss and released the fastenings on her gown. "You will have to shed your underpinnings, I'm afraid. I'll turn my back."

"You intended me to go all along," Priss accused as she shed her gown and chemise and shivered at the air caressing her bare flesh, wishing it were Gavan instead.

Shameless—she was utterly shameless and couldn't manage to feel a shred of remorse for it.

"Of course I did. Your presence is as important as mine now that word has got out about your medallion, and speculation is running rampant that the book has been found also." She whirled around and gasped at the sight of Priss. "You are the one who looks like a priestess. It shows all your beauty." Picking up the remainder of the gold pieces, she wrapped torques around Priss's arms and settled a *lunula* similar to hers on her head. "I don't think a gorget will do at all. The medallion is more meaningful. Everyone will want to see it." She handed Priss a plain gold wire choker. "Here, slip the pendant on this."

Giddy with the speed with which Gwyneth had taken over, Priss stood mutely staring at her reflection in the cheval glass as Gwyneth freed her hair from its chignon into a mass of wild curls falling over her bared shoulders and down her back. She looked unreal, like some primitive warrior queen. "A brush," she said weakly.

"Absolutely not, Priss. Your hair is perfect as it is." Gwyneth settled a hooded cloak of soft white wool over Priss's shoulders and donned another. "We have pockets—a concession to modern times. Put your pistol in there."

"Gwyneth, I don't think we should do this," she protested on a wave of sudden panic. "Gavan is right; we should allow the people their celebration without our interference . . . Gwyneth, I cannot go out in public like this."

"What Gavan forgets is that we are part of the people . . . and of course you can. You look magnificent. Now we must hurry before

Gavan finishes his meeting with the castle steward."

Taking a fortifying breath, Priss followed Gwyneth down small corridors and back stairways to a door set into the stone enclosure of a small private garden. "Maire will be waiting for us outside with her two grandsons. We will be perfectly safe, Priss, you'll see."

At the sight of the two tall, robust men flanking the stooped woman with a hat of ostrich feathers and butterflies perched on her head, Priss ordered her doubts to silence and slipped her hand into her pocket to feel the reassuring metal and weight of her pistol.

Precious sauntered up to her and wound his long body around her legs, purring loudly.

"Go back, Precious," she whispered. The cat leaped up, barely giving her time to catch him. "All right, you may come along," she said, finding comfort in his presence.

They would be all right. Surely they would.

The night was unseasonably warm and clear, as if nature herself had blessed the gathering far below Gavan on the shore of the lake. The moon hung high and mottled silver over the small meadow, its glow mingling with the golden red light of a hundred torches and casting a quicksilver sheen on the wooden circle. Oddly, a gentle mist almost as luminous as the moon, swirled and roiled gently over the ground.

Even so far above the festival, he could hear the babble of voices rising and falling in the musical cadence of their native tongue.

A distance away, near the trees ringing the meadow, a couple wandered and kissed and slowly sank to the ground, obscured by the mist as music played—a flute here and a trumpet there. The strains of a violin wafted through it all in a haunting melody.

Gavan wouldn't have minded being among them rather than isolated on top of a tower. The thought didn't surprise him as it would have in the past. He was changing, becoming more relaxed, less bored, more vital. The return of an old memory seemed just that—a memory rather than a wall in his mind, shutting in a part of him.

He glanced impatiently at the doorway leading onto the tower roof. Where were Priss and Gwyneth? He couldn't imagine Priss missing such an experience. Gwyneth would never allow an indisposition to prevent her from watching the festivities.

He glimpsed a blond mane of hair hanging loose in a bounty of curls bobbing through the crowd and thought of Priss. Of her hair that was always hanging haphazardly from whatever restraint she imposed upon it. Of the color like wheat in the sun. Of how it gleamed richly in any light.

His fingers clenched on the battlement. No one in the district had hair like that. No one in the world had hair like that . . . except Priss. No one else would be carrying a large black cat that stuck out like a banner against her white clothing.

"Daisy, come," he commanded. Foreboding urged him across the roof, down the stairs, into the great hall. He shouted for his horse, and a footman scurried to do his bidding. He donned his cape and called for men, then cursed as he remembered that all but a few of the servants were at the wooden circle.

Everyone . . . Priss . . . Gwyneth.

A stableboy rode his horse right up to the entrance and leaped down, handing Gavan the reins.

He bounded up into the saddle and spurred the horse on, Daisy running easily at his side and a sense of doom nipping at his heels.

Someone was watching, perhaps following him. The Reverend Price glanced over his shoulder and saw nothing but robed people from all four St. Aldan villages milling around trading stories and songs and strings of verse.

Someone was watching. He scanned the throngs of people and saw nothing out of the ordinary—no strange faces, no watchful stares. Nothing. It was his imagination—a product of the moon and the circle and the poems and songs recounting the days when ignorance and war and darkness ruled the land.

He was the one watching. Watching Lady Gwyneth and the Whitmore chit weaving through the villagers in their heathenish garb. Watching the villagers being beguiled by the hat maker's beauty and the medallion at the base of her throat.

He had to act soon or it would be too late to save his poor misguided flock.

The night was warm, prompting many to

discard their robes for the comfort of their everyday clothing. Certainly Lady Gwyneth and Miss Whitmore were not overly uncomfortable with their bare arms and traditional costumes, though they at least preserved modesty by not removing their cloaks. A mixed blessing, for while the unseasonable weather allowed him to better distinguish identities without the concealment of hooded robes, he sweltered beneath his own Druid costume, unable to remove it for fear of being recognized.

He ignored the discomfort—a small price to pay to end the blasphemous practices the earl and his sister condoned. For the first time in his life, he experienced hate for the woman who was both his superior and his curse.

He knew what he had to do. He'd known yesterday after seeing the medallion around the Whitmore chit's neck. Hours of prayer and planning had overwhelmed reluctance with purpose and a scheme that could not fail to reward him with the book.

He'd thought to take only one of the women, but now he knew they both presented a danger. And two would bring results faster than one.

He signaled the three men loyal to his cause, waited for them to reach him, and outlined his final plan while wrapping cheesecloth around his nose and mouth, concealing his features. One man would remain concealed in the trees, waiting to aid him. The others would accompany him into the lion's den itself.

He again turned abruptly at the sensation that someone watched. Nothing met his gaze but shadows of the trees and moonlight painting a trail on the lake.

"Gwyneth, we are being watched; I'm certain of it." Priss glanced uneasily over her shoulder, seeing nothing but people.

"Well of course we are being watched. You draw stares with your beauty, Priss. In that rig and with Myrddin's token hanging at your neck, you command attention."

"We must return to the castle," Priss insisted. "Something isn't right." She knew it wasn't, could feel the bore of a single stare as surely as she felt the balmy air and heard water lapping at the shore not far away. "You've done what you intended. You have greeted everyone and recited a legend and made me the newest curiosity."

"Not yet," Gwyneth said. "I must recite *the* legend before I go. It is expected. . . ." Gwyneth's voice trailed off as a group of villagers stopped her and began to converse in Welsh.

Shivering, Priss stepped back away from the throng, seeking Maire's grandsons then searching the shadows at the edge of the nearby woods, searching for the source of her unease, searching for the danger instinct insisted lurked in the autumn night.

She rubbed her temples as the noise faded, trying to soothe the hammering behind her eyes as she strolled within the perimeter of the meadow, her gaze analyzing each shape of tree and branch and rock, her instincts warning her not to stray so far from the crowd. So far that even the light from the bonfires no longer reached her.

But as she began to turn toward the circle, a form separated from the shelter of a tree and took one step toward her. Her heart drumming in her throat, she backed away, toward the wooden circle and the light and protection. She jumped and cried out as a hand touched her arm.

"Priss, really," Gwyneth said. "Do stop being so gloomy. This is a night for happiness and celebration. And since you are the one who insisted we remain together, the least you can do is not wander so far from the festivities—"

Gwyneth silenced with a squeak as something white appeared around her throat.

Precious yowled and jumped from her hold.

Suddenly, Priss could not breathe and clutched at the weight around her own neck. An arm, she thought in panic. Strangling her. Another strangling Gwyneth. Men in hooded robes, white against shadow. . . .

The pressure eased, allowing her to breathe as she was dragged backward, into the trees. Fear seized her as she remembered the day at her shop and later her cottage, of how helpless she'd felt against the intrusion into her safe world, even though they'd defeated the intruders.

Not again. Not ever again.

All the lessons she'd ever learned from Willie and Drew charged into her mind with a surge of energy. She ordered her limbs to go limp, creating a dead weight. Her captor cursed as he staggered. Pulling her elbow forward, she jammed it back into his midsection as she stomped on his instep.

She lurched to her knees from the momentum of his sudden release and immediately dug into her pocket for her pistol.

Something black shot past her and leaped up on the shoulder of the man holding Gwyneth. Precious—his back arched, his fur standing on end, his eyes a feral gold in the darkness.

Gwyneth gave a muffled screech and kicked her legs out in front of her, throwing her attacker off-balance, then whirling around to face him, her hands lashing out at him like a child flailing to defend herself against a bully. Precious clawed the man's face and ear, his feline growl sounding unholy mingled with the music and the chatter a distance away.

The man threw Gwyneth away from him and dropped to his knees, cursing hoarsely as he batted at the cat.

The pistol flew from Priss's hand as a man's arm snaked around her waist and hauled her back. She raised her own arm, turning her hand to dig her fingers into his eyes.

He cried out and pushed her hard to the ground, knocking the breath from her.

Priss crawled on the yellowed grass, groping for her weapon.

The other man struggled to his feet and began to circle Gwyneth while kicking at the cat winding between his feet and swiping at his calves.

Cold metal grazed Priss's fingers. A hand gripped her hair and pulled without mercy, nearly breaking her neck as she was dragged backward. She twisted, ignoring the pain, and held up the pistol and cocked it. She didn't move, didn't waver as he stilled and opened his hand.

Dispassionate with shock and anger, she aimed between the eyes above a cloth covering the man's mouth and nose. "Tell your companion to leave her alone," Priss ordered, dimly aware that the voice sounded strange, too hard and vicious to be her own.

"Stop," he ordered. "Release her."

Sounds of the struggle ceased. *The leader*, she thought. He was their leader.

"Gwyneth, your pistol," Priss said, with a cold calm that frightened her.

Fear strengthened its hold on her as she spotted another shadow approaching at a run across the meadow from the forest a distance away. Five men—they could not possibly fight five men.

Gwyneth appeared at her side but facing the other direction, holding her pistol steady on her attacker. "Priss," she hissed from the side of her mouth, "I don't remember what you told me about how to use a pistol."

"Pull back the hammer and pretend," Priss whispered back.

The two men running toward them from different directions distracted Priss. The man she held at bay bent at the waist and charged. She sidestepped, just barely avoiding him.

Gwyneth cried out and fell backward. Something shoved at Priss's back, knocking her down. Four men loomed over her and Gwyneth.

They were lost.

With an odd detachment, Priss noted that the fifth man lay slumped against a tree, seemingly unconscious. She didn't recall striking him or firing her pistol. Had Gwyneth?

As if by mutual agreement, she and Gwyneth acted out of desperation. They screamed. *Why hadn't they screamed before now?* Priss wondered. They might have been heard over the celebration. She prayed they would be heard now.

In the distance, the noise of the villagers increased with the sound of commotion—shouts of warning and squeals and cries as the crowd parted suddenly. Horse, rider, and dog appeared, riding hard through the aisle created by people skittering out of the way, hooves thundering, the rider's cape flying out behind him, then a moment of utter silence as the horse jumped the boundary of the wooden circle, flying through the air as gracefully as an eagle soaring over a mountaintop.

One man separated from the group standing over her and Gwyneth and loped toward the one lying against the tree.

Hooves hit the ground with a spray of dirt and thundered toward them.

The three men scattered.

The rider leaped from his saddle as the horse reared to a stop.

Gavan ... catching one man and whirling

him around, slamming his fist into the man's face, letting him fall to the ground, whimpering in pain. Gavan . . . tripping another man and avoiding a vicious kick aimed at his knee, then ordering Daisy to guard the criminal. Gavan . . . stepping over her as if she were a pebble to meet the third man and deliver a blow that resulted in a grunt and a satisfying crunch of bone.

Gavan . . . saving them.

Precious jumped on one man's chest and added her growls to Daisy's.

Gavan hauled one man, then another over to lie beside the third. Fierce and angry, he stood over them, his fists clenched as if he would pommel them into oblivion if they so much as moved.

The greyhound bared her teeth as a man reached up to stem the flow of blood from his nose.

"Oh my stars," Gwyneth gasped.

Priss sat up quickly and searched for the other two men. They were gone.

He'd lost his opportunity and now he would have to call in at least two more men to aid him. No matter. There were a few others in the villages who were faithful enough to remain home rather than celebrate *Samhain*. They would take up his cause. They might even do it without insisting upon being paid for the privilege of serving God.

He shook his head, puzzled that two women hampered by close-fitting skirts and one aristocrat had been too much for him and his cohorts. Ironically, the arrival of his lordship galloping across the meadow had provided diversion enough for him to escape.

It wasn't proper for ladies to struggle so, or to carry pistols. And who ever heard of an earl brawling with several men without a single thought to soiling his hands?

At least they couldn't have recognized him. A blessing he'd had the wit to conceal his face.

He narrowed his eyes on the man lying face down across the horse he was leading through the woods. Another blessing that he'd recognized the tall, loose-limbed body and blond hair of William Whitmore running toward him from across the meadow. Knowing he had been provided with another opportunity, he'd cut Whitmore off and rendered him unconscious with a well-aimed rock, just like David against Goliath. It had been his favorite Old Testament story.

But he could not give in to excessive pride. He must remember that if Whitmore had not been so intent on reaching the women, he never would have been so easy to take.

His mouth dry in the aftermath of fear, he glanced over his shoulder, squinting to see the revelers who had gathered around his lordship and the ladies in the distance. It had been a close escape. A moment's hesitation would have seen him captured with his men. But, no matter. William Whitmore would serve his purpose just as well as the ladies would have. Otherwise, Whitmore would not have been served up to him so easily.

Confident that he had put enough distance

between himself and the others, he pursed his lips and began to softly whistle an old hymn as led the horse carrying his hostage into the trees.

Chapter 21

"Gavan, how did you find us?" Gwyneth asked.

"It is never difficult to find trouble," he said grimly as he motioned for several men to carry off the unconscious form of a man he recognized as one of his footmen. In his rage, he'd broken the man's nose and jaw. He would be getting no answers from him for a while.

"Are you hurt?" he asked.

"Of course not," Gwyneth said as she stood and brushed off her costume. "We did very well for ourselves."

"Priss?" he said, addressing her for the first time.

"No, I'm not hurt," she said, eyeing him warily as she rose from the ground.

"Yet," he gritted out as his gaze traveled over bare shoulders, close-fitting toga, and wild blond curls, "I have a strong desire to throttle the both of you."

"Really, Gavan," Gwyneth began. "You needn't have charged in like some avenging knight. We—"

"Yes, you should," Priss contradicted. "I feared we would have to shoot, and Gwyneth didn't know how and I only had one shot." She stood in front of him, only feet separating them, her face pale in the moonlight, her arms at her sides as if they were too heavy for her to support them. Her damned black cat purred and rubbed his side along Priss's leg.

A bruise darkened her throat.

Too furious to speak, he raised his hand to the mark on her throat, afraid to take her in his arms lest he crush her with his relief. Another man ran forward leading Gavan's horse.

With every muscle in his body restrained, he reached for Priss's hand, pried her fingers open, and removed the pistol from her grasp.

"We shouldn't have come. It was stupid of me," she babbled. "I cannot imagine what I was thinking. I knew better. I was just so curious and a bit excited and—"

"Be quiet, Priss," he said, wanting badly to shake her . . . or kiss her.

"I can't seem to," she said. "I shouldn't have done it. I should have remembered that someone wants—"

"I don't think it very nice of you to take all the credit for coming here, Priss," Gwyneth said. "Please recall that I gave you little choice."

"Be quiet!" he ordered with forced calm, then reached for his sister and jerked her toward him as he pulled Priss close with his other arm, holding them tightly, his body shuddering with the release of the fear that had almost felled him with its force when he'd seen them struggling with—

"I'm sorry, Gavan," Gwyneth said, having the grace to at least tremble. "It was all my fault. I thought we'd be safe."

"And I didn't think at all," Priss said fiercely.

Another shudder rocked him as Priss burrowed into the shelter of his embrace, her arm wrapped tightly around his waist. "Don't either of you do that again," he said gruffly. "Ever."

He turned toward the man standing patiently with the horses. "Help Lady Gwyneth mount," he ordered.

Gripping Priss around her waist, he lifted her to sit in the saddle sideways and mounted behind her.

"My lord." A servant from the castle stepped forward, unspoken questions in his eyes, as if he wanted to ask why the ladies had been attacked, yet knowing it was not his place. "We will be riding back with you."

"Finish your celebration," Gavan said. "You should not suffer because of the ill-advised actions of my sister and Miss Whitmore."

"Begging your pardon, my lord, but with the ladies gone, our celebration is over. We'll be riding with you."

Studying the man's face, he saw only concern and sincerity. The villagers stood behind him, each holding a makeshift weapon, hastily torn from their wooden circle. Touched beyond description by the sight of those splintered pieces of wood, he met each grim face, reminding himself that his people were loyal. Loyal enough to rip apart their ceremonial circle to defend him and his family. Loyal enough to end their celebration early to protect them.

Yet some of his people had not been loyal. Some of them had attacked his sister and Priss. He'd recognized them as his footmen. Zealots whom he often caught preaching to the other servants rather than performing their duties.

It confirmed the suspicions that had been growing with every thought after the day he'd taken Priss into the village.

Nodding his permission to the footman, Gavan wheeled his horse back toward the castle.

Priss rode silently in front of Gavan, comforted by the strength of his arms around her, soothed by the sure grip he had on the reins, sheltered by the power of his body, which seemed to surround her. She wanted to sink back against him, indulge the weakness that attacked her limbs and her mind. But guilt held her straight and admonished her with cruel memories.

"I always cause problems when I behave impulsively," she blurted, knowing if she did not say it now, she would not have the courage later.

"And so, you try to be very careful in everything you say and everything you do," he said tersely. "And we are discussing this . . . *why*?"

"Because it's all my fault, Gavan. Because Gwyneth attended the festival for the best of reasons. I went along with her because I have never learned to restrain my impulses."

"Don't learn. It is against your nature."

The ferocity of his statement unraveled her. Don't learn? Her impulse had caused nothing but trouble, yet he didn't want her to go against her nature? Surely he didn't know what he was saying.

"My nature causes trouble for those I care for most," she argued, then clamped her lips together, afraid to go on, yet knowing she must. Gavan cared for her, perhaps was coming to love her. She'd known when he'd held her so closely with his sister, as if she were of equal importance. She hadn't expected that. She'd expected only anger and censure, not the trembling relief she'd felt as he'd crushed her against him as if he would never again let her go.

Gavan didn't believe in love. He didn't believe in anything, she reminded herself.

Yet, his actions indicated otherwise.

She waited for some sort of denial to surface, for her mind to scoff at her for wishful thinking. Nothing came but the same sense of certainty she'd had the other night that he did care, that he had suggested marriage and insisted on keeping her at Castell Eryri for that very reason. That he just hadn't admitted it to himself yet. The idea of it calmed her, cleared her mind of all but Gavan and the possibilities presented by her realization.

If there were to be any chance for them, she couldn't be continually on her guard against herself. How many times had she slipped her hold on her tongue and her actions since meeting Gavan? He deserved to be warned about her "nature," just in case she was right about his feelings for her . . .

Just in case dreams did come true.

She sat more stiffly, averting her gaze from the anger still in the clench of his jaw and the tightness of his mouth. "When I was sixteen, I loved a man so much that I took every opportunity to undermine his wife and keep them apart." She spoke quickly, not wanting him to interrupt her, knowing that if he did she might never be able to finish. "Theirs had been an arranged marriage and he had immediately left her after the wedding. I'd read their letters, which more than once mentioned an annulment, and I schemed to help it along. My actions caused her to become quite ill and later to be attacked and nearly killed by footpads. To make matters worse, I stole a letter that was important to him, so sure that I knew what was best and could protect him. I threw myself at him while his wife lay unconscious on a London street." Rubbing his arms, she choked back a sob. The shame seemed worse now. Worse because it was the man she loved hearing the story. "They forgave me and expressed such faith in me that I have tried very hard to deserve their faith and friendship."

He said nothing as he drew her back against him, her cheek pressed to his chest.

She looked up at him, bemused by his small smile and gentle touch. "You aren't angry anymore? Why aren't you? How do you do that?"

His chuckle rumbled against her cheek.

"You are so angry with yourself that it would be a waste of effort for me to add to it." Shifting the reins to one hand, he cupped her chin and dropped a light kiss on the corner of her mouth. "You tie yourself in knots trying to control yourself, Priss. And I, for one, am quite taken with your impulsiveness. When you are measuring every word, you are rather like your hats before you add the butterflies."

She peered up at him, afraid to meet his gaze fully, acutely aware that she was naked beneath the single layer of clothing, that her fears and her heart were naked as well. "It frightens me how easy it is to cause trouble without meaning to."

"When Gwyneth was that age," he mused, "she fell in love with her dance master and went to great lengths to 'bewitch him.' I believe that was the phrase she used."

"But she hurt no one."

"She terrified the poor man out of his wig. His betrothed wasn't too pleased either. She left him for a while, which was rather awkward since she was three months gone with child."

"You make it sound so trivial." Suddenly it seemed trivial—a thing in the past that was done. She'd been so afraid others might view the incident as she did, with disapproval and censure of which she'd already served herself a full dose over the years. But Gavan was treating it as a common occurrence during adolescence.

"Nothing is trivial when you're young and foolishly believe the world belongs to you," he said softly, as if he were speaking to himself. "We hurt others and receive forgiveness from everyone but ourselves."

It comforted her as nothing else had. Oddly, it seemed to give her permission to lay past mistakes to rest. For that she loved him even more and prayed that he did care, that her perceptions were right.

She closed her eyes against the sudden onslaught of doubt and vicious reminders of her own foolishness. Once before, she'd been so sure that a man loved her. So foolishly, stupidly sure. She'd survived being wrong that time.

Shivering, she hunched her shoulders and leaned into Gavan, seeking his warmth, seeking reassurance in his nearness and the way he dropped a light kiss on her forehead and inhaled deeply, as if he were drinking in her scent.

In that moment nothing was more frightening than the thought that she might be wrong. That if she was, she would not survive.

Gavan didn't like the way her flesh chilled as they rode slowly toward the castle. He didn't like the way she clung like a child to him, while her gaze darted right and left and ahead in fear as conversation gave way to silence and the return to fearful thoughts.

"I assume Gwyneth told you about my debacle with a woman?" he said suddenly, surprising himself.

"I . . . yes. But you don't have to—"

He silenced her with a wry look. "Priss, I think it is better to speak of anything right now than to dwell on what has happened to-night," he said bluntly.

She closed her eyes and nodded. "Yes, anything is better than that, but—"

He pressed two fingers to her lips. "Enough, Priss. I'd rather you hear the truth than that claptrap Gwyneth spouts about how a woman destroyed me. Besides, one secret deserves another," he added with a trace of humor, struck by the absurdity of riding home, surrounded by men wielding makeshift cudgels, in the aftermath of an attack on the two people he cared most about.

Cared. Perhaps more.

He gathered her closer and kissed the top of her head. He'd never liked the idea of dredging up what was dead and buried. But Priss was still trembling, and he would do anything to distract her from her lingering fear.

Not absurd at all.

"I was twenty when I saw Julia at her come-out and knew I was in love," he said in a monotone. "It seemed the same with her. We were both right. I was in love with her beauty and the seduction in her eyes. She was in love with the idea of my wealth and position. What Gwyneth does not know is that Julia and I were married in London. We left immediately and celebrated our wedding night here."

He paused, waiting for the struggle to begin, against his own reticence, against his unwillingness to resurrect past humiliation. Nothing came but the words—only words describing what no longer had relevance in his life. "It was a disaster. She hated me and she hated my home and despised my sister. I was so busy trying to learn in one day how to redeem myself that I didn't realize she was packing. She returned to London and obtained an annulment after leaving me a very nasty note. After that there seemed no point in telling Gwyneth. She was barely an adolescent and it would have served no purpose."

She peered up at him. "An annulment? But how—"

He stared straight ahead, at the castle rising above them, at the gates opening to admit its master. "I told you our wedding night was disaster. She was within her rights."

"Oh. I think I see ... but, I cannot imagine you being a disaster in ... I mean ..."

"Thank you for that." He sighed as they entered the outer courtyard and the gates squeaked shut behind them. "At least I now know that the month I spent soaking up every drop of spirits in the district and employing more than one 'tutor' to fill in the gaps in my education was not wasted."

Her eyes widened in proportion to her realization of what he meant. "You mean you ... that I ... that you have been ... since that month?"

"You have corrupted me, Priss. The monks will never have me now."

"That would have been a horrible waste," she blurted as only Priss could do.

Touched beyond description by her candor, he lowered her to the ground and dismounted. "And while we are on the subject of confessions, I suppose I should tell you that you are to be courted. By me. I haven't the slightest idea of how to go about it, so I beg your indulgence." With Gwyneth and a dozen men milling about, it was the best he could do just then to let her know he would never let her go.

Gwyneth slunk away the moment her feet hit the ground. Gavan let her go. Nothing he could say or do could top the attack on her and Priss. Nothing he could say or do would diminish his wrath for the ones responsible.

He guided Priss up to the master suite and saw her into her bedchamber, remaining in the doorway, unwilling to let her out of his sight, yet afraid that if he didn't, he would take her on the floor, touching all of her, reassuring himself that she was here and safe and whole.

She stood uncertainly in the center of her bedchamber, staring blindly at air, as if she didn't know what to do next. Leaning against the doorway, he stared at her in the darkened room, at the magnificence of her, at her bare shoulders and lush form outlined in the white gown, at the gold torques on her arms and the diadem crowning her untamed curls.

"I think they wanted to kidnap us," she said suddenly as she rubbed her arms. "They were trying to carry us off."

"And ransom you for the book," he added.

"They failed."

"Yes."

"They will try something else . . . soon."

"Yes," he said as he entered the room, strolled toward her, unable to leave her looking so lost and uncertain. Unable to have her out of his sight, knowing that they would again be attacked in one way or another, knowing that they had been fortunate so far and might not be again.

She sobbed once and ran to him, wrapped her arms around his waist, lifted her face to him. "I'm a coward, Gavan. And I'm frightened."

So was he. The image of those men trying to carry her and Gwyneth off loomed in his mind like a demon shadow threatening to rob him of all he had found since meeting Priss, threatening to deny him all that mattered to him.

He wrapped Priss in his arms and held tightly as he stared down at her, at the trust he saw in her eyes. Trust in him. And he saw need and caring and another kind of fear that had nothing to do with evil men and their greed. Fear that he would not kiss her, that he would let her go.

He couldn't let her go. He had to kiss her . . . and more.

He had to make her his. Had to make her understand that she was his.

Control left him as he covered her mouth with his, harshly, desperately, urgently, needing to touch her and feel her against him and beneath him, needing to be inside her, holding her fast. She met him with equal desperation, her embrace tight, her hands clutching his waist, then fumbling at the fastening of his trousers.

He tore the toga at her shoulders, releasing

it, his breath snagging at the realization that she wore no petticoats, no shift, no stockings. He shrugged out of his jacket and shirt, allowed her to slide his trousers down his legs, until she was on her knees.

He followed her down, faced her, plundered her mouth, grazed his hands over her body, lowered her to her back and shuddered as she opened for him, pulling him down, frantically urging him closer. He plunged into her and felt her close around him, her legs encircling his waist, holding him inside her, arching her hips, consuming him with her heat. He plunged again and again as her hips matched his rhythm, as her breath mingled with his in kiss after kiss.

He rolled to his back, taking her with him, mindless with the feel of her breasts, her belly, her legs imprinted on his body. She sat astride him, circled her hips, rose and fell upon him, took his hands and guided them to her breasts, sobbing in pleasure as he stroked and teased her nipples.

Her hair fell over him, caressing his flesh, tormenting him, driving him to reach for the deepest part of her. He gripped her waist, held her as he arched upward, as she slid up and then down and cried out, her head thrown back. Her chest heaved as she strained to take the last bit of him, tightening around him, bathing him in her passion.

He pulled her down, holding her with one arm, pressing his other hand on her bottom, pressing her closer than air, thrusting upward, wringing cries from her until she quaked around him once more, quivering inside, draining him until he died of pleasure in her arms.

Hours passed, perhaps only minutes, as he held her and she held him, reluctantly returning to the world they'd left behind.

He cursed as he felt the carpet beneath him, saw the window hangings framing stars suspended in a black sky underlit by torches his men had set in the courtyard below to discourage intruders. And he felt Priss's hair blanketing him, her body lying over his, warming him as she slept, her head tucked into the crook of his neck.

He didn't want to move.

But he had to move. Whoever was after the book was becoming desperate. He would not wait long to make another attempt. Gavan guessed the man would make a move tomorrow.

And tomorrow, Gavan would end it once and for all.

Chapter 22

~~~~~❦❧~~~~~

Dawn washed the sky with shades of rose and gold and palest lavender on the east horizon. From the west an icy ceiling of silver-gray clouds slowly slid toward the mountains of Snowdonia. Enchanted mountains, Priss thought as she wandered out to the walled garden that sat at the end of the cliff upon which Castell Eryri was built and overlooked the narrow valley and Yr Wyddfa beyond.

Nothing was more imposing than Gavan in his shirtsleeves standing at the very edge, his legs braced apart, his hands on his hips, his head thrown back as he watched a pair of eagles circling high overhead. The great birds dipped and soared, their wings outspread, then swept low as if communicating with Gavan.

"Lord of Eagles," she mused as she approached him. *Lord of Destiny*, she thought, knowing it was true.

He lowered his arms and turned to her with the smile that never failed to tease her imagination. Today, it awakened memories as well—of the night before, of how the simplest look or touch played havoc with her control, of the way they fell upon one another as if every time was the first or, perhaps, the last.

There would be no last time if she had anything to say about it. Right or wrong, she knew that she would fight for him as fiercely as he had fought for her and Gwyneth last night.

"I liked the toga better," he said, as his gaze seemed to penetrate her gown of dark blue wool.

"It is beyond repair," she replied, remembering how it had become that way.

"I'm sure Jenny can repair it," he said. "She and Burns arrived last night."

"Yes, with the contents of my workroom and my stables," she said with a smile. "Jenny was in my bedchamber when I awoke."

"Are you hungry?" he asked, and waved his hand toward a table set up to take advantage of the view.

She walked over to inspect the fine damask cloth and settings of china and silver and crystal, the bowl of fruit and vase of dried flowers. "Do you do this often—break your fast at dawn in the garden?"

"Weather permitting," he replied.

She nodded, perplexed that she felt so awkward, that he appeared to feel awkward, too. "I'm famished," she said, meeting his gaze. "You left me last night," she said, giving up on ever being able to tame her unruly tongue.

"And you were so deeply asleep that you

will never know how difficult it was." He sat in a chair and tugged her down to his lap, then nibbled at her lower lip.

"Then why did you not stay?" she asked, meeting each nibble with her own.

"I had work to do." He captured her mouth in a hard, fast kiss.

She pulled away from his mouth and stared at the great mountain in the distance, suddenly awkward again with the reminder of the question she'd not had the chance to ask the night before. The question she needed to ask, though she couldn't imagine why it seemed so important to her.

"You said that it was claptrap . . . about your being brokenhearted," she stammered as she stared down at her hands. "You are not still in love with her . . . with the woman you married?"

He sighed and covered both her hands with one of his. "I never was in love with her, which I realized quickly enough. When she left, I was relieved—not a sign of enduring devotion. For that matter, I did nothing to convince her to stay."

"You didn't refuse her transport home?" she asked as a thrill danced up her spine.

He turned her head toward his, compelling her to meet his gaze. "No, I didn't," he said gravely, his eyes seeming to say more, telling her something he could not say.

"You didn't kidnap her in her nightgown and bring her back?" she asked in a near whisper.

His mouth twitched, then settled into a somber line. "I can't imagine why I would do such a thing."

"You kidnapped me," she said, trying hard not to allow her imagination to run wild at the implications. "Why?"

He opened his mouth then shut it with a perplexed frown, as if he weren't quite certain of the answer.

Gwyneth arrived, with her hand covering a wide yawn. "It appears no one can sleep," she said, as if she found a woman on her brother's lap every morning at dawn.

Reluctantly, Priss left Gavan and sat in the chair next to him, wishing that Gwyneth would disappear so that she could pursue the answer Gavan had yet to give. So that she might know once and for all if her heart was lying to her about Gavan's feelings for her.

Gwyneth sat across from her, a beatific smile on her face.

A servant appeared with a large serving platter laden with fish and ham and rashers of bacon. Another carried breads and cakes, and a third brought in pots of tea and coffee.

"I have been thinking," Gwyneth said, as soon as the servants left.

"No wonder none of us could sleep," Gavan said with good nature though his expression was tense and the crooked smile that usually accompanied his quips was little more than a grimace.

"It occurs to me that whoever has been attacking us has focused on Priss and me. It must mean that William is safe." Gwyneth glanced anxiously from her brother to Priss.

Priss stared down at her hands in her lap, fighting tears as Gwyneth's statement brought her own fears close to the surface. "I'm certain he is," she said quietly, praying that it was so.

"I sent Bow Street Runners out to find him the day before we left Priss's cottage," Gavan said.

"You've found him!" Gwyneth exclaimed.

"No," Gavan said. "He seems to have vanished off the face of the earth."

"Willie is proficient at losing himself when the occasion warrants. I'm certain he'll appear soon," Priss said thickly, not quite believing it.

Gwyneth jumped up from her chair, her fists clenched at her sides. "You think he might be dead," she cried. "But he isn't. I know he isn't. He promised to return to me." Whirling, she faced the vista beyond the cliff and pressed her fingers to her mouth.

Gavan set down his cup of coffee. "Priss, if you know where he is or have any ideas—"

"I don't," she said, and blinked her eyes. "If I knew, I would have sent for him. He should be here."

"Yes, he should," Gavan agreed. "This began with his discovery of the book, and I am damned tired of seeing you both threatened at every turn and fending off criminals to—"

A footman appeared with a piece of paper on a tray. "A message, my lord."

"Who brought it?"

"It was stuck to the gates with a knife, my lord."

Taking the note, Gavan nodded in dismissal and unfolded the parchment.

Priss's heart leaped into her throat at Gavan's silence and control, like the calm before the storm. He'd been expecting this. He'd known something would happen today.

"It would appear that Whitmore is no longer missing," he said as he very slowly crumpled the paper in his hand.

Gwyneth didn't turn, but kept her back to them, stiff, as if she were afraid to move or speak.

Priss held out her hand and met Gavan's gaze.

"No, Priss. Whitmore is alive, and that is all you need to know at the moment."

Gwyneth sagged to the ground and began to weep.

"I am his sister," Priss said. "Gwyneth is the woman he loves. We have a right to know." Her voice was steady, her words clear. She felt as if something were dying inside of her. Gavan would have immediately told them if all was well. That he hadn't indicated only one thing.

Willie may not be alive for long.

Her hand shook as she kept it open, palm up, waiting for Gavan to give her the note.

"Whitmore is being held for ransom—for the book," Gavan said tightly. "I can't risk you and Gwyneth knowing where he is being held, Priss. I will take care of it."

"We will take care of it together," Gwyneth cried as she shot to her feet and stormed over to the table. "The book was written by our ancestor. The legend involves Priss as well as you. It's our fight, too."

"I would like to avoid a fight, if at all possible, Gwyneth."

"A bit unrealistic, don't you think?" Priss said, repeating what he'd said to her under very different circumstances. "We have fought at every turn whether we wished it or not." Anger sat like a crouched animal in her stomach, waiting to strike. Waiting to know where to strike. "I do not understand why the book has taken on such importance beyond scholarly investigation."

"Our nemesis thinks to destroy it," Gavan said. "He sees it as a danger to society."

"But we don't have the book," Priss said.

"Then I will either convince him that it is irretrievably lost or pound it into his head with my bare fists," he said with a gleam of relish in his eyes. "The man is simple in his approach. His actions have all been straightforward and obvious. I doubt he will think we would value the book above Whitmore's life."

Gwyneth paled, and her hands twisted in her skirt. "Gavan," she said, and bit the corner of her lip. "I—"

"No, Gwyneth," he said, slicing his hand through the air. "Not another word. I will take care of this as I see fit. There will be no giving in to this man or any other who seeks to impose his will on others. And there will be no book burning in my district, in spite of my earlier declarations to the contrary. In fact I will go so far as to admit that I am glad the book is out of reach at the moment. If I were to give in now, we would be subject to all manner of chicanery every time someone does not agree with me."

"But—"

"I will not argue with you," he said. "You will have to trust me."

Priss clutched the gold medallion as anger found a target in Gavan's steady voice, his calm, his knowledge of where Willie was being held. Her knowledge that Gavan would go alone to help Willie expanded it to fury. "So you would again play the avenging knight and risk the lives Gwyneth and I hold most dearly. Hardly a noble endeavor if you think about it."

"I have thought about it," he said savagely as he rose from his chair, knocking it back to totter on two legs and fall over. "I have done nothing but think of how you and my sister have been in danger, how even home isn't safe for either of you. I have thought of nothing but finding the man responsible and twisting his neck, slowly, so that I may wring every last ounce of revenge for threatening the lives of those *I hold most dearly.*"

The last words almost shattered her, almost gave her the answer she sought. But not now. Not when anger ruled her. "And you have been secretly plotting to save us all, as if Gwyneth and I were too scatterbrained to understand the degree of danger. I would imagine that you even know who is responsible."

His scowl deepened.

"You *do* know, and you're keeping it from us," she accused. "What right have you to keep it from us?"

He gave her a hard, predatory grin that held nothing of humor. "Consider it the modern version of *droit du seigneur*," he said flatly.

She rose and flattened her palms on the table, glaring at him. "You expect us to sit quietly in the ladies' solar while you go off to save the day."

"I expect you to trust me," he said in a low, savage voice, "and if you cannot manage that, I expect you to obey me. I know exactly what is at stake here." He turned toward the door leading into the great hall. "Now if you will excuse me, I have things to do."

Priss sat stiffly, saying nothing, staring straight ahead as he strode from the garden, then jumped up and ran after him, jerking the medallion from around her neck as she caught him just inside the door to the great hall. "Gavan, take this. It might help . . ." Her voice trailed off as she stayed him with a hand on his arm and tucked the golden circle into his hand.

He stopped but didn't turn, didn't speak, his profile sharp and noble and proud.

"Understand this, Gavan," she said, hating the sudden tremor in her voice. "I trust you, but I know how things can go awry, how fragile life is and how easily it can be ended. You know how impossible it is to stand by while those you love are in danger, how when you love someone you feel that no one can protect that person better than you."

His body stiffened. The muscles in his arm under her hand clenched and his mouth tightened, as if he were struggling against himself, against words that wanted to come. "You are not going with me," he said harshly.

"I realize that," she replied quietly. "And it occurs to me that your pompous male attitude is exactly why I have avoided marriage. Nevertheless, if you and Willie do not return in one piece, I will never let you forget it."

His mouth twitched though he still didn't look at her. "That sounds very much like a promise, Priss. Do you plan to remain after this is over?"

"I love you too much to do anything else," she stated, watching him, her hand still on his arm.

"Ah God," he said hoarsely as he closed his eyes briefly and inhaled deeply. His hand covered hers on his arm, squeezing tightly. "I will keep that firmly in my pompous male mind, Priss," he said, his voice softening around the edges, caressing her with unspoken promises.

Infuriated that he did not say more, that he did not give voice to the promise when he was surely going into danger, she whirled and returned to the garden, not looking back, the sound of his receding footsteps pounding her frustration home one blow at a time. She'd had enough of his reticence and the droll humor he used like a shield. Enough of living on assumptions and conjecture and hope, and dying a little each time fear and doubt chipped away at her illusions. Enough of wondering and waiting and needing to know for certain. Foolish or not, improper or not, she would have answers from him before the day was out.

All she had to do was see to it that the end of the day saw Gavan and William standing whole and well before her.

She slowed to a walk as she approached Gwyneth, fortified by determination.

"Priss, we can't just let him go," Gwyneth said. "What is wrong with you?"

"Sit down, Gwyneth, and take a few deep breaths."

"What? Has the entire world gone mad?"

"Sit . . . now," Priss hissed, then turned to summon a parlormaid and give her some instructions.

Gwyneth was sitting by the time she turned back to the table, staring at Priss with undisguised admiration. "I am impressed," she said with a conspiratorial grin. "I never could lie well."

"I did not lie once, Gwyneth. I simply told him what I felt he needed to know."

They said nothing more as they waited, the seconds stretching into minutes and those seeming like hours.

Jenny arrived at a dead run. "Miss, I cannot find them," she panted.

"Gavan hid my pistols, the wretch," Priss said.

"Priss, have you taken a good look at the walls in this castle?" Gwyneth said guilelessly. "Swords and battle-axes and lances everywhere. Gavan keeps them in prime condition as a matter of pride . . . and Gavan and I used to take lessons together; it is tradition carried over from the ancient warrior queens, you see.

I can wield a sword and dagger far better than I can shoot a pistol.''

Hooves rang in the cobbled courtyard. Gavan was leaving. From the sound of it, he was at least wise enough to take several men with him. All the better. Several men on horseback would raise more dust to follow than one.

''Has Burns saddled our horses?''

Jenny nodded, her hand on her chest as she caught her breath. ''The twins with men's saddles, just as you said.''

Priss exchanged glances with Gwyneth. They rose in unison and hurried through the hall, stopping only long enough to pull several swords and daggers from the walls.

Gwyneth eyed another weapon and reached for it.

''It would take two of us to swing that one, Gwyneth.''

With a regretful sigh, Gwyneth left the claymore behind.

After attaching their weapons to their saddles, Priss showed Gwyneth how to make her skirts into pantaloons and swung into the saddle astride, for once in her life certain that she was doing the right thing.

They followed Gavan at a safe distance, keeping to the trees and moving cautiously. The twins did what they did best, keeping close to one another and stepping lightly, Priss leading the way on Tweedledum.

''Oh my stars,'' Gwyneth said in a loud whisper as Gavan turned off the road and headed toward the waterfall. ''The cave.

They're holding Willie in the cave."

Priss stared at her, puzzled by the note of panic in her voice. "What aren't you telling me, Gwyneth?"

"There is only one entrance and there are no windows."

"I don't expect there are," Priss said, wondering what she was missing.

"Priss, Gavan cannot tolerate the cave. He has not gone inside since he was ten."

"He cannot tolerate enclosed places?" Priss asked.

"I don't think that is it. He doesn't mind the carriage, or a small room. It seems to be confined to the cave. I've deduced that it either is because something dreadful happened to him there or that it is due to the idea of being beneath a mountain with no escape route if it should cave in."

"Then we must hurry, Gwyneth."

"This way, Priss." Gwyneth tried to turn Tweedledee in the opposite direction, but the horse wouldn't budge without its twin.

"Gwyneth, you said there is only one entrance and it is over there; I can see it."

"There is only one entrance that others know about," Gwyneth said. "So, get your dratted beast moving in this direction."

Priss turned her horse and cursed Gavan for being such a . . . *man*, and prayed they would not be too late.

Chapter 23

The cave entrance was little more than a narrow slit on an inside fold of the mountain slope, appearing like just another shadow among many. But Gavan knew what was inside—stone walls and unnatural light and memories of pain and betrayal. Memories that suddenly rushed at him from all sides, urging him to leave this place, to leave the past beneath the mountain.

Perspiration beaded on his forehead as he told himself that he was a grown man and he had no need to fear the return of emotions that had devastated him as a boy. The best way to defeat a fear was to confront it. Fear of memories that he'd spent a lifetime trying to forget. Memories that had changed his life and destroyed a young boy's magic world. But this time, he knew exactly what he would find inside and why. This time, the only harm that could be done to him would be physical. This time he would understand what was happening and why.

He instructed his men to wait half an hour,

then storm the cavern if he had not returned. Leaving his horse tethered to a tree, he inched toward the entrance and turned sideways, easing inside. Voices from the past seemed to close in on him from all sides, as unrelenting as the stone surrounding him, and as cold.

Images rushed at him like bats flapping in all directions, screeching for him to go back, to not risk the revival of old dreams and old pain. He inhaled slowly, exhaled even more slowly as he sidestepped through the passage, feeling his way, his hand connecting with nothing more solid than chill, damp air.

Memories . . . only memories . . . a foolish thing to fear.

As if he'd been here only yesterday he remembered the way to the massive cavern, finding one corridor, then another, then the steep incline where footing could be lost with one misstep and one would slide and roll directly into the underground lake—a pond really, but underground it appeared larger than it was, and tributaries snaked through a myriad of corridors.

He moved deeper into the tunnels, reciting scientific knowledge and rational explanations for everything around him. The formations that had once captivated his imagination were nothing but moisture, laden with minerals that dripped from the ceiling and collected on the ground and dried into shapes. The underground lake he'd described to Priss was nothing but more minerals—phosphorous—that naturally gave off a glow. The past was nothing compared to the present . . . and the future. His future, with Priss.

Their future together. Though he could neither touch nor see, nor hold it, he believed in it. He knew it was real.

Priss—he would think of Priss, remember how she looked the first time he'd seen her. How she'd tasted the first time he'd kissed her. How she'd received him the first time he'd made love to her. Priss draped in white and gold, her hair like a beacon leading him to her.

His foot slipped. He recovered. It might be wise not to think of Priss being ethereal and seductive.

Again, he touched only air and stepped to the right, to the ledge that descended like a natural staircase into the main chamber. *Think of Priss. See her in your mind rather than your father. Remember her words rather than those once uttered by a broken man.*

She loved him. Oddly, he believed it, believed in what she offered him. Believed that it was real and strong. And oddly, he felt stronger, more at peace, as if he was meant to come here, meant to see whatever lay beneath the mountain like a sleeping dragon. . . .

As if he were meant to confront the beast and tame it. As if something inside him knew that it had been holding all that was best of the boy he had been in safekeeping. A boy who had believed in miracles and magic and things that could not be seen or touched.

Priss loved him. A miracle.

Water rippled and lapped at stone walls and

floor. The air itself glowed with unearthly light and cast luminous colors on the walls in ever-changing patterns. Stones rose from the underground lake in a worn path across the water.

The high ceiling and large chamber and shimmering light from the phosphorescent water illuminated the Reverend Price standing at the head of the altar.

He studied the familiar formations rising from the floor and hanging from the ceiling, the rectangular stone altar littered with the remains of offerings from long-ago rituals, the lake that seemed to stop at the boulder in front of the far wall. All thoughts of the past receded, leaving only calm deliberation in Gavan's mind as he assessed the situation, his gaze focused on the altar, on the man standing beside it. . . .

The Reverend Price, seeking to protect his flock by taking the book and destroying it. A noble intention implemented in the wrong way.

Price stood behind a chair where Whitmore sat, a noose around his neck attached to his hands tied behind the back of the chair and his hobbled feet. Tricky. Rigged as it was to the bonds at Whitmore's hands and feet, any wrong movement would strangle him. Yet Whitmore wiggled his foot subtly, a signal that he was working his bonds free, that the situation was not wholly in Price's control, that perhaps he had been waiting for Gavan to arrive before acting. Whitmore might well have fought savages in America, but he was not foolhardy. He knew when to wait for and accept aid.

Price held a knife to Whitmore's throat—far more dangerous than a pistol. One small twitch of Price's hand could sever Whitmore's jugular and windpipe, killing him before anything could be done. A second man—a villager—stood to the side with a musket trained on Gavan. A third lay belly down on a ledge above him to his left, also holding a musket. It surprised Gavan that Price had commanded such loyalty from even these few villagers and the footmen captured the night before.

Three men, all advantageously positioned. Less than desirable odds. Still, if he could divert the men with conversation while Whitmore continued to work at his bonds, there might be a chance.

"You are alone?" Price asked in the way of greeting, his voice echoing through the labyrinth of tunnels and chambers.

"I am," Gavan replied. "Are you all right, Whitmore?" William blinked his eyes in deference to the blade at his throat and extended one foot a bare inch to show Gavan his progress.

Better and better, Gavan thought. Four fists were better than two if it came to that.

"You haven't brought your men?"

"I think enough people have been hurt by this, Price."

"Quite right. There has already been too much damage for such a small book."

"And more to come, I warrant," Gavan said. "If I give you the book, you will have to kill me and Whitmore so that no one will know who is responsible for the harm you've done."

"No," Price said with a trace of panic. "Not unless you present me with no choice by initiating a fight. All I wish to do is remove the book before it can influence and tempt my flock. My work will be done then and I will accept whatever punishment man imposes upon me. I understand well that the letter of the law must be honored as well as the spirit of God's law." He cleared his throat and inhaled deeply. "*Where* is the book, my lord?"

"Admirable, I'm sure, and I imagine a man of your . . . devotion, would find honor in martyrdom."

"There are worse things. Now, I will have the book, if you please, my lord."

Gavan stifled a snort at the cleric's form of address—an important revelation to keep handy. Price might have become a crusader of the worst sort, but he was still susceptible to authority. "If you wanted it so badly," Gavan said, "you should have presented your case to me." He narrowed his eyes, searching Price's countenance for signs of madness. He saw none—another point in his favor.

"I present my cases to you on a daily basis and you never listen," Price said. "I couldn't expect that you would comprehend the danger the book presented to the villagers and tenants."

"Ah, yes, the danger," Gavan said as he surveyed his surroundings, needing to keep Price talking while he found a way to free Whitmore. "May I sit down?" he asked as he sat on a familiar outcrop, stretched out his legs, and leaned back on his elbows. "Now, we were discussing the danger of the book, were we not? It would corrupt the people, convince them that the old ways have not died out, that Myrddin is merely frozen in stone rather than reduced to dust in a hidden grave. The book might even reveal how to free the sorcerer so that he could lead them, perhaps even use his magic to restore Wales to glory once more. Obviously, you feel that must be avoided at all costs."

"You understand?" Price said. "I didn't think you would."

"Did you perhaps neglect to think at all?" Gavan asked conversationally as he stared at the lake, at Price's reflection wavering and glowing unnaturally. Price's minions were also reflected in the water, affording him a clear view of every movement in the cavern.

"Of course I think. I cannot rest for thinking of the threat to my flock, to their immortal souls."

Whitmore opened his mouth to speak and shut it again as the blade of Price's knife drew blood at the movement.

"Would you be speaking of the villagers?" Gavan asked, then continued without waiting for an answer. "You are referring to human beings are you not? The same human beings to whom God granted free will?"

Price nodded warily, then drew himself up to his full height. "You would dare to counsel *me* on Scripture?"

Movement from a small chamber behind

Price caught Gavan's eye, chilling him as he identified a blue frock and a long, wayward strand of golden hair. Priss. And behind her, Gwyneth. He should have known they would not be able to sit idly by.

The sight of each wielding a sword froze him with both horror and fury. He clamped his lips together and gritted his teeth against the churning in his stomach and the roar rising in his throat. Price might not intend to murder him or Whitmore but Gavan had seen how viciously he and his men had treated the women the night before and suspected that the cleric had little regard for them. He doubted Price would hesitate to be even more vicious toward them if given the opportunity.

He forced himself not to look in the direction of the small tunnel, at the two wide-eyed women huddled behind a stone formation. Shifting his gaze to the water, he narrowed his eyes with singular intensity, willing Priss and Gwyneth to look at their reflections in the water, to move back before they were caught.

Priss pulled Gwyneth back until they were out of sight, their reflections in the water only a chilling memory in Gavan's mind.

He would throttle them both yet.

"Enough of this," Price said. "The longer you delay, the less inclined I am to believe you wish to resolve this without violence." Gavan shrugged, fighting the frantic urge to take action, to do something, anything to end this, to get Priss and Gwyneth and Whitmore out of here. But he couldn't give Price any excuse to committ violence as he'd just threatened. He might not think he believed in violence but his previous actions said otherwise. "Not at all. I am merely curious since your father—and your predecessor as curate of the parish—taught me that only faith given freely is true faith. That one cannot force another to believe or disbelieve. And that faith cannot be destroyed by anyone but the one who holds it. Did he teach you differently?"

Price's mouth flapped as it always did when he could not find a valid response.

Gavan glanced at Whitmore, relieved to see him wiggle his other foot in signal. Blood trickled from the knife-prick on his neck.

"Do you enjoy torturing him, Reverend Price?" Gavan asked as he nodded toward Price's captive.

"I have done all I can to avoid causing harm of any kind," Price said stiffly.

"Then I suggest you either slit Whitmore's throat and be done with it or remove that knife before he slowly bleeds to death from a dozen cuts. Your hand is shaking badly."

Price moved the knife away from Whitmore's neck a fraction of an inch. "I beg your pardon, Mr. Whitmore," he said stiffly, and wiped at the blood on Whitmore's neck.

"I never thought I would see the day that a Price would offer up a sacrifice in a Druid temple," Gavan remarked, keeping one eye on the place where Priss and Gwyneth hid and the other on Price. The other two men were so intent on him that they noticed nothing else. "You were aware that ceremonies took place here when the Druids were forced to practice their beliefs in secret?"

"I'm not . . . it isn't."

"It is." Gavan's voice nearly broke on those two simple words, on the memory they resurrected. His heart jumped into his throat as Priss crept along the passage wall nearer and nearer to Price. "One wonders why you chose this particular location. Why not hallowed ground? It would provide spiritual protection, would it not?"

"I would never desecrate the parsonage with the book," Price huffed. "I chose this place because it is where such abominations belong, and because it affords me protection from a surprise attack by your men."

Gwyneth disappeared, then appeared again on the ledge, inching toward the second man.

Rising slowly, Gavan strolled toward the minister, taking one stepping-stone at a time across the water to keep Price's attention fixed on him, chafing at the need for patience, for calm. "Perhaps you don't consider members of your flock as human beings. Perhaps you consider them to be sheep, without minds," he said in a low, soothing voice as he secured his balance on a sloped stone.

"My lord, do not be reckless. I would not have your death on my conscience. Now, please give me the book, and we will be done here."

"I don't have the book, Price. It has been lost since our coach was waylaid on the road to London." He stepped to another stone. Only one more to go. "I assumed the men who attacked us took it."

"They didn't." Price's eyes took on a wild gleam. "You *must* have it."

"Do you dare to call me a liar?" Gavan asked silkily as he fixed him with a cold stare.

"No, my lord. I only meant—"

Suddenly, Whitmore's hand shot up and grasped Price's wrist, twisting it until a snap echoed in the chamber and the knife fell to the ground. Gavan leaped the remaining distance across the water and dived for the knife as Whitmore's face reddened from the noose tightening around his neck.

Price kicked out at him, catching Gavan under the chin. Seeing stars, Gavan rolled and rose to a crouch, waiting. Price kicked again and shouted at his men as Gavan caught his foot and jerked, toppling him onto his back with a thud.

Gavan glanced at the man trying to aim and fire without hitting Price. "Fire that and you will bring the roof down upon our heads," Gavan warned as he reached up and pulled the noose away from Whitmore's windpipe, slicing the rope in two with one quick swipe. "You are on your own, Whitmore," Gavan said as he lunged for the man falling from the ledge to his right with a knife in his shoulder.

Gwyneth laid the blade of her sword along the neck of the man on the ledge, then shrieked a warning as the second man tossed down his musket and charged at Whitmore.

Price jumped to his feet, surprisingly agile for his lanky build. Gavan lurched to the side and cracked the edge of his hand on Price's neck. Price staggered and fell into the water headfirst.

"Gavan!" Priss called out.

He pivoted and grunted as the man with Priss's knife protruding from his shoulder butted his head into Gavan's stomach. Gripping the man's arm, he twisted hard. The man screamed as fresh blood poured from his wound. Gavan twisted harder until the man's eyes rolled back in his head, and he fell, unconscious, draped over an outcropping.

Gavan turned and ran for the water, groping for the feel of a solid form. Nothing. Cursing, he shed his coat and jumped in. A head bobbed up a few feet away. Reaching out, he hauled a gasping Price to shore.

Priss ran up to him with rope she'd found behind the altar and straddled Price's back. "Help Gwyneth. I'll see to him."

Nodding, Gavan searched for the source of sound bouncing off the walls and found Gwyneth and William standing over a prone figure, shouting at one another.

"You had no bloody business coming here," William said.

"I had as much business here as you did," Gwyneth retorted.

"I did not simply stroll in—"

"Neither did we. We sneaked in the back way."

Shaking his head, Gavan pulled Priss off of Price's back and secured the ropes more firmly. "You're hell with knife, pitchfork, and pistol, Priss, but your knots leave a great deal to be desired."

"You're welcome," she snapped as she crossed her arms over her chest.

"I will not thank you for interfering," he shouted above the din. "You could have gotten us all killed if Price or one of his men had seen you."

"And you, of course would have defeated all three with a flick of your wrist, I suppose."

"Whitmore and I would have managed. Dammit, you promised to remain at the castle."

"I would never be so stupid as to promise such a thing."

"She didn't promise, Gavan," Gwyneth said. "You simply assumed you would be obeyed."

"I am in charge," he roared. "Lord of the castle, or so I've been told. I *expect* to be obeyed."

"Well," Priss sniffed, "I am certain you will be when your orders make sense."

Whitmore tossed Gavan a length of rope and took one himself to tie up the man he and Gwyneth had defeated. "Price had enough rope in here to truss an army," he commented calmly. "I think he was disappointed when you arrived alone. He was talking about David slaying Goliath and turning the hordes of Philistines back." He grinned. "You were the giant, of course."

Gavan secured the third man. "Which of you ladies will sacrifice your petticoat to ease this man's suffering?"

"I would as soon let him bleed, the traitor."

"Gwyneth, you were not raised to be blood-thirsty," he admonished.

"No? There are any number of warrior queens throughout history, Gavan. Do you suppose they attained their positions by being adept at embroidery?"

Silently, Priss lifted her skirt, tore a ruffle from her petticoat, and pushed him out of the way. "I will see to his wound. After all, it is woman's work."

He stood back, watching her deftly press a folded square of muslin to the bleeding wound, then wind strips around the man's shoulder to hold it in place. "Very nice work," he commented blandly, then turned to his sister. "Gwyneth, I have men waiting outside. Will you tell them to come in and collect"—he waved a hand over the three men lined up on the floor—"these."

"You had men," Priss said, rounding on him, "yet you came in here alone? I was mad with worry, not knowing how many men Price had—"

"Priss!" Whitmore said quietly. "Let's have a little hush, shall we?"

She snapped her mouth closed.

"You'll have to explain to me how you do that," Gavan said wryly, and hauled Priss into his arms. "Later," he added and lowered his mouth to hers, needing to feel her, taste her, and know she was unharmed.

Gavan's men made short work of carrying Price and his followers out of the cave, leaving them alone in the great chamber glowing eerily and casting swirls of color on the rock walls.

"Shouldn't we be going?" Priss asked anxiously.

He shot a glance at her, knowing she always fell apart after a crisis, no matter how calm and methodical she'd been while it was occurring. But she was not pale or trembling in reaction. She was anxious for him.

"Not yet," he said, fixing his gaze on his sister as she fidgeted and avoided looking at him. "Where is it, Gwyneth?"

"Where is what?"

"The book. You know—the one Whitmore found and you took from the coach. The one you've been translating at night."

"I cannot imagine where you got that idea," she said with a sniff.

"I should have known," Whitmore muttered.

"Well, you weren't supposed to know; that was the entire point," Gwyneth said with an indignant glare as she released her skirt from her waistband, turning her makeshift pantaloons into a skirt once more, and fumbled with a pocket sewn into her petticoat. "When I have not been translating it, I have carried it on my person at all times." His sister displayed no shyness or reluctance to expose her underclothing and limbs in Whitmore's presence.

He really was going to have that talk with Whitmore—

Gwyneth clutched the book to her chest. "I tried to tell you of it at least twice, Gavan, but you would not allow it and instead made obscure references to my continuing to do what

I felt was right. I knew then that you knew and did not want me to mention it yet." She nodded once and with vigor. "Admit it; I did well."

"You did well," Whitmore said on a sigh, and pried the book from her hands by bending down to kiss her. "I would not have wanted this to fall into Price's hands. I have an aversion to men who presume to know what other men should believe."

"See that it remains in your hands until we return to the castle, Whitmore," Gavan ordered and again looked at Priss, alarmed by her silence.

She stood a few feet away, watching the proceedings with interest. And calm. Obviously, she was not going to fall apart.

"Come along, Gwyneth," Whitmore said as he took her arm. "We will wait outside for them."

Gwyneth dug in her heels. "But Gavan must leave here. He is—"

"Out," Gavan said.

"Now, Gwyneth." William clasped her hand and pulled her into the tunnel.

Turning to Priss, Gavan stared at her, at the way she stood so still and silent like a child waiting to be chastised.

He smiled and advanced on her as the sounds of footsteps on stone faded completely.

They were alone at last.

Silence but for the gentle lap of water against the cavern floor. Silence but for the sound of her heart beating as Gavan walked toward her. Silence but for her hopes and dreams and the gentle breath of magic in the air.

Priss's courage was failing her, bleeding away with every moment that passed in silence. She couldn't allow it, yet she was held mute and bound and terrified in the face of Gavan's calm and the strength that was always with him.

"Stop!" she said, the words echoing as if spoken by some unearthly being lurking in the shadows.

He halted and stood tall and proud, watching her with the intensity and stillness of a predator.

She took a deep breath, swallowed down the fear clogging her throat, stilled the uncertainty cowering in her mind. "You will never find a better woman than I to make you happy," she said, her voice wobbling and her knees threatening to give way.

"I believe that is why I insisted that you marry me," he said quietly.

It annoyed her, his lack of reaction or expression. Annoyed her enough to blurt out the rest in defiance of better judgment. "You love me and you know it." Her voice was stronger, firmer, as if her soul spoke above her fears. "If it takes the rest of my life, I will prove it to you."

His mouth angled up at one corner as he sighed . . . in regret, it seemed.

Her heart sank slowly, painfully, to her feet. She stared down, feeling as if his silence was drawing the last drops of blood from her body. *Regret in his eyes . . . sadness in his smile*

. . . in the words he did not say . . . would never say.

She would not survive this time.

"I wish you were not so honest and fair, Gavan," she said, hearing the words escape her flat and hollow, as if she had already died. "I wish that you could have lied to me about this at least. I could have married you then and been quite happy believing the lie. There is a great deal to be said for illusions, I think."

"No, you couldn't, Priss. Your love would have turned to hate eventually." Gavan stared at her with a somber, brooding look she could not decipher. "I want to show you something," he said, and held out his hand.

Feeling as if only her body moved, she took his hand and followed him to a rock wall, waited as he pressed his shoulder to a large wheel-shaped stone and rolled it away, revealing the entrance to another chamber.

She halted just inside, staring without really seeing at the water that flowed in a wide luminous stream from the main cavern, at the ethereal glow shimmering on the walls, at the formations of stone and hardened minerals standing as if arranged in a certain way.

"It's like staring at clouds and seeing something other than clouds," Gavan said.

She could not bear to see what wasn't there. Not any longer. "I see rocks and water," she said as she glanced dispassionately at a formation rising from the stream, glowing water pouring from two holes near the top.

"Phosphorous makes the water glow," Gavan agreed, then pointed at the stone pillars that looked nothing more than a blur through her burning eyes. "Those are formed by water dripping and collecting and evaporating, leaving only minerals behind—"

"It is what you see and what you know," she said sadly, grieving for the man who had somehow lost his imagination, grieving for the emptiness it had left behind. Perhaps they were a good pair after all. Perhaps they could live together sharing their belief only in what could be held and seen and touched.

"I *know* the scientific explanation"—he strode to a formation—"but I *see* a sword here. There, a stack of books. And there, in the water, a winged dragon breathing fire." He walked to another formation within a niche in the wall. A formation that stood like a man, tall and handsome and a bit forbidding, his robes falling in folds to the floor, one arm held upward, the other bent as if it had once held something—a book perhaps.

She blinked at the thought, tried to discard it. It *was* too much like looking at clouds and seeing something more than white puffs scudding across the sky. Too much like seeing what could not possibly exist and believing it did exist. . . .

Like believing that Gavan loved her as much as she loved him.

Numb to everything but her own misery, she angled her head and watched him because it was the easiest thing to do, because she needed to finish dying before she could walk away from him.

"I found this hidden chamber when I was

eight. Until then, only my father, and later Gwyneth, knew of it. This is where your brother and Gwyneth found the book, fallen behind Myrrdin's robes." He touched the raised arm. "Here was the medallion." He paused to stare at the figure, his touch lingering on the arm. "I see Myrddin here, Priss. I always have."

Her scalp prickled and every inch of her skin tingled, as if enchantment were washing over her, as if she were slowly, painfully uncurling from a long sleep. "But how can you," she whispered, the words coming from the hope she'd left lying on the floor in the other chamber, "when you don't believe in—"

"Magic?" he said as he skimmed his hand over each shape, tracing the details wearing away with the years. "I believed once, Priss. I did not return here because I knew I would believe again if I walked these tunnels." He paused and lowered his head, looking like a small boy just then, alone and lost. "I didn't want to believe in magic. I didn't have to believe as long as I stayed away from here. I thought I hated everything to do with the cave and the legends that robbed me of my father."

Stunned by the pain in his voice, she sat down on an outcropping, barely breathing as Gavan moved through the chamber, entranced by how much he appeared to belong here.

"I used to come here to explore and weave fantasies," he said as he crouched in front of her, sifting through a small pile of rubble that had crumbled from the rock shaped like a sword. "I came here to think and to explore, imagining that I searched for the Grail. This was my very own castle, full of wondrous things like dragons and magical light that seemed to me the very stuff of dreams." His fingers poked through the stones he'd piled up in a pyramid, scattering them. "But even then I knew the difference between imagination and reality. We'd been raised in the Church, schooled in Scripture. I believed in my parents and what they taught us. I accepted on faith what we were taught because it seemed right and honest and fair. I trusted my father in all things."

Rising, he turned and angrily tossed a handful of pebbles into the water. Phosphorescent drops sprayed upward like tiny strings of light. "I found Father here," he said softly, "in the robes and trappings of an archdruid, chanting to idols and symbols of Druid gods, and reading aloud from a large book that held spells and incantations and old rituals. And when the spells failed, Father crumpled to his knees and wept in despair, as if his life no longer had meaning."

Light played on the figure of Myrddin, making it seem as if he reached out to them, but Priss said nothing, afraid of what Gavan might tell her, afraid that if she interrupted him, he would tell her nothing more.

Gavan lifted his head, his throat convulsing as he stared at the figure of a man formed in stone. "I told Father that he was a fool, that magic never existed. I used my faith in God as a weapon to taunt and defy him." His voice broke and he hunched his shoulders.

She reached out to him, then drew her hand back, afraid to express even that small bit of hope and love. "You felt betrayed," she whispered. "You felt as if he'd lied to you."

"A boy of ten does not expect his father to lie," he said heavily, "much less live a lie. I stood here and listened to his explanations, to his despair and guilt . . . but I didn't hear him. Not really. Not then." His shoulders heaved. "After that, I refused to believe or trust in anything at all. My father had lied to me, and I could no longer even believe in the faith I had in God . . . until I realized that my faith was real and not to be abused. But by then my father was dead, and I could not tell him that what he'd taught me was right and good. By then I had forgotten how to trust myself. I was empty. My life was hollow."

Hollow, like her, if Gavan could not love her. "It's very difficult to trust oneself, Gavan. And so much easier to exist without risk than to face any mistakes we might make." Her breath caught as she heard her own words, recognized the truth of them. "If your father had truly believed in the old ways, he would have shared them with you. Instead, he shared with you the only belief he did trust."

"Magic exists, Priss," he said as he stepped toward her. "But not through spells and incantations and animals that no longer walk the earth or fly through the air." He reached for the single, thick braid hanging over her shoulder, watched the end of it curl around his hand. "Magic is you, Priss." He dropped the braid and turned away to pace restlessly in front of her, as if he were nervous, afraid.

As afraid as she in that moment that the wrong word spoken might destroy what seemed too fragile to survive in the world beyond the cave.

Gavan halted, stared down at her, spoke softly. "Magic is knowing from the first moment I saw you that you are unique in all the world, that you would enrich my life with that special quality. It is looking at you and being so completely bewitched by you that I must hold you and make love to you. It is not caring if I am bewitched because you brought happiness into my life and I want to return the gift in full measure."

Tears burst from her on a loud sob. Turning away, she wept, great wrenching sobs that shook her body. For happiness and for relief and for dreams fulfilled. She hadn't realized how uncertain she'd been. He hadn't said he loved her but it didn't matter. He'd said so much more. He'd said what was most difficult for him to say, to admit, to accept. Magic . . . he'd said that she was magic. That she made him happy.

"Priss . . . don't," he said hoarsely, a wealth of pain in his voice, as if he could do nothing else but share the pain that caused her to weep. She raised her head and saw him standing so rigid and proud, saw his expression so stiff and controlled, saw his eyes revealing what she'd never thought to see.

Love, unrestrained and unadorned. Love, raw and hurting in its uncertainty.

"I was so afraid, Gavan," she said as she

wiped tears away with the back of her hand. "Afraid that you would be lost to me. That I would say or do something stupid that would drive you away. Afraid that you would be taken from me by Price. Or the cave. Afraid that nothing I could do would keep you safe. That I would have to go through every day of my entire life with only my memories of you."

He lowered to one knee in front of her, enfolded her in his arms, held her so tightly that she felt as if, in that single moment, she had become a part of him. He angled back and crooked his finger under chin, lifted her face to his. "I have it on good authority that no one can protect me better than one who loves me. You see, I am unhurt—proof that you were right."

She gave him a watery smile, her sob turning into a laugh. "And you're not writhing on the floor in fear."

"I never writhe on the floor in fear," he said. "And contrary to what Gwyneth might think, I am not afraid of enclosed places. I simply hated *this* place."

"Still, it must have been difficult for you to revisit your memories."

He gave her a tender smile. "Not difficult at all. I just kept repeating to myself that you loved me. That losing you was the only thing worth fearing."

More tears flowed and laughter bubbled up at the same time. "Then you *do* know that you will never find a better woman than I to make you happy."

"To fill the empty places inside myself, Priss."

"And you know that the true magic is love."

Again he nodded. "Magic that dwells in the heart and in the endless possibilities conjured by the mind . . . you fulfill me, Priss. You complete me." He smiled wryly as he glanced down at his position on the floor of the cave. "And since I seem to be on bent knee I suppose I should tell you that I can no longer blind myself to what I feel. I love you, Priss. You love me. I must insist that you marry me."

She arched her brows at his arrogance.

"Please?" he said with a cocky grin. "I need your clutter and nonsense and honesty in my life. I need to awaken every morning with the taste of strawberries on my lips. I need the excitement and unpredictability you bring to each day. Without it, I will have no life at all."

She wrapped her arms around him, too happy to do anything else. "You need me, my lord, to keep you humble." She raised her face and kissed the corners of his mouth.

He rose, bringing her with him, lifting her off her feet and twirling like a child, his laughter ringing off the stone walls in the music of happiness. And then he halted and slid her down his body, and stepped back to lead her into the main chamber. He reached for the coat he'd shed before saving Price from drowning, pulling a golden circle on a ribbon from his pocket and tying it around her neck.

From the adjoining chamber, dragon and sorcerer watched from their places in eternity as Priss took the step toward Gavan that would bring them together like the ends of a circle—hands intertwined, mouths meeting in the unspoken language of love . . . hearts joining for all time.

Priss and Gavan emerged into the sunlight and found Gwyneth leaning against an oak tree, Willie leaning over her, kissing her as if he couldn't get enough of her. They broke apart as Gavan cleared his throat, Gwyneth giving him a defiant glare and Willie arching his brow as men did when sharing a moment of commiseration or understanding.

Gavan sighed and swiped his hand over the back of his neck. "Did your book mention that Myrddin's legacy would be claimed by both of the St. Aldan heirs?" he asked wryly. "Or was it full of prophecies about the end of the world?"

"The book," Willie said with a look of disappointment, "is nothing more than an epic poem of love . . . unsigned. It contains no proof that Myrddin existed."

"Does it matter?" Priss asked.

"Not at all," Gwyneth murmured. "We know the truth and that is all that matters." She grinned impishly up at Willie. "And I think an epic poem of love is exactly what *should* be in the book."

The ground rumbled and quaked. Dust billowed from the cave entrance as it collapsed in on itself, leaving nothing but a shadow on the slope of the mountain. Willie opened the book and pointed to a drawing, identical to the shadow right down to the rocks piled on the ground. The pages crumbled in his hands, turning into dust scattered by the breeze.

Willie opened his hand, allowing it all to escape him as they each stared at the other, knowing nothing needed to be said, no regret felt for the loss of the book or the cave. They were the real keepers of magic. They and each man and woman who knew love, saw it in the eyes of a cherished mate, held it in their hearts, touched it with passion shared.

"No, it doesn't matter at all," Gavan agreed as they all turned and walked, four abreast and hand in hand, toward the road home, leaving Myrddin and the dragon to rest in peace.

Epilogue

Seven weeks later

Evergreen boughs and mistletoe draped all that was left of the wooden circle in the meadow in honor of the approaching Christmas season. Snow glistened on the ground radiating an ethereal glow in the twilight as souls from the four villages, the farms, and Castell Eryri gathered to celebrate the solstice and the marriages of the earl of St. Aldan to Miss Priscilla Whitmore and of his sister, Lady Gwyneth, to Mr. William Whitmore.

"And not a moment too soon," some whispered with smiles and happy sighs, "for our lady is surely growing thick in the waist."

Priscilla laughed. "Indeed, not a moment too soon," she murmured in Gavan's ear as she patted her barely discernible belly. "You are well and truly caught now, my lord."

"Thank God," he said fervently. "I am well and truly saved from myself."

"Really, Priscilla," her mother said with no

real admonishment. "I'm certain I did not raise you to be so . . . earthy."

"Of course you did, Mother. You raised me for this very moment, and for this very man, and he would have me no other way."

Drew Sinclair-Saxon winked at Priss. Harriet Countess Saxon, stood beside her husband and smiled. Viscount Dane grinned as his wife gave a robust laugh. "There is a great deal to be said for earthy, Mrs. Whitmore," he remarked.

"It discourages misunderstanding, among other things," Gavan agreed. "I insist that Priss speak her mind in all things before she has the opportunity to think."

"I will if you will," Priss retorted.

"Agreed," he whispered, and leaned over to kiss the corner of her mouth, his hands slipping inside her fur-lined cloak to pull her close. "Fairy silk," he said, as his fingers tangled in the yards of gossamer fabric from which she'd fashioned her wedding gown. Like all her creations, she'd embellished it with golden butterflies scattered here and there. Caught at the crown and drawn through a circle cut out of a small bit of nonsense she called a hat, her hair drifted around her head and down her back with more golden butterflies seeming to hover around her head in flight.

Magic. She was magic itself.

"I never thought to see it, but I vow Willie is completely befuddled by all this," Priss said as her brother and new sister-in-law wove through the crowd, exchanging blessings with one and all.

"He hasn't a clue as to what has hit him," Gavan agreed. "But I have no doubt that Gwyneth will explain it to him quite dramatically."

"Well someone must. He has lived in the past—literally—for far too long. Gwyneth will see that he takes a good look around the present from time to time."

Gavan arranged the hood of Priss's cloak over her head, then opened his greatcoat and wrapped it around her, enfolding them both in warmth. "And you, Priss, will bring magic into my life every time you walk into a room, every time I hear your voice, catch your scent in the air, feel your—" His voice snagged as he stared down at her, drowning in the love she showed with every look and every touch and every word.

Daisy barked as a torch was held to an immense stack of wood and tinder, flaring instantly into a bonfire that created its own circle of warmth and light in the meadow. Precious meowed from the relative comfort of a large sleigh and flopped down on the back of the seat to stare haughtily at the humans foolishly milling about in the cold. High above, inside Castell Eryri, lay the runt Gavan had chosen from Lady Dane's menagerie and the rest of the litter presented to him as a wedding gift from Priss. She'd known without being told how much he'd wanted them all.

Priss laid her cheek against his chest and wrapped her arms around his waist, swaying to the hymn a few villagers had begun to sing and the others were picking up a voice at a time.

"A wonderful day, Gavan," she murmured sleepily. "I don't want it to end."

"There will be more, Priss. Many more." He held her and swayed with her, his head bent over hers, smiling at the memory that had replaced all others in his mind. . . .

The villagers gathered inside the church and spilling out of the doors, straining to hear and to see a new tradition begun. A Lord of St. Aldan marrying for love alone to a true lady who created sunshine with a smile. A new vicar presiding who spoke the old language and honored the best of their ancient traditions. A ceremony of faith and commitment within the church followed by a celebration of nature and the magic of love in the meadow below the walls of the ancient keep.

Magic thriving in a look between lovers, a kiss between mates, love expanding with every moment shared.

Destiny fulfilled as it was meant to be.

A fantasy, a love story, a summer of change...

The China Garden

By LIZ BERRY

CHN 0599

Dear Reader,

As we all know, every bride is beautiful—but a bride left at the altar is a force to be reckoned with. In Tanya Anne Crosby's latest Treasure, *Happily Ever After*, we meet Sophie Vanderwahl. She's been waiting for three long years for her wandering fiance to return. But when she discovers his indiscretions, she sets off to find him—determined to give him a piece of her mind. So she boards handsome Jack MacAuley's ship, and begins a journey of discovery—for Jack is everything her husband to be is not...handsome, irresistible, powerful and faithful in his love.

A modern-day Montana cowboy, a peerless heroine, a love story you'll never forget...this is what makes up Cait London's latest Contemporary romance, *Sleepless in Montana*. Hard and haunted, Hogan Kodiak is an outsider in his own family. Love has burned him in the past, and he's determined not to let sassy Jemma Delaney under his skin. But when passion overcomes caution, Jemma and Hogan embark on a romance that just might shake the Kodiak family to its very core.

In Avon Romance, we're first off to Scotland with Kathleen Harrington's *The MacLean Groom*. Rory MacLean is ordered by the king to wed Joanna, the fair daughter of the rival MacDonald clan, only to discover that his bride has run off!

And if you love Regency-set love stories, don't miss Margaret Evans Porter's *The Seducer*. Highborn Kerron Cashin is tantalized by the local innkeeper's daughter, Ellin Fayle, but when they're caught in a compromising position he must decide if he should be honorable and wed the country lass.

Enjoy!

Lucia Macro
Lucia Macro
Senior Editor

Avon Romantic Treasures

*Unforgettable, enthralling love stories,
sparkling with passion and adventure
from Romance's bestselling authors*

❋❋❋❋❋❋❋❋❋❋❋❋❋❋❋❋❋❋❋❋❋❋❋❋❋❋

Avon Romances—
the best in exceptional authors
and unforgettable novels!